CHRONICLES OF THE CROWNED

the STAR
of
Zephyria

B. L. VANG

Content Warning

Emotional Abuse
Suicidal Thoughts
Alcohol and Alcoholism
Slavery
Mentions of dead bodies
Brief mentions of racism

Contents

Dedication

To my mother, who not only allowed me to write my whole life, but encouraged me. Also thank you for letting me rant about the book that was so bad I had to write a better one.

Prologue

The soft, muffled sound of people shopping drifted through the streets, mixing with the irresistible smell of sizzling food. One merchant was shouting for half price on gold, another one boasted about their fried dough. Children's laughter rang through the streets as they ran after each other with wooden swords.

Within the last year, the kingdom had expanded greatly due to the king's conquests. Many religions, tribes, and trades came pouring in, making a home within the capital. This was the first outing the prince took outside the outer palace wall since the last conquest. An older woman who was selling spells for finding your one true love caught his eye.

Amir looked down at the woman from atop his horse. Her face was weathered from the years, and despite the shroud over her head, he could still see the crown of gray that was her hair.

"A potion for the young prince?" She held up a potion bottle that glowed pink.

"No." He shook his head, waving her on, urging his horse forward. He didn't believe in love potions, especially as the second prince. He would not choose his wife.

"Then a reading, my lord!" She grabbed his horse's reins, halting the horse.

Amir blinked a few times, confused on how this old, frail woman could be so forward, so bold with a prince. Even as the prince of the second wife, everyone knew who he was. He kept his tone under control as he looked her. She was dressed in beggar clothes, and her shop was a few loose boards that were strung together with a handful of rope.

"No, nothing." He shook his head as he tried to pull his rein free from her. Readings were nothing but a scam in his mind.

"Of course not, my lord." She bowed her head a little. "You are too strong-willed for something such as readings." The old woman smiled at him. "How about a blessing for you, my lord?"

"I have done nothing to earn a blessing," he said, now slightly annoyed. He knew where he stood, and no blessing would change his fate.

"Children are always a blessing to their parents," she said firmly.

The grim expression on his face grew deeper. A hollow feeling crept into him as he thought about the blessings she spoke of. However, looking at the old woman, seeing the sparkle in her eyes, he couldn't tear himself away.

He gave a single nod with a heavy sigh. "Very well, woman. Give your blessing."

She released the rein and put her hands together as if she was praying. "May the woman who is from the stars be a light to you." She then raised her hands up with the palms facing the sky, as if she was expecting rain to fall down into them. After a few moments, she lowered her hands and grinned at the prince. "Love will find you, my lord. When it does, may the creator continue to bless you."

"Thank you." Amir nodded to the woman before he urged his horse on. *What nonsense*, he thought. His queen was to be chosen by the king. When they finally made it closer to the outer palace wall, he turned to his personal servant. "Lysander?"

"Yes, my lord?" A young, blond man stepped forward, but still stood behind Amir.

"That woman, what tribe is she from?"

The young servant shook his head. "My prince, I asked if anyone knew her…"

"And?"

"No one knows, my lord."

He nodded. *She was just some merchant who was passing by*, he thought. "Thank you."

It wasn't a long walk before they reached the outer palace gate. Amir dismounted his horse, allowing the stable hand to take the beast. As he went through the gate, the soft sound of his footsteps echoed as he crossed the stone floor. The smell of fresh jasmine wafted through the air as he continued to walk through the outer palace. It once was a lush, beautiful garden, a paradise, but as he turned to look at each of the buildings, he saw the cracks in them. He walked by several of the higher ranked concubines and their servants, most who sneered at him.

He turned back to look at the palace walls, seeing more dust, webs, and cracks within them. The servants were supposed to take care of the outer palace, however with so little money given, it was not a high priority to keep it in good condition. Especially when the king stopped visiting.

Amir shook his head as he walked into the garden of the courtyard; it was in the middle of the outer palace, called the heart. There, he found his mother, talking with someone. It was a man who looked as old as his father. He was well-built in simple leather armor, *dir*. His hair was covered by cream-colored head wrapping, only his medium-length beard showing. He stood straight as he talked to her. Though his skin was tawny and touched by the sun, Amir could see that he was not a Zephyrian. Amir's mother didn't seem to mind this as she smiled genuinely at the man. She was wearing a dusty-pink lehenga today, one with white thread woven into it. She shined like a pink rose in a sea of broken rubble.

Out of the corner of her eye, she caught sight of Amir and motioned him to come over to her. He obeyed, giving a bow to her once he approached.

"Amir," she said in a tired voice, "this is going to be your new guard, Zeke. His tribe has joined our people recently."

Amir raised an eyebrow to the older man as he straightened himself. "My guard?"

His mother nodded. "Yes, your father came by today while you were out. You'll require a guard by you from now on."

His face morphed into a glare aimed at his mother. "Why?"

She gave him a pained smile. "You are to go to the inner palace and live there."

"No," he snapped, not meaning it to sound as harsh as it came out. "I will not leave you."

"It has already been decided." Her voice was strained as she quietly dismissed Zeke, who left without a word.

"Why does he want me? I am not his first born, and you are not his first wife." Amir didn't like mentioning that his mother was second wife, but he was angry.

Her eyes had averted him, and after a moment, she met his again. "Your three older brothers are dead." The strain in her voice, the tears welling up in her eyes told him it was true. Although Amir had to question whether those were tears for his dead half-brothers or losing him to the inner palace.

"How?" He knew the answer, but the question still came out.

"The war," she said softly. "You are to gather your things and join your father in the inner palace tonight."

He shook his head. "I won't leave you," he repeated.

She snapped her fingers. "Lysander," she called. Out of the shadows came the young, blond servant. He was only a few years younger than Amir. "Gather all of his majesty's things and have them moved to the inner palace. Immediately."

"Right away, my lady." He bowed low before leaving.

"Lysander!" he called out, but it was to no avail. Lysander made no attempt to return.

"Amir," she said coolly, "I am still in charge of this palace. They will not listen to you here."

He narrowed his eyes at her, holding back his own tears now. "Ma," he never called her that name out loud in public, "I don't want to go there. He cares nothing for us."

"I know." She cupped his cheek, her voice shaking. "But I know you will be a wonderful king." A single tear rolled down her cheek as she swallowed hard. "Be a better king."

He swallowed back some tears, nodding to her, grasping her hand, and kissing her palm. "I will visit as often as I can."

She said nothing as they began to embrace each other under the jasmine vines, silently crying.

The smell of nightfall was always crisp, but tonight, Amir couldn't help but think it smelled of salt and sulfur. It didn't take Amir long to scale down the side of his room—he was grateful Lysander had packed some things which were dark, so he could be hidden under the night sky. His father had told him to not escape, threatening him, ensuring the outer palace was heavily watched, so he couldn't see his mother. But at this point, Amir couldn't stand to be in the inner or outer palace.

He knew of a tree that had low-hanging branches which lead to the direction of the villages. Amir made light work of climbing it and watching for guards as they paroled the area. As stealthy as a cat, he dropped down, doing a roll as he made contact with the ground. He made a mental note about this weak spot in the palace's security.

Once he was out of the palace's vicinity, the sounds of the village became alive. Merchants were still selling wares while some of the food vendors had gone home for the night, but Zephyria was the central hub for all places in the wild desert they called home. The kingdom had expanded greatly over the years from war, and it showed with all the different tribes that were settled in.

As Amir walked through the town more, he found there was a celebration on the edge of the town's limits towards the open desert. In the middle of a mass of people was a large bonfire. The light of the fire danced across the people's faces as they danced. Despite how lively the celebration was, the atmosphere was calming and inviting. A little man walked up to him, pushing a stick with lamb meat on it into his hands. Amir stared at it for a moment before taking a bite. The fat coated his tongue, the smokiness from the flame allowing him to taste the layers of flavor. As Amir made his way around the crowds, the sounds of laughter, coins, and meat sizzling carried throughout the desert sky. Upon looking closer, he noticed some of the people donned necklaces with pendants of the sun.

He looked at the desert sky, seeing the wispy clouds and showing that spring-time was truly upon them. Amir was a stranger in the celebration, but the people were not questioning it; they allowed him to join in with them without second thought.

"Oh, I'm sorry," Amir said as he bumped into a young girl. As he looked down, he was met with sparkling, green eyes. She was younger than him, and her hair was covered with a pale blue cloth as many of the tribes that joined in the last few years had donned.

She smiled up at him. "Hello."

"Hello..." He looked around to see if he could spot her parents.

"You're not one of us, huh?" She glanced him over, puzzled by his dark clothes.

"I came for the festival," he said quickly.

She raised an eyebrow at him, clearly not believing him.

Great, he thought. *This eight-year-old is on to me.*

She relaxed into a smile. "Welcome, we are the Ātash People. Today is an important day for us."

"What is it today?" There weren't any festival times he knew of with the major religions in the kingdom.

"The Feast of Lots," she said plainly.

"What is that?"

Her smile turned into a smirk. "The Feast of Lots shows we are free people."

"You live in Zephyria; no one is free when under a king," he snapped. He didn't mean for it to come out so harsh, but it was proven to him today after the deaths of his brothers. Freedom was an illusion when it came to the king's will.

"We are always free, even in slavery," she said as if it was an indisputable fact.

"I don't think that's true." He looked at her as if she was crazy.

The girl continued to smile at him. "It's okay, it is our faith which keeps us strong." A woman called out, and the girl immediately straightened up. "I have to go, have a good night! Try the naan!" The girl waved goodbye as she ran off.

Amir watched as she ran over to an older woman, possibly her mother. He returned his gaze to all the other people still laughing, twirling in the dances, the music playing loud with praises. These people were happy, even though they were foreigners in a strange country. They sang, ate merrily, and just as the young girl said—he felt free with them.

"*Free regardless of wherever they are,*" he mused to himself. "Always free."

"Always free!" someone heard and echoed to the crowds, raising their glass. A loud yell was exclaimed from everyone.

Amir left feeling warm and determined. He would choose his own way of being free. He vowed to see his mother again, to find a way to bring her into the palace with him.

This would not come to pass, for Amir would never see his mother again. Death took her within the year of Amir's departure, and not a year after his mother's death, the king would die.

Making Amir the king of all Zephyria.

CHAPTER 1

Same Wine, Different Bottle

SEVEN YEARS LATER

THE AIR WAS FILLED with the loud clang of swords and the pained grunts of the men locked in battle. *Parry and strike!* Another clang from a sword, but this time, the sword made a scrapping sound before hitting the ground. The man stood towering over the fallen man. He had sun-kissed skin, a closely trimmed beard, and a full head of hair that didn't go past his ears. His smoldering, amber eyes narrowed at his opponent who was breathing heavily.

"Are you done, Hamid?" he asked, his chest rising and falling. His voice was full of humor as he pointed the tip of his sword at the young man's chest.

The young man gingerly nodded, saying nothing.

The man with the beard rolled his eyes. "So young and inexperienced."

"It's not in our people's customs to learn how to fight with swords," he said as he wiped the sweat, which just left a dirt smudge where a beard wasn't.

The man now narrowed his eyes. "That is not true." He pointed his sword at the older man, who stood at attention by the door. He had silver streaks colored throughout his hair, and showed no emotion on his face. "Zeke is from the same tribe, and he is one of the best fighters we have."

"Zeke is a monster," Hamid grumbled.

The man laughed, offering his hand. "I agree." The young man took the offered hand.

The young man bowed. "Thank you for the lesson, your highness."

A male's voice rang out, followed by a slow clap. "Amir, did you beat our poor guards again? So soon after coming home from the war?"

Amir looked over and saw his dear friend, Darius. He was dressed in a silk dhoti, a traditional, ankle-length lower garment for men, and a tunic. It must have taken his seamstress, if not a team of seamstresses, multiple days to complete the garment with all the jewels and embroidery on it.

"You're all dressed up." Amir eyed his friend before grabbing a towel one of the servants gave him. Slowly, he started to rub the sweat off his chest and neck.

Darius gave an offended look. "Sire, do you not remember that today is the start of your party?"

"So you got ready at this time of day?" He looked up at the sky; it must have been just after high noon by now.

"I have to ensure that the party will go well." He smiled. "After all, your parties don't set themselves up."

"That's what Lysander is for," Amir mused as he grabbed his shirt that was draped over a chair. Another male servant ran up to Amir with a tray full of cups and a pitcher.

"Water, my lord?" he asked, his head bowed low.

"Yes, of course." Darius smiled, taking a cup and pouring the water. He took a sip first, then poured a glass for Amir.

"What is that?" Amir narrowed his eyes a bit at Darius.

"I'm ensuring you don't die." His friend laughed. "Next time, I'll let you drink poison since you're so ungrateful."

"How do I know you're not going to poison it yourself?" Amir teased back before he put on his shirt.

"I wouldn't be so crass as to poison you. That is a coward's way of killing someone."

Amir nodded, draping his arm around his friend's shoulder. "Yes, so you have told me many times over the years."

"It bears repeating." He smirked.

Amir laughed, shaking his head. "I don't think so, my friend." Just then, a blond man walked up to them, bowing his head.

"Your majesty."

"Lysander, how are the party settings going?"

"They are going well, my lord," he said, then hesitated.

Amir narrowed his eyes at Lysander. "What's wrong?"

"The queen doesn't want to host the women's side of the party."

Amir stood up straight, unhooking his arm around Darius and staring down at Lysander who was still bowing low. "What do you mean?"

"She said, and I quote, my lord, 'There is no point in being part of this party if all he is going to do is get drunk with his friends. The women don't get drunk, and I don't want to do it.'"

Amir's eye twitched. "Where is she?"

"In the queen's drawing room."

"Thank you, Lysander. Be sure to put Darius to work, since he is already ready for the party."

Darius looked offended as his hand went to his chest.

"As you wish, my lord," Lysander said.

Tabitha was his queen, and though she was a raving beauty from a well-bred royal family—one of the many his father conquered—she was quite a stubborn woman. Amir didn't hesitate as he entered her drawing room, seeing she was sitting there with her ladies and drinking some tea.

"Leave," he commanded, and everyone vanished from the room, leaving the queen sitting there as she continued to sip her tea.

"Well, husband, how do I have the pleasure of seeing you today? It has been some time since I last saw you. I had begun to think I was widowed." She tucked a piece of her raven hair behind her ear, showing her glittering jewelry.

He ignored her contempt. "What do you mean by telling Lysander that you aren't going to host your side of the party?"

Tabitha's mouth pinched, her brows furrowing. "That little rat, Lysander."

"You cannot punish Lysander. He is my servant, and you have no power over him."

"I have no power over anything," she spat. Her brown eyes were glaring at him from behind her teacup.

"You are the queen, you have power."

"I am just a pretty rose in your garden of women. A rose has no power over anyone."

He pinched the bridge of his nose. "Again, I don't even have any other mistresses or wives in my life. I barely have time for *you*. Any more women and I wouldn't know what to do with all of them."

"To have your babies, of course," she snapped, averting his eyes, looking at the corner of the room.

He sighed, wanting to rub the back of his neck. Tabitha had been married to Amir before his father had died, an arrangement set up with another king to make peace. During the entire time of marriage, they produced no heirs. As time went on, Tabitha's touch grew cold, and her accusations of him with mistresses grew tiresome. Rumors began to spread about her that reached the king's ears. Still, he stayed loyal to her.

"I don't have any other women," he said once more through gritted teeth.

"I don't believe you." She looked back at him furiously. "I know what they all say about the war camps. They bring women in for you. Women are thrown around the camp as dirty rags once you're done with them."

Amir groaned internally as he pinched the bridge of his nose once more. He knew that there were bad stories from the camp, but most of them were unfounded. They did often try to set him up with a woman, which he soon found out was a carried over tradition from his father. He always went and let the woman go. What happened to her afterward, he didn't always want to know.

"See?" she snapped again, this time sitting up straight. "You must have a woman in your mind. Someone from your new kingdom. After all, you are home from war, having conquered the weak king in the east. I heard he gave you a gift. A new bride."

"No," he said bitterly before narrowing his eyes at her. The gift was horses, including one young war mare. "But I promise you this, Tabitha: if you do not host your side of the party, I will toss you back to your family as a disgraced woman."

"You wouldn't dare," she hissed through her teeth.

"Try me," he said with an eerie calm in his voice.

They stared at each other for a long minute before she sighed. "Fine, but I will only do five days, then I am done."

"Fine," he replied before leaving.

CHAPTER 2

When Drinks Don't Mix Well

WHEN THE KING RETURNED home from the war, the days were filled with never-ending extravagant celebrations. Each day brought new excitement and entertainment from all corners of the world, honoring the victorious return of the king. As the final day of the festivities arrived, Amir had opened his personal chambers to a myriad of men, celebrating and rejoicing with them. He extended invitations to some of his top guards, allowing them to join as guests rather than workers. Of course, this didn't sit well with everyone, but he was the king.

Soft tunes from harps and flutes danced through the air, mixing with the soft chattering of men. As per tradition of Zephyrian law, the men and women were separated during the parties. Amir always thought this was so each gender could gossip about the other. He inhaled deeply, smelling the mix of wine and dried leaf smoke. As Amir took a sip of his wine, some men whispering to one another piqued his interest.

"She must fall on her hands and knees for him when he comes home from war," one man said.

"I heard she is not so kind to him when he sees her," another man snickered.

"Perhaps she is used to being *alone* and she no longer answers to him," a third man joked.

"After all, she is the most beautiful woman in all of Zephyria." The first man laughed before taking another drink.

Slowly, Amir placed his drink down, letting the alcohol coat his tongue as he allowed the words being said about his queen settle. His jaw was set, tightening as more words were exchanged between the men. Tabitha's coldness had reached others' ears, outside their own private exchanges. Amir knew he never spoke of it, leading him to believe it was the servants or Tabitha herself spreading the rumors.

With a slight raise of his hand, his man-servant came rushing towards him.

"Lysander, tell Tabitha I wish to see her."

Lysander seemed to want to say something, but thought better of it. "Of course, my lord." With a quick turn, he sent another servant rushing to collect the queen.

Within five minutes, the younger servant ran in, clearly out of breath. The palace was no small feat to run from one end to the other in such a short amount of time. The king had since abandoned his glass of wine. "Where is she?" he asked directly, looking forward at his guests, never at the servant.

Silently, Lysander gave a questioning look at the young man, who violently shook his head, sweat beading down his face. Lysander took in a deep breath and whispered to Amir.

"She is not coming, my lord."

Amir sat up straight, his chest rising and falling, his jaw tightening. The smell of everything suddenly turned putrid. It was a whim that he had asked to see her, yes, but something in Amir snapped after days of trying, only to be met with the news that she could not receive him without any explanation.

Lysander was quick to send two men to Tabitha, hoping she would come this time with the extra presence. Another few minutes passed, but nothing was heard from the servants. Tension hung in the air; everyone could feel and see the anger in the king's face.

Finally, the men came rushing in. They held out a note to Lysander. They looked pale as they bit onto their lower lips. Lysander closed his eyes for a moment, trying to control his breathing. He knew what it probably said. It was not a good plan for Tabitha to decide that she simply didn't need to come when Amir summoned her *twice*. Then to send a note in return? Lysander steeled himself for what was to come next, praying to his gods that it would work in his favor.

"My lord," he said, bowing as he presented the letter of paper to his master on a silver platter.

Amir ripped open the letter and quickly read it. Once he finished, Amir crumbled up the letter with one hand. For a few moments, the entire room froze, waiting for the king to lose his composure. But then he softened his face, smiling to his guests and making a grab for his goblet, downing it in one swallow.

"Please, my guests," his smile grew broader, "don't stop enjoying yourselves!" Amir threw the letter off to the side and snapped his fingers. Music began to play louder, and people talked with one another once more.

The king, though smiling, had a dark look in his eyes. Lysander quietly picked up the letter. With great discretion, he read it behind the curtains where the servants hid.

Oh dear husband who loves me so much,
I am afraid I just can't make it to your little party. You have instruct-
ed me to take care of my end of the party, which means entertaining
the women. By now, you have sent two men to retrieve me. I am not
a dog you can whistle, and off I go. I am not a servant that needs to
bring you a sandwich, should you feel as if I am your forever indebted
servant. So I wish you, dear husband, to have fun, for I shall have

husband, to have fun, for I shall have mine tonight.
Tabitha, your loyal rose in a garden of flowers

Lysander felt sick to his stomach as he groaned silently. Tabitha was playing a dangerous game with the king, though he was normally gracious with his wife. Lysander knew of all the rumors that swirled around the queen and the king, but tonight of all nights, she should have gone to him. Lysander knew that the queen had not received the king's company for more than a few seasons.

"Lysander," one of the servants said in a hushed voice, "what do we do?"

"Keep his glass full, and see to it that the other men do not talk about the queen."

"How do we do that?" another one asked.

"Feed them, get them drunk—whatever you have to do in order to keep them from talking. If they so much as start saying the word *queen*, ask if they want a refill."

"But Lysander, we aren't supposed to talk to them."

"The king's mind is occupied with Tabitha tonight; he will not notice you interrupting the guests. Just make sure to be discreet about it."

The gold glittered, the silver platters moved around the room as if they were magical, and the candles set the place aglow. The torches outside gave the palace a warm glow. Joy had thought the gardens looked beautiful with all the flowers in bloom, despite it being winter, as she walked through them. They were a desert country, so having a garden this lush showed the wealth of the king.

This was the fifth and final day of the party. It also was what Joy's uncle had thought was the most vulnerable for the palace's safety. She looked at his stern face as he continued to survey the area for any potential danger lurking.

"Uncle Zeke," she cooed, looping her arm with his. "There is nothing that is going to happen. The other men on duty will take care of everything."

"Hmm," he muttered, his eyes still scanning their surroundings.

It was the only day Joy and her Aunt Mari were allowed to come to the palace's festivities with the king's return. Joy was going to relish in it. Even though she was in her twentieth year, and well into the age eligible to marry, she remained shut away from the world. For this occasion, she was allowed to wear a dark, muted red dress with a high collar and wrist-length sleeves, her long, dark hair hidden beneath a beautiful shawl. Compared to the other women, she and her aunt were the most modestly dressed in the room.

"Stay close to your aunt," her uncle said in a low, warning tone.

Joy's smile faltered as she gave a silent nod. Whether there was danger or not, she was always commanded to stay close to a family member.

"Remember the king required that we come today, we could not refuse the king," he said in the same tone. "I have to go to the king's side where all the men are meeting. Please don't leave the side of your aunt."

"I know."

The scent of roasted lamb wafted through the castle, making Joy's stomach ache for some food. She wondered if Aunt Mari would let her eat. As they walked through the halls and rooms, dozens of women were dressed in colors of all kinds. The servants, on the other hand, wore white. Everything felt like a royal wedding. Music danced through each room, wrapping around Joy, making her feel alive.

"Joy!" A familiar voice rang out. "You made it!"

Joy's gaze fell upon a young girl with olive skin and long, light brown braids cascading down her front. She wore a simple lehenga in a vibrant shade of red that hugged her round figure. With her plump cheeks and round face, Joy couldn't help but think she looked like a ripe apple. Cassia was younger than Joy by several years, but since Joy was unmarried, she couldn't be selective with friends.

"Cassia!" she exclaimed, embracing her friend.

"I can't believe you made it! I thought for sure your uncle wouldn't let you come," she said, giggling.

She gave a half-smile, looking back at her aunt who was busy talking to one of the other members from their tribe. "I was allowed to go as long as I was under the watchful eye of my family. My uncle Zeke was told he *had* to attend the party with his family."

"Why?" she asked curiously.

Joy shrugged. "I'm not sure, but I'm happy I can come and see the palace. Even if it is the only time I ever will be here."

"Oh, me too," her friend swooned.

"Have you seen the king?" Joy asked, giving a small chuckle. Cassia always tried to see the king whenever he rode through town. Joy knew that Cassia wished to be a mistress to the king one day.

"No," Cassia's lips turned up into a pout, "I haven't even seen the queen, either."

"Oh?" Joy stood on her toes, looking around. "Is she here?"

Cassia gave a nod. "Of course, but rumor is that with every passing day, her mood gets more and more foul. I'm not sure if I want to meet her."

Joy knew of course that Cassia's true goal was to get close to the *king*, but the queen was considered the fashion standard of the kingdom, so it wasn't unheard of to want to see the queen.

"If she is in a foul mood, it might not be a good idea to see her."

"I know, but I want to see how beautiful she is for the festivities."

"Is she beautiful?" Joy asked. "I know nothing about her."

"Joy, how have you lived here for all this time and not seen the queen? She visits the village once a week."

Joy gave a shrug. "I only ever go inside the village when my aunt is with me."

"Do they hate the royal family?" she asked.

"Shh!" Joy slapped her hand over her friend's mouth. "Don't say such an awful thing. My uncle works in the palace as a guard."

Her friend nodded before Joy took her hand away.

"But," Cassia whispered in her ear, "they didn't want to come to the party, did they?"

Joy gave a nod. "My aunt and uncle said I would gain nothing but a yearning for a lavish life by attending." She chuckled, knowing that she didn't want that kind of life. She wanted to be free in a different sense. She loved her maternal guardians, but sometimes she felt smothered.

Her friend gave her a raised eyebrow. "Are you okay?"

Joy giggled. "Of course."

Her friend continued to keep her eyebrow raised. "Are you sure you don't want a lavish life? You could become a mistress with me."

Joy rolled her eyes. "I don't want to be constantly watched by everyone. What if I mess up or sneeze at the wrong time?"

"Then it would become fashionable to sneeze at the wrong time," Cassia said as she laughed.

Joy rolled her eyes, giving a gentle push to her friend.

"Doesn't your family have someone in mind for you?"

Joy rolled her eyes. "Oh yes," her voice went gruff, "*gentle Hamid will make a fine husband for you.*" She paused, returning to her normal voice. "That's what my elders keep saying, but I don't want to marry Hamid."

"I thought in your culture, you had to listen to the head of the family?"

Joy gave a stern nod. "Elders actually, and we do—but the head of my family is secretly my aunt, and she said she didn't like the look of Hamid, so…" She trailed off with a grin as she shrugged. "I got out of marriage to Hamid."

Both girls let out a laugh together when a sudden commotion erupted in the room. Joy turned to see what was causing the disturbance. The queen herself had entered the grand hall, flanked by her ladies-in-waiting. Queen Tabitha's eyes scanned the room, her expression a mix of indifference and boredom.

Cassia gasped and clutched onto Joy's arm, giving a squeal as she jumped a little in place. "She's here! The queen is actually here!"

Joy couldn't tear her eyes away from Queen Tabitha, who seemed to float through the crowd with an air of regal grace. The whispers grew louder as the guests took notice of the queen's presence. Some spoke in hushed tones of admiration while others expressed curiosity about her rumored foul mood.

As Queen Tabitha neared, Joy felt a rush of excitement mixed with apprehension. She wanted to see the queen up close, to witness firsthand the beauty that had captivated Cassia as well as so many others. The queen moved swiftly through the room, disappearing as quickly as she showed up.

"Come on." Cassia pulled Joy to the other end of the room, trying to follow the queen.

"My aunt," Joy said softly, looking back at where she was.

"She is talking to one of your other aunts." She waved a dismissive hand at her.

As they wandered through the bustling halls of the palace, Joy couldn't help but overhear snippets of conversations from guests and servants alike.

"Did you hear? The queen snubbed the king at his own party!" an overweight, garish woman said behind a fan.

"They say the king is furious. Who knows what he'll do," another equally overweight garish woman honked.

"I heard she's been sending letters to her secret lover." A small, petite woman snickered with the women.

Joy's curiosity was piqued. She had never paid much attention to rumors before, but it seemed like these were spreading faster than a fire.

"The queen has another lover?" the first lady asked as she licked her lips.

"Oh, I doubt that she has another lover." The second garish lady waved her hand in dismissal.

"What would happen if she did?" Joy asked suddenly without thinking.

"Probably nothing," one woman answered mindlessly. "It's common knowledge that the royals have many lovers."

"Really?" Joy asked softly as she turned her attention back to the queen, who now seemed to be smiling genuinely at her guests.

"Yes," the first one said, "but I think it's only acceptable to have eunuchs, or women as the queen's lovers, therefore they don't produce an heir by accident."

"And the king?"

"He will have tons of mistresses." The first lady fanned herself. "Better chance to produce an heir."

"Does our king have tons of mistresses?" Joy asked, tearing her gaze from the queen.

Cassia thought for a moment, putting her finger to her lips. "Not that I heard."

"Oh no," the third woman shook her head, "he has nothing."

"Not even an heir with the queen." The second lady laughed.

"Probably why they have marriage problems." The three women cackled as they made their way closer to the queen.

"Oh, I see." She nodded, swallowing hard. Joy knew that she couldn't stay away too long. Her aunt would eventually go looking for her. "I better go back; my aunt will be wondering where I went."

"No, stay." Her friend pulled on her hand, trying to keep her there. "She is probably still talking. You can break the rules sometimes."

Joy pulled her hand free. "I need to keep my promise." She gave her friend a quick smile, then ran back to her aunt.

CHAPTER 3

Gilded Cage

THE SOUND OF HOOVES clattered against the uneven street of cobblestones and hardened dirt. The shouts from the soldiers were loud, and there was a distinct murmur through the town as Joy and her aunt walked through the marketplace.

"What is going on?" Joy asked as she turned, standing on her tiptoes. She adjusted her rusari, a square and diagonally folded cloth that is knotted under the chin, as she was trying to see the commotion.

"Joy, stay here," Aunt Mari's voice warned.

"Uh, okay auntie." Joy wanted to see what was going on, but dared not defy her aunt when she used that voice.

"The queen is gone!" a villager shouted as he ran by, flailing his arms about.

"They are looking for another queen in our village!" another one shouted as he ran by them in the other direction.

"The queen can be anyone!" a woman cried with joy.

"The queen is gone?" Joy asked. She was surprised that her uncle hadn't mentioned this.

Aunt Mari said nothing, never looking up from deciding which fish she wanted for the Summer Harvest that was coming up.

"Auntie," Joy repeated. "Is she really gone?"

Her aunt finally nodded. "Yes, we must hurry home now." She quickly chose her fish, then paid the vendor. The man nodded, wrapping up the fish, then draped a cloth over his stall before running off towards the crowds.

Joy blinked at where the man had run off, before she turned back to her aunt. "All right, Auntie."

As Joy grabbed the basket full of food for the festival; a throng of people began to rush towards them. Joy got swept away with them as if they were a powerful river.

"Who is going?" someone yelled.

"Wait," Joy tried to push her way through the crowd. "Auntie!"

"Please take my daughter!" a woman cried out.

"No, take my daughter to the palace."

"Auntie!" Joy yelled out, trying to reach out. She scanned the crowd, unable to see her.

"Everyone, stop moving towards us! We will go around and pick out the girls. We were given instructions on who to take," one of the soldiers said in a loud voice.

Joy frantically looked around for her aunt, realizing the crowd had closed in on her. She saw a sea of wide-eyed parents and young women linked to their arms. Joy tried to take slow breaths as her uncle had taught her when she panicked, but the hairs on her arm raised.

"All the young unmarried women need to step forward!" another guard yelled out.

Without warning, someone shoved Joy into the open space. She, along with a dozen or so women, was now in the middle of the crowds, surrounding a wagon and the soldiers.

"Joy," her aunt gasped behind her. Mari's eyes grew wide before looking to the guards. They were counting each one, pointing to each as they walked by.

"Auntie!" she exclaimed. "They pushed me in here, please believe me."

Aunt Mari saw the guard walking towards them before she looked back to Joy. "They have seen you now."

"No, I don't wish to be queen. Uncle will save us."

Aunt Mari looked at Joy, her eyes brimming with tears.

"You cannot run, Joy," she said in a hushed tone.

"But..." She looked around. "They are taking the girls to the palace. What am I supposed to do? I don't want to go."

"They will kill you if they find you running. They must not find out you are from the Ātash People, it is not safe now."

"But Auntie..." Joy clutched her aunt's hand.

"Keep yourself hidden, you cannot show who you are." Her aunt gave her a soft smile. "You must live." In one swift movement, Aunt Mari stripped off Joy's shawl.

Joy's eyes went wide as she immediately reached for her hair, trying to cover it. For the first time since she had bled, her hair was exposed. "Auntie," she breathed.

"May the will of the Ātash People protect you," she said, a tear still escaping as it rolled down her cheek.

"Here is another one!" The soldier who was stalking towards her earlier made a grab for her.

"Get up here." The leader of the soldiers was on a horse. The stomping of the hooves made Joy nervous.

"No," she stammered, shaking her head. "I can't." She started to reach for her aunt, but realized Mari had melted into the crowd.

"Come on," another soldier said in a calmer voice as he extended a hand to her. Cautiously, she took it.

Each woman was ushered into the wagon one by one, as if they were cattle. There were women of all ages, some with wisdom showing in their hair, some of them with their baby fat in their face, and some around her age. They were of all colors, races, and body types. Joy didn't know what was going to happen to her, steeling herself for all that was going to come in the following days.

"Excuse me," Joy said to the girl next to her. The woman was in loose-fitted clothing that hid little from the bosom up. "What is going to happen to us?"

The woman smirked. "We are going to the palace to replace the queen, of course. If you don't win, you become a mistress."

Joy's eyes widened. She didn't relish becoming a mistress, and was even less excited about becoming a queen.

It wasn't long before they entered into the inner palace walls. When the doors of the wagon swung open, light poured in, blinding Joy for a moment.

"Come on," one of the soldiers snapped.

One by one, they exited, allowing Joy to see the amount of wagons full of women. Though Joy wasn't able to determine the exact number of women that were pooling into the courtyard, it seemed more than the party the other night.

"Welcome everyone!" A dark-haired man smiled with his arms raised. "You have all been chosen to join the contest for the king's hand."

A murmur went through the crowd.

"However," the man said, "women must be of eligible age, so anyone born after the age of the Oryx is allowed to stay. Anyone born before the year of the Camel must go home. You will not be punished; nothing will happen to your family. Please return to your wagon."

Slowly, young women made their way back to their wagons.

"Additionally," the man smirked, "anyone caught lying about their age will be dealt with swiftly."

Small gasps were heard in the crowds before more young women made their way to the wagons.

"Wonderful!" The man clapped his hands. "Please follow the guards of your wagon to your respected rooms."

As they entered the grand palace, they were immediately ushered into a lavish room adorned with plush pillows in every color imaginable. The walls were draped with sheer curtains, creating a warm and inviting atmosphere. Plates overflowing with an array of delicious foods lined tables in the middle of the room, tempting their taste buds. Some of the women already present were dressed in exquisite gowns, each one more stunning than the next. It was like stepping into a world full of luxury and wealth—and it made Joy want to escape. They hadn't taken her name yet, so maybe she could still escape...

"Joy!" Cassia exclaimed, grabbing onto her friend. "You're here!"

Joy gave her a half-smile as she swallowed hard. Though she knew of Cassia's dream of being a mistress, she didn't imagine seeing her here.

"Isn't it wonderful?" her friend swooned.

"To be paraded around the palace like prize livestock? No," she said bitterly.

Cassia waved her off. "You worry too much. This is going to be wonderful for your family."

"How? My uncle and aunt are alone now."

"Your uncle is hardly ever home, serving the king," she waved a dismissive hand, "and your aunt has other relatives. I'm sure they are fine. Plus, we get money if they choose us."

"Choose us for what?" Joy's eyes narrowed. She was feeling more sick by the minute, unsure if it was the overwhelming smell of perfume or the smell of the lavish foods.

"For mistress," she said, matter-of-fact.

"I thought we were here to be queen." The queasiness seemed to be making the room swirl a bit.

"Only one can be the queen, silly." She gestured to the room of beautiful women. "Guessing by the state of how many women are here, I know I won't be chosen for queen, so I am going to settle for mistress like I always planned.

With luck, he won't visit me, and I can live a lavish life while sending money to my family."

"Is that what *you* want?"

"I can't do anything to change my fate, so I am making the best of it." She shrugged before turning to one of the female servants walking by. "Hey you," she said, snapping her fingers, "I need a refresher." She held up a silver goblet.

Joy had just noticed it in her hand and wondered when she obtained it. They just got into the room not long ago. Cassia had changed her voice to a lower tone that Joy had never heard before. The servant looked at Joy and then to Cassia as she silently nodded.

"Anything for you, ma'am?" she asked Joy.

Joy shook her head. "No, thank you."

The servant's mouth tugged at the corners slightly before she left.

"Cassia," Joy chided. "I don't think you should treat them as if they are your servants yet."

"Why not? I am going to be a mistress."

Joy winced. "They are humans, too."

"Slaves aren't human." Cassia scrunched up her nose before walking off.

The sickness of her stomach increased as she heard her friend. Cassia being born a Zephyrian, she never knew slavery. However, the Ātash People had been slaves under different kings before.

Joy's eyes roamed over the room, taking in the colorful array of handmade pottery, vibrant woven rugs, and delicate embroidered pillows scattered across every surface. She couldn't help but run her fingers over the intricate designs, marveling at the skill and artistry of each piece.

A gilded cage, slavery dipped in gold, she thought.

CHAPTER 4

Queen's Opening

"H EY YOU!" JOY LOOKED up and saw a woman who was lying down on some pillows snapping her fingers at the servants in the same fashion as Cassia had earlier. "I need a refill."

"Is it common for people to treat them like slaves?" she muttered to herself.

"Some of them *are* slaves," a woman in a royal blue saree with embroidered crystals said as she walked up to Joy. Zarak (goldish dust) glittered on her face and hair.

"But they are humans," Joy said firmly.

The woman smirked, giving a shrug. "Are slaves human?"

"Yes," she said as her jaw tightened.

The woman rolled her eyes as she started to walk away. "I can see where you will end up in this contest."

"I hope home..." she said softly.

The woman laughed loudly, saying from over her shoulder, "Good luck, kitten."

Tears threatened to fall, but Joy wouldn't allow it. She noticed that the other women here seemed too eager to leave their families, their freedom. She took another calming breath, her hands still wringing.

Joy quickly found a dark corner, untouched by anyone. She arranged the cushions into a makeshift bed, trying to keep from crying. Joy was taken from her home, her family, everything she loved—only to become a pleasure toy for some king.

Her eyes dulled as she watched the women interact with one another and the servants. She pulled the pillow closer to her chest as one woman threw a drink onto the ground. Several women snickered in her direction; Joy wasn't sure if it was at the woman or the servants scrambling to clean up the mess.

Her eyes grew heavy; Joy didn't even remember when she fell asleep. It was very late into the night when Joy was shaken awake. In her slumber, her eyes fuzzy, she saw the female servant Cassia had mistreated earlier. The room was dark, but she could make out her face clear enough.

"How may I help you?" she whispered.

The servant said nothing, motioning her to quietly follow her.

With careful steps, she tiptoed out of the room and into the grand hallway. The marble floors made no sound as she walked barefoot, making her way down the long corridor. They stopped at the end of the hallway where a dark, heavy curtain swept the floor.

Behind it was an outdoor terrace, bathed in the soft glow of moonlight. The cool night air brushed against her skin, carrying with it the faint scent of jasmine. She took a moment to breathe in the peacefulness of the night. Her skin prickled with the late coolness as she saw that she was high up in the palace, where below her was a lush garden. It was a sin to kill oneself, but how tempting it looked. She felt the cool of the stone ledge under her fingertips.

"Joy," a familiar voice said to her.

With a jolt, she turned around, and this time, she couldn't stop the tears. "Uncle Zeke," she sobbed as quietly as she could.

"Shh child." He made a quick grab for her, pulling her into a hug.

"Oh Uncle, I am frightened," she sobbed into his uniform.

"I know, child." He soothed her hair.

"What am I to do?" Her voice trembled as she clung onto him.

"I'm afraid, child, there is only one thing you can do."

"What is it?" She looked up at him, tears running down her face. "Auntie said I couldn't run from this."

"She is right, and I'm sorry, but I must ask more of you."

"What?" She wiped her tears away, trying to calm down.

"You must not say you are related to me."

"Why not?" She took a step back from him, confused. "Auntie said something similar. She said I must hide who I am."

"I am afraid that there are those who wish to do harm to the Ātash People. Free as we might be under Zephyria Law, we are still foreigners in this land. You must hide yourself, to protect yourself."

"I will do as you ask, Uncle..." She swallowed back some tears, nodding. "How will I keep people from learning who I am? Cassia is here and she knows that I am from the Ātash People."

His brows furrowed. "I doubt she will say anything, but I know they will be moving the women around in the coming days. There is a chance she won't be close to you. The advisors don't want sabotage."

"Sabotage? Will the women do that?"

Zeke nodded. "To be queen? Many women will do anything for such a position."

"What happened to the queen, Uncle?"

His lips pursed together. "I cannot say."

"But you know?"

He nodded.

"Okay." She nodded, steeling herself as she rolled her shoulders back. "What shall I be called?"

Her uncle looked up at the stars. "Estella, may the heavens look out for you."

"Estella," she repeated, the name foreign to her ears.

"Please know I think of you as my own daughter," he urged. "I want you safe, and right now, it is not for our kind."

Joy nodded. "I understand Uncle...um, I mean Zeke." She took a breath. "May I know who is against you?"

"In time." He kissed her forehead. "Now you must return to the room. We cannot meet again. They know I have a niece. I will have to say you moved on to get married. That way it isn't a lie."

"What if I need you?" Her eyes welled up as tears continued to threaten to fall once more.

"I will figure out a way, my child—" He shook his head. "Estella," he corrected. He gave a low royal bow to her, then disappeared behind the curtain.

Joy—or rather Estella—looked up at the sky, silently praying. She was alone, and there was very little she, or her family, could do about it. She worried for her auntie, but she supposed that her uncle could tell her about how she is doing. She sobbed as quietly as she could, knowing that she couldn't get caught, but she didn't want to cry in the room with the vicious women.

As she cried, letting the tears fall into the palm of her hand, someone stumbled onto the terrace. Estella instantly stopped crying, clutching her hands to her chest. The shadow was the shape of a man, and he tumbled through the curtain, probably thinking it was a solid wall.

"Goodness," she whispered, "are you okay?" He was tangled up in the curtain, on the floor like a spider caught in its own web. He also reeked of alcohol. "Sir?" she asked more sternly.

He burped. "Excuse me," he said, his words slurred.

She did her best to not grimace in front of him. "Sir, let me help you." She tried to help him on his feet. He flailed his arms around as if he was swatting a fly as he stood up.

"*Lanat beh*," he swore, trying to free himself.

Estella gasped. "Sir!"

In his drunken state, still covered by half of the curtain, he stopped moving and seemed to be staring at her. He really couldn't see her, but he was looking directly at her with the curtain on his head. "I'm sorry," he apologized. "I didn't know someone was here."

"I was just leaving..." She raised an eyebrow at him. "Are you all right? Do you need me to call someone for you?" She knew it would mean she would be in trouble, but she didn't like leaving someone in trouble.

The man swayed slightly. "No," he waved her off, the curtain still on his head, "I just had a bit too much to drink."

"I can see that," she remarked.

He chuckled. "You're feisty."

She wasn't being feisty; she was just honest with what she saw. "Are you sure you don't need me to call you someone?"

He shook his head vigorously as he swayed more, giving another burp. "I'm okay."

"Very well..." she said cautiously.

He swallowed hard, probably trying to suppress another burp. "Go ahead and go on." He motioned with his hand to beside him. "I'll be fine."

She bowed, though he wasn't in a state to see it. "Very well." She started to walk out, then stopped, turning back towards him. "Maybe don't drink so much. If you have a problem, drinking won't make the problem go away. It will still be there in the morning, but even worse because you'll have a headache."

He snorted. "Then what am I supposed to do?" He was still swaying, much like a tree in the wind.

"Play a game of chess," she suggested with a smile. "Good night." With that, she left.

"Chess?" he mused some more. "Why chess?"

"Sire!" a man hissed. "There you are!" The man pulled down the curtain and gave a worried expression to the drunk man. "Your highness," he groaned.

"Lysander." The king smiled, grabbing him by the shoulder. "I might have had a little too much to drink." He held out a finger, wagging it around. "Are you sure I have to marry someone?"

The servant nodded, careful with his facial expressions. "Yes, my lord."

"And," his smile turned into a smirk, "a girl spoke harshly to me."

Lysander's eyes widened. "Who?"

He shrugged. "I don't know. I didn't see who it was. But she…" He paused, looking far off. "She told me something strange."

"What was that?"

"To play chess." He chuckled before falling on top of Lysander, gently beginning to snore.

Estella sat there, bored. It had been a few days now since she had come to the *pretty cage* as she had affectionately begun to call it.

The ones in charge began to do a census on all the women, ensuring that no one was too young—or as they said, born before the year of the Camel. As promised by her uncle, after the census, they mixed up all the women. Cassia was sent to another room. Some of the women remained, but for the most part, everyone was shifted.

Now they were in the massive ballroom where the party was held, only to feel like it was ages ago.

"Did you hear that the mothers are allowed to help us get ready for the mask ball?"

"What ball?"

"Were you not listening to the eunuch? He said there would be a ball in two years when the king comes back from his travels."

"Why is he traveling?"

"He's returning his now ex-wife to her family." The woman snickered.

Estella had heard some about what happened to the queen in the last few days. From what she heard, the former queen, Tabitha, was banished back to her hometown. The king sent a letter that said he is no longer married to her by his own decree.

Estella sighed, leaning against her hand.

"I heard she had a lover," one woman chimed.

Not again, Estella thought.

"Nooo," said the first woman with a smirk. "I heard it was because she disobeyed him at the party in front of all his men."

That's a new one, she thought.

"And," the first woman continued, "he had already threatened her to obey him or he would send her back to her father."

The first woman chuckled. "Her sin is our blessing." The other woman joined in on her laugh.

"Ladies!" the blond man at the front of the door shouted. "I have an announcement."

All the sounds of squeals and laughter died and everyone was staring at him. "The king will be away for some time, and you all will have to get ready while he is gone. Be prepared." He bowed. "That is all."

The sounds resumed as everyone was more frantic.

The same pair of ladies walked by Estella again. "I bet he went to deal with his divorce so we don't go into war."

"I hope he doesn't come back with her," the other woman said.

"Oh, I doubt it," Estella said in a low tone. "After all, why bring all these women here?"

"You there!" a voice called out.

Estella looked up to see the young man with blond hair walking towards her. He was fit, but wore higher ranking servant clothes.

"Yes?" She stood up.

He looked her over, his eyes trailing over her body like she was cattle for sale. She knew he was the eunuch everyone talked about, but it made her skin crawl being looked over as if she was some piece of livestock.

"What is your name?" he finally asked.

"Jo—Estella," she said softly. "Estella," she repeated.

"Do you not have any family members?"

She shook her head. "No."

He nodded. "Okay, come with me."

"There is no need," she said quickly. "I have no family jewels, and since the king won't be here for a while, I don't see the need to rush."

He stopped walking and gave her a confused look. "The king is being kind to the women."

"Excuse me?" She blinked at him.

"He is spending time away from the palace to ensure that the women have complete devotion to preparing for what is to come next in the next year."

Estella continued to blink at him. "What is the year-long beauty treatment exactly?"

"My name is Lysander." He smiled before showing her into a bathhouse room. "We need to prepare you for the meeting of the king," he repeated.

Guess that is my answer, she thought. "Isn't it just us meeting him and him throwing away the losers?"

"That is a very cynical way of thinking." There was a hint of a smile on his lips.

"It's true, isn't it?" She smiled at him.

Lysander looked her over once more, but now it was more as a person. "I won't lie. I don't know what is to become of the women after the contest."

"So all he has to do is look me over and I can go home?" There was a glow to her cheeks as she said this.

"Oh no." Lysander shook his head. "If you fail becoming queen, there are several things that might happen. You become a mistress, a nun, or a servant. As a servant, you might become a mistress, but a nun can never hold a position of power."

"You mean I am stuck here?" There went the last dash of hope that perhaps she could go home.

"I'm afraid so. Did your family not tell you that before they sent you?"

She shook her head, "They didn't send me, I..." Her words trailed off as she looked to the side.

He nodded in understanding. "Fear not," he lifted up her chin, "I have a plan."

She took a deep breath. "What? Are you planning to have me escape?" she asked hopefully.

He shook his head, giving a nervous smile. "No, I don't want to die."

"Then what?"

"Let me make you into a queen."

CHAPTER 5

A Daughter Returned

TWO MONTHS SINCE THE PARTY

AMIR'S HEAD HURT. HE wished he could take a strong drink, but something about the girl who told him to play chess instead of drinking his problems away made Amir rethink his life. It also didn't help that he was bored, waiting for the groveling to end.

He had stopped listening to Tabitha's parents after the fifteenth apology. They were a king and queen from a small country that got swallowed up in the wars of his father's time. Though technically owned by Zephyria, they were their own country.

"Please, sire," the father begged once more. "She will mind, I promise you."

"Give her one more chance," the queen pleaded. "Marriage is forever, and it's about forgiveness." Amir knew her argument was more valid than the king's. However, it didn't sway him.

He gave a yawn and picked up a date, chewing on it.

"Sire," the king begged.

Amir swallowed the date and gave the king a deadpan expression. "I am not leaving her here because she misbehaved once. She misbehaved in front of my entire kingdom one too many times. There are countless rumors about her and some mysterious lover." He held up his hand to the small king. "I know there is no lover, however I can't ignore how many rumors have swirled. She has produced no heirs in the last six years of our marriage, and finally, plans are already in motion."

"What plans?" the queen asked, her brows furrowed.

Ah, he thought. *They haven't heard the news.* Amir smirked as he took another date. "Right now, in my palace, there is a contest on who will be my next queen. Dozens upon dozens of women are in my palace going through beauty treatments fit to become queen as we speak."

Tabitha's mother gasped, covering her mouth. The king's face grew red.

"My lord," his voice held warning, "if you truly plan to divorce my daughter and leave her here, I will—"

"What?" he cut him off. "I took your army." He paused, smirking. "Actually—my father took your army, and I saw no reason to change that fact. You have nothing to go to war on. We keep your money pretty tight with taxes, so there is no way for you to pay for another country's army."

The king said nothing, his chest rising and falling, his face growing paler the more he thought about it.

"Surely—" the queen started.

"Surely nothing," he cut her off. "The queen is hereby stripped of her title, and is not allowed to step foot in the capital ever again. Doing so will get her hanged like a dog," he paused, pouring a small amount of honey on his date, "or worse."

The queen's hand went to her throat; the king said nothing.

"Don't worry," Amir's smirk grew wider, "now you have a daughter who will take care of you in your old age." His voice grew more sinister. "Forever."

Tears welled in the queen's eyes and the king made a tsk sound.

Amir took a handful of dates as he got up. "Now, if you excuse me, I would like to retire."

Once in his room with his servants and guards, he sighed. "Hamid," he said in a low voice. From the shadow came a young guard.

"Yes, my lord?" He bowed low.

"You were there. Tell me what you think, honestly. I don't want the *it's not your place* business."

"I think that your father made some enemies over the course of his reign."

Amir nodded, scratching his chin. "I agree, I will have to visit them."

"Sire..." Hamid started.

"Yes?"

"What about the capital?"

He rolled his eyes. "I am going back at the last possible moment."

"May I ask why, sir?"

Amir scratched the back of his neck before taking off his shirt. "Growing up in the outer palace, I saw many women come in and parade like peacocks around my father. They would dress up every day, waiting to see if he would come by to pay attention to them. Looking back, I realized my father liked the attention from them. However," he groaned, "*I* hated it. They were always trying to outdo one another. They would sabotage each other at any chance they got."

Amir softly landed on his bed, allowing the soft scent of lavender to fill the air.

"I gave them the palace to get ready," he said finally. "To perhaps bond with one another instead of trying to kill one another. I don't want to be cooed at like a cat in heat."

"Cats purr, my lord," Hamid corrected.

Amir let out a bellyful laugh as he sat up. "Thank you, Hamid." Amir knew he was young and didn't know the rules, but Zeke recommended him as a guard on the trip. Most servants and guards wouldn't have spoken their minds, much less corrected him.

"I think I will take a bath. Someone please tell me where it is."

"Would you like your normal wine with your bath?" a female servant asked with her head bowed low.

Amir stared at her for a moment, not because he was interested in her physically, but because he once again remembered the random girl on the terrace who had told him to stop drinking. He remembered a vague shape of her. She was shorter than him by a good margin, but she looked at him directly. Probably because she didn't know who she was talking to.

"Sire?" the maid asked.

"Oh," he blinked a few times, "no, I will just soak off the journey."

"Then your wine after the bath?" she asked, hopeful.

Amir internally groaned. *How much do I drink?* "I'll take on a game of chess. Find someone who is good at the game."

Amir saw the confusion written on the servants' faces. This wasn't normal behavior from him, and for some reason, it bothered him severely that he was predictable. What bothered him more was that he was a heavy drinker without realizing it.

After a few long, tense moments, the maid nodded. "O-of course, my lord."

Amir made a mental note to take Lysander with him next time. He left him, thinking it would be better to see who was the right fit to be queen. Lysander had been with Amir before he was king, and therefore knew how to handle anything he asked.

His bath didn't take longer than normal, but it felt longer. Probably because there was no wine. When he came out and into his room, he found a disheveled old man in his room.

"Who is this?"

The servants were sweating profusely. Hamid stepped forward, also sweating. "He is the only one in this village who said he knew how to play chess."

Amir raised an eyebrow at the old man. He had aged, weathered skin that looked like he had spent too much time in the sun. Amir wasn't prejudiced about people for the most part, but was there no one else who knew how to play chess in this town?

"Are you ready, your majesty?" The old man's voice sounded strained.

Sighing, Amir nodded, taking a seat across from him.

"I already checked him, sire," Hamid reassured.

"All right." He waved him off. "Black or white?"

"I'll give you the white, majesty." He gave a smile, and Amir noticed some of his teeth were missing.

"Very well." He moved his knight first.

"Hmm..." The man put his finger to his thin lips, and stared at the board. Amir waited. And waited. The man took his time as he stared at the board. Amir knew chess wasn't always a fast game unless you played with someone who really didn't know how to play.

Another minute passed as Amir stared anywhere else but the board. He craved a drink— one was even offered to him, his servants probably noticing how agitated he was.

"Good sir," he said, annoyed. "Please choose a spot. It is the opening move."

The man nodded. "Thus, it is the most important."

"What?" He sat up straighter, leaning in ever so slightly towards the man.

"The opening move tells you how the rest of the game will go. Do not fret, my lord, the game will move on much faster once I make my first move."

"Why is the first move the most important? Isn't the finishing blow important?"

"Ah," the man grinned, "how do you get to the finishing move?"

"What?"

"In order to get to my king, you must move all the obstacles in your way first. You cannot do that unless I plan poorly. My goal is to make sure I defend while I attack you. I must be diligent not to waste my moves, or sacrifice my men needlessly."

Amir looked down at the board, seeing only his right-hand knight move to the right, above the furthest pawn.

"Tell me, my king," the old man asked thoughtfully, "why did you choose the knight to go there?"

"Uh…" He didn't have an answer. A king shouldn't share their weakness, but he felt as if he should tell the truth. "I don't know."

The man nodded, pointing at each piece. "It is a very passive move, your highness. Not one played too often. Many novices play this move thinking it will help them win. You are a king, you have played before. I am sure against many people who are not as good as yourself."

Amir gave a single nod.

"However…" The man finally picked up a piece, moving the pawn which was in front of his king piece and placed it two squares ahead. "Chess allows me to see how the man thinks."

Amir moved his piece, and the man followed through it. Piece after piece, they moved, until—

"Checkmate, my lord." The old man gave a smile that almost resembled pity.

Seven moves. It took all of seven moves for this weathered old man to checkmate him. Amir was not the best player, however there seldom were games where he lost. Especially as a man, a king.

"How?" he asked softly.

"You played to play my lord, not to win. Chess is involved in all parts of life."

"I wonder if that's why she said to play it," he murmured to himself, looking away.

"Oh? Your wife?"

Amir looked back at him surprised. "No, a woman told me to stop drinking and face my problems with chess."

The man chuckled. "A smart woman, she is. If she is not your wife, send her to me. I would like to see what her opening move in chess would be."

Amir gave a gentle smile to the man. Though he didn't know who she was, he too wanted to see her play against this old man.

"Shall we play again?" Amir asked.

The man nodded. "It would be my pleasure, my lord."

CHAPTER 6

Lessons

WITH EVERYONE GATHERED, LYSANDER had instructed the main gardeners to teach about proper garden etiquette—especially when with the king. Most of the palace dwellings were in the inner palace close to the king, and it was instructed that no one was to enter the glass dome without permission. However, the outer palace was overshadowed by the inner palace, which was built in the last king's reign, and connected through the gardens.

Many of the girls were yawning, clearly bored with the lesson they had to learn. Happily, none of the mothers were allowed at this lesson. However, Estella was quite taken with the lesson. She heard the king had planted some of the plants in the garden, so it was important not to pick anything. Only the king knew which were his plants. Not even the gardeners knew for certain.

"Please be aware of not going into the king's private area unless you are invited by the king himself. We are not even allowed in there to tend to them."

"What? That seems silly. He goes to war," one girl who had her arms crossed sneered.

The man nodded. "I agree, but the king has expressed that if they run wild, or die, so be it. No one is to tend to them but the king himself."

"Why?"

"It is not for us to question," the man frowned at the girl, "he is the king." He finished answering the other girls' questions and moved on to what kind of flowers were in bloom at the time of the king's return.

Then a small clang rang out. Lysander stood in front of a long table, bowing. "My ladies, it is time to eat. All the food has been tested, so please, feel free to eat it."

A loud sound of squeals came from the girls as they ran towards the table. Plates clanged against each other and giggling ensued. Estella slowly made her way to the gardener who looked a little cross.

She bowed her head and smiled at him. "Thank you for the lesson."

The man blinked at her. "Uh..." he stammered. "You're welcome."

Her smile broadened. "One day if we are free, please tell me which is the king's favorite."

The man nodded as he swallowed hard. "Of course, I would love to."

"Excuse me, I have to get some food. Thank you, once again." Estella turned and got in the long line. It seemed as if some of the girls were afraid it would run out if they didn't shove others to the back. She looked ahead and saw Cassia now dressed in an expensive velvet dress, which was different than most of the girls around her.

"Checking out the competition?" The girl next to her chuckled.

Estella looked at her, seeing that she was dressed in something that looked like it was dipped in gold, but it was definitely fake. She had a thin figure and a very thin, long face.

"No," she shook her head, "I saw an old friend."

"Friend?" She snorted. "There are no friends here. Just competition."

"Wouldn't it be better to make some friends here since we all will be living together? It isn't as if once one gets chosen, we go back home."

The girl looked her up and down. Estella was wearing a powder blue dress that was made from cotton. It was lightweight and not flashy in any way. "I can see who is going to the nunnery."

Estella decided not to answer that, even though she wanted to. She never thought herself a great beauty, but she certainly wasn't ugly just because she had on a plain dress. She relaxed her shoulders and went back to the food.

She slowly picked out what she wanted; happily, the kingdom had similar tastes in food that she was used to. No pork, no seafood, and lots of beef to eat. Though her family wasn't against the consumption of alcohol, there was a rule about getting drunk. She would have to be careful about some of the foods she suspected had alcohol.

She thought back to the man from the other night. He was absolutely drunk, and though she wouldn't dare to rat him out, it was a rather shocking sight. She hoped he wasn't the person who handled the money. He was dressed in a simple tunic from her memory.

"Estella?"

She looked up and saw Lysander's furrowed brows.

"Yes?"

"What's wrong? Are you ill?"

She quickly shook her head. "No, I feel quite well."

His furrowed brows didn't lessen, but he seemed to look her over as a concerned mother would have. "I cannot have any of the women sick, so I need to make sure you're all right."

She gave a reassuring smile to him as she grabbed a piece of tandoori naan. "I'm very well, thank you."

He nodded, though reluctant, before looking over the rest of the women.

Estella looked around the room where they were all placed. The room was decorated in bold colors and some heavy curtains. It was some sort of a tea room to accept private guests. It had a more feminine touch to it, and Estella wondered if it was one of the previous queen's rooms.

Lysander walked up to the women. "Gather around." He snapped his fingers and several servants came out with small tables; then another set of servants came out as they placed some items down. "Everyone, please sit at the tables."

All the women sat down; once seated, Estella saw that it was a small wooden box and a stylus of some sort next to it.

"Open the boxes," Lysander commanded.

They did so, and inside was the small wooden box with wax laid out. Estella had never seen anything like this before.

"These are known as wax tablets. They are going to be used to teach you all how to write. As a queen, there will be expectations of you writing letters and invitations. You will have to read as well, should the king send you an invitation for your eyes only. These things are important for you to understand."

One of the girls raised her hand.

"Yes?" he asked.

"Is this for us to keep?"

He nodded. "These are reusable. It's a way for us to not use all the parchment. I have to teach each room separately."

"This is pointless." One girl crossed her arms. "Those of us who know already should be automatically qualified to be queen."

Lysander frowned at her. "The former queen had all the poise and learning of what is right, and yet she still lost her crown. Be careful, little one, for your tongue might also make you lose your crown."

Her hand went to her throat, her eyes widened.

He turned back to all the women. "Learning is an important part of being queen. I am not saying you need to know all of the books in the king's library, but you need to be able to write and read some. Those who already know how to read and write may choose not to come to the classes from here on out. But do not be fooled into thinking it will give you an advantage. You never know what kind of information you learn from anywhere."

The girl gave a soft tsk before she pressed her lips together. Estella knew very little of writing and reading. She knew numbers and math, since the women in her tribe were in charge of all the money.

Lysander clapped his hand. "The other end of the stylus is meant to rub out any mistakes you make. Let us begin with the letters."

CHAPTER 7

Advice

THREE MONTHS SINCE THE PARTY

IF AMIR KNEW HOW much trouble divorce was, he might have reconsidered it. Not only did he have to leave Tabitha with her parents, he had to, under advice, pay a visit to all the records of the country to make sure there were no hidden surprises. He gave a yawn from the lack of sleep. He had been playing with the old man since he arrived, and when he wasn't playing with him, he was trying to find new ways to beat him.

A knock came on the door. "Come in," he said quickly.

A small woman came in with a silver tray with parchment on top of it. "A letter for you, my lord."

Amir looked to his left, took the letter, and began examining the seal, seeing it was a sea green with some fancy swirls on it. "Hm, the King of Zerzura has sent a letter." He quickly scanned the contents and then slammed his fist down on the table, sending chess pieces flying. Amir stared at the letter, rage bellowing inside him.

"Sire?" Hamid asked, picking up a few pieces that flew far.

"It appears I must visit Zerzura as our next stop. Ready the horses."

"Right away, my lord," he said quickly before leaving.

Amir looked at the pieces that were toppled over, though in truth he wasn't actually looking at the chessboard. He was going to have to deal with that problem with the King of Zerzura later; for now, he had to figure out how to stay away from his garden for the next year. His plants wouldn't survive if he stayed away too long.

"Kaulu," he said quickly in a low voice, "please bring me paper and a pen. I need to send Lysander something."

The maid brought a letter set to him, which included his wax, ink, and parchment. He quickly jotted down the thoughts he had, sealed it, and handed it to the maid. "Send this to Lysander immediately. He is the only one to open this letter. Understand?"

The maid nodded before running off.

A soft knock came on the door, making Amir look at it. It was the old man.

"Hello, my lord." He smiled.

"Hello."

He gave a bow of his head. "I heard you are leaving today."

Amir nodded.

"I was wondering, my lord, one more game?"

Amir smiled. "Yes, of course."

"Thank you, my lord. It has been so long since I have had someone to play with. I truly enjoy our games."

"I will have to visit often to play with you." Amir reset the board, picking up some of the pieces that Hamid didn't get, as the old man sat down.

"Yes," he nodded, "please bring your wife when you come back."

Amir raised an eyebrow. "I have no wife, remember?"

"But you will." The old man looked at the board, seeing he was white this time.

Amir shrugged. "Perhaps, if the right woman can be found."

"Ah, that is tricky." The old man looked at each piece before finally settling on a pawn, moving it one space ahead.

The king countered it, placing his pawn close by. "I am sorry you do not live in my country. I could set you up in a nice place."

The old man shook his head as he moved another pawn. "No, my lord, I am happy here. It is nice to be happy with little than be miserable with much."

Amir chuckled, moving another piece. "You plan to win again."

"I always plan to win." The man smirked.

Amir smiled, then an idea came to him. "What would you think of me having a contest for my future wife?"

"Isn't that what you're doing?"

"I mean having them all play chess, to see who is able to play against me."

"Chess would be a good way to check if they can think through or," he paused as he moved another piece, "if they will lose." It was checkmate.

Amir stared at the pieces. "There were several possibilities for that last move you did."

The old man nodded.

"But it won?"

"It's all about thinking things through." He pointed to the pieces. "This piece could have gone, but it also could have been this piece." He pointed to another piece on the board.

"But that one I could have won."

He nodded. "Yes, so have your man-servant set it up exactly like this, and hopefully you will find the mystery woman who told you to play chess."

"What if she doesn't solve it correctly?"

The old man chuckled. "You will find her."

CHAPTER 8

Opening Move

THREE AND A HALF MONTHS SINCE THE PARTY

ACROSS FROM HIM SAT a new opponent; this man was quite younger than the old man from the other village. It was interesting how one girl's comment, one he is still yet to meet, made him take up chess in a new way.

Amir smiled gently as he looked at the board, deciding to play one of the techniques he had learned from the old man. There were quite a few pieces still left on the board, and if he didn't play it right, the game could be extended. If he did play it right...

"Checkmate." Amir smiled, leaning against his arm.

The man stared, mouth agape, at the board. Then he grinned at Amir. "That was quite impressive, my lord."

Amir sat up straight, still smiling. "Thank you for playing with me. My guards will escort you back to where you want to go."

The man stood up and bowed respectfully before leaving.

Amir looked back at the board, seeing how the man played right into the trap. Just as he had when the old man played it against him.

"Sire, shall I clear it for you?" one of the maids asked with her head bowed.

"No," Amir waved her on, "I would like some paper and a pen. I need to send another letter to Lysander."

"Very well, your majesty." She left and quickly returned with the items he had requested.

Amir quickly jotted down his thoughts, and drew a small picture with it. He hoped that it would bear the fruit he wanted. He knew Lysander would understand, but not being there made his stomach upset.

"Send this to Lysander post haste. He will know what to do."

The maid nodded. "Very well, my lord."

When Lysander received the second letter in front of everyone, he quickly opened it. However, there was a horde of women who suddenly wanted to be closer to him. Word had quickly spread that he was the right-hand man of the king. He wasn't exactly trying to keep it a secret, but he also wasn't going around telling any of the women or their mothers.

He pinched the bridge of his nose before making a quick exit to the servant area. With each room, a curtain had been placed for the servants to prepare drinks, food, and the likes for the royal family.

He began to read the letter again, and another servant came up to him.

"What is it, Lysander?" they asked.

He groaned looking at the other servant. "He wants to find the girl from the other night."

"How? You asked every servant, and they all said it wasn't them."

"Yes, which means it's one of the women." He glanced behind him, peeking through the curtain, seeing all the women chatter among themselves.

"Do you think the king believes she is one of the candidates?"

"I believe the king would think I would have found the woman if I was able to; now he is trying a new method."

"But that means they were out of the room in the middle of the night." Sweat beaded down the other servant's face.

Lysander nodded. "I don't think it was for anything nefarious, but he wants us to—" he cut himself off, looking around. "Get these things ready in the other room. We will do as the king requires." Lysander gave the other servant a list of the items.

The servant ran off, leaving Lysander, who took a deep breath before exiting the curtain. When he looked out, there were dozens of hungry eyes staring at him. Fear crept into the pit of his stomach as each woman wondered what he had retrieved from the king.

"Ladies," he smiled the best way he knew how, "we will be returning to our rooms now." Several claps rang out, bringing out servants, guards, and the likes, moving the girls back into their rooms.

Estella looked at Lysander before she left, seeing the way his smile was plastered on.

"What do you think happened?" one girl whispered to another.

"I don't know, but if that eunuch thinks we will go away quietly, he is wrong."

The girl softly gasped. "Do you think he found another woman in his travels?"

A girl behind them scoffed. "I hope not. We will squeeze her out."

A few of the girls who were listening nodded. Estella wanted to roll her eyes at the pettiness of the other women, but dared not make a single movement that would suggest she wasn't on their side.

Once they reached their room, the women grew loud. No longer whispering amongst each other, they were theorizing out loud.

"If she comes here, we will give her the silent treatment."

Another girl cackled. "How about the leftover scraps with every meal?"

"Oh, I like that," another girl chimed in. "We don't share any of the blankets with her."

Estella stared in earnest at the women, not because she wanted to join in on the fun, but because she couldn't believe they were being so cruel to a woman they hadn't even met. If she did exist at all.

The girls went on for what felt like hours, talking about the cruel things they were going to do to the new girl if she came into the room. Others talked about what they were going to do to make themselves outshine the others. Estella grew tired after a while and began to practice her writing. Lysander had given all the girls lessons in writing and reading. Estella knew a little of reading, but she didn't know how to write. It was easy to lay low that way. Most of the women in her room already knew how to write, and even read.

The room quickly silenced when a knock on the door came, making every woman turn their head towards it. Lysander, his hands folded, stepped in a small bead of sweat on his brow.

"From here on out, the king has a series of tests for his future queen. You are prohibited to share what the challenge is with others. In doing so, you will be asked to leave and placed into a nunnery." Lysander's face grew serious, his eyes narrowed. "Do not think for one second that we will not find out if you do."

Estella's spine tingled as she looked at him. If looks could kill, that one would. If a servant, the right-hand man of the king looked like that, she wondered what the king looked like.

"Now," Lysander relaxed into a soft smile, "I shall call out a few girls at a time to come with me for their challenge. Please be ready. No need to change." He grabbed a piece of parchment from the servant on his left. "Kali, Ashley, Vashti, Jade, Simran, and Estella." A hush went through the room. "Everyone will be called eventually, but this is the first set. Remember, no one talk about the challenge."

Estella was surprised she was called upon first, but she stood up, smoothing her dress.

"Come," he said in a cool tone.

The sound of their shoes echoed off the stone flooring. The other women dared not to say anything after Lysander's speech. Estella looked at the paintings on the wall as she walked with everyone, noting that it was a collection from many different places. Most of these were not normal Zephyrian-type paintings.

These were more realism than bold colors with landscapes. The colors weren't muted, but the brushstrokes were more about the subject than the whole painting. Lysander starting speaking again, and this snapped Estella back to the subject at hand.

"One by one, you will go into the room, and there, I will discuss what to do for your challenge. Those outside will wait for your turn." He turned to one of the women. "Vashti, you are first." The woman was decorated in gold and white linen, her silken, black hair cascaded down her back as she stepped forward.

If Estella didn't know better, she would have guessed that she was the queen.

"I am ready," she said in a silky voice that was deep and seductive.

Lysander was unfazed as he turned and led her through the doors. Once the door closed, the other girls began to whisper to each other.

"What is it?"

"Do you think we have to eat something?"

"What if they make you read something out loud?" another girl said with horror in her voice.

"What if we have to build something?"

"I doubt we have to build something, but remember he likes the gardens. What if we have to name all the flowers?"

Each girl chattered for a few minutes, then the doors opened once more. Vashti walked out with elegance in each step and her head held high. However, Estella noticed the slightest quiver in her lip, as if she was upset. She wondered if she would fail at whatever test they had set up.

"Next will be Ashley," Lysander said in an even tone.

Ashley bit her lower lip as she stepped forward. She was dressed in a deep blue saree with silver jewelry and silver thread on her outfit. There was a glamorous air to her, as if she was a princess, but not the queen just yet. The second wife perhaps.

"I'm ready," she said softly.

They walked into the room, Lysander closing the door behind them. Some of the girls tried to look into the room, but nothing was seen. When the doors closed, they looked at Vashti who said nothing as she stood there.

"Vashti, can you really not say anything?"

She simply shook her head.

Estella looked her over, noticing that there was no physical change in her. There was nothing on her perfectly clean hands. Her outfit was the same, and not even her silken hair had been disturbed. Estella looked back at the doors, wondering what was behind them to make Lysander make such a threat to them.

After another minute, Ashley and Lysander came out of the room—Lysander looking more annoyed and Ashley looking as if she wanted to cry.

"Remember," Lysander stated, his voice cool, "do not discuss the challenge and do not even talk to those who have taken it. The king has commanded that it be kept a secret." The two women clung to each other and nodded silently. Lysander smiled brightly. "Now, on to the next."

It took a long time to go through each one. Not everyone was gone for the same amount of time. Some of them took longer and some took less time. Estella was the last one to go, and based on all the looks of the women, there was much to be nervous about.

"Ready, Estella?" Lysander asked, but this time, his smile was slightly more genuine.

She nodded, swallowing hard.

He guided her into the room, closing the door, and in the room, where sheer curtains hung up everywhere. The balcony door was open, and it made them dance around softly, allowing Estella to see that there was a small table and two chairs set up in the middle of the room. Lysander made no movement, just continued to smile at her.

Estella walked over to the table, and looked at it. Her eyes widened as she saw what was on the table. A chess board, mostly completed. Some of the pieces were on the side, showing they had been taken. Some of them were still positioned where they started.

"What is this?"

"The king requests that the ladies must be able to finish this."

"Why?"

He gave a shrug. "Not for me to say. The king's will is his law."

Estella nodded. "Which one am I?"

"Black," he simply said.

"Black?" She furrowed her brows as she looked at the table. There were a few possibilities, and though the game would continue, she doubted that the king wanted to play a game with her or any of the women. She wasn't a great chess player, and though she had on occasion beat her uncle at chess, she didn't know all of the plays.

Slowly, she sighed, picking up the bishop, and moved him to the appropriate spot. "Checkmate," she said softly.

"What?" Lysander moved to her. "What happened?"

"Checkmate," she repeated.

"What does that mean?"

"It means I won, white lost, and if I was playing against someone who was a sore loser, I would be playing again."

Lysander stared at the board in amazement.

"Is that the challenge?"

He nodded, his mouth slightly open.

"Lysander?"

He closed his mouth and looked at her. "Yes?"

"What else is it?"

"Nothing, it was just the game."

"Oh..." She looked to the door. "Why the big secret?"

"The king wrote he wanted to see who could solve it."

"There are a lot of smart women here, and I was the last of the first group, surely you expect some of them to talk about it." She paused, looking at the board once more. "Should I put my piece back where it was?"

He nodded. "Thank you, Estella."

"Of course," she smiled. "If there is nothing else, I will return and then go back to my studying."

"Yes, let us get you back to the room."

True to their word, no one spoke about the challenge. However, once all the rooms and all the women had finished, Lysander mentioned to another servant in front of them, probably on purpose, that several of the women had solved the challenge. Everyone knew what the challenge was, but no one spoke of it.

CHAPTER 9

We Shall See

FOUR MONTHS SINCE THE PARTY

LYSANDER PACED BACK AND forth, chewing on his thumb nervously. He paused, looked over to his left, and immediately went back to pacing.

"Will you calm down, Lysander?" Amir asked as he looked at the chess board that he had all the women compete against.

"Sire, you are here—and in a guard's uniform no less!" His voice went into a high-pitched squeal.

"Technically, I am in Zeke's uniform."

"That's another thing!" He looked over at Zeke who was standing in attention, dressed in some plain training clothes. "Zeke, say something to his majesty."

"What would you like me to say?" he asked in a monotone voice.

"Anything!" he sobbed.

"Lysander, calm down," Amir said in a low, calm voice as he moved another pawn.

"You say that, but you're not supposed to be here. And to come back for your garden is—" Lysander cut himself off. Nothing he could say was going to be appropriate considering his status.

Amir looked at him for a long moment, wondering if he wanted to finish his sentence.

Lysander cleared his throat. "I'll prepare everything for you." With that, Lysander left the room with only Zeke and Amir in it.

"I think the women are making him gain a backbone." Amir smiled, shaking his head as he went back to his game.

Zeke said nothing as he stood there.

Amir looked at him, raising an eyebrow. "Speak, Zeke."

"It is not my place."

"I told you repeatedly, it is *my place* to tell you to speak plainly."

"Yes, my lord." Zeke bowed his head. "I think Lysander is worried about your well-being."

"I am worried about my plants."

"Yes, my lord."

"What else?"

"I think the women have made a difference in the palace. It is more lively than before."

"You don't say that like it's a good thing."

"Everything in moderation."

"Is that what your creator says?"

"Yes." He kept his head bowed.

"What else does your creator say?"

"Sire?" Zeke looked up for a moment, then remembered himself, standing at salute.

"You're part of the People of the Sun god, aren't you?"

"Not quite, my lord." Zeke didn't like to correct the king. "Of the Ātash People, is what we are known as."

"Tell me more about them."

Zeke opened his mouth to answer.

"A bunch of pagans," Darius said as he walked into the room. "I heard from that man-servant of yours that you were back."

Amir gave a pointed look to his friend. "I am to assume you threatened him in order to get that information."

Darius placed a hand on his heart. "How cruel, I am your friend. I deserve to know where you are."

Amir rolled his eyes as he placed another pawn on the side. "He isn't supposed to tell anyone. I would hate to punish him because you threatened him."

"He's a servant, it is fine."

Amir's eyebrow twitched. Though he always knew there was a status difference, he thought of Lysander as a trusted servant, a loyal friend. "My friend," he said, giving a glare from the side of his eye, "do not threaten my servants and go against my law."

Darius nodded. "Very well."

Amir moved the last piece, making a checkmate, then getting up from his seat. "Now, if you excuse me, I have a garden to tend to."

Darius smiled at his friend. "Always with that garden. If you made love as often as you tend to that garden, you might have had some heirs by now."

Amir rolled his eyes, smiling as he walked into the hallway. He was dressed as a guard, and as he passed one of the inner court gardens, he heard a woman's voice.

"Once there was a farmer, who was neither rich nor poor. He just was."

Amir stopped, seeing several women gathered at the feet of one woman who was perched on the fountain in the middle of the garden. From what Amir could see of her, she had dark hair, placed into a high bun and covered with a veil.

Strange, he thought, knowing veils weren't a Zephyrian tradition. The woman was facing away from him, so he couldn't catch a good look at her face.

"This old man once had a horse, a beautiful stallion who was strong and well-trained. One day, after a storm, the gate that held the horse broke. The horse ran away. The villagers came by to see what had happened. One of the villagers had said, 'What horrible luck.' The old man simply replied, 'We'll see.' He shrugged and went on to repair his fence.

"Just as the old man finished the fence, the horse came back, this time with a harem of horses. The villagers, of course, came by and heard he had more horses now. 'What great luck!' a villager announced. The old man closed the gate to the horses, and gave a shrug. 'We'll see.' Confused, the villagers went back home. How could more horses be bad? They can be eaten, used for labor, and they can be traded. Nothing was wrong with owning more horses.

"It was then, after the horses had been there for some time, that the eldest son of the old man began taming all the horses. One by one, he tamed each one. Until he came upon a young colt who was difficult to ride. The son made one more attempt to tame this wild beast. He gripped the horse and rode that colt. Unfortunately, that colt had more power than the son thought. The horse threw him, and the son broke his leg. The doctor quickly came to set the leg. Along with the doctor came all the villagers. One of them said, 'Oh farmer, you were right. It wasn't good luck to have all those horses. Your son is left broken.'" She paused.

"Go on." One of the women leaned forward.

"Yes," Amir silently whispered to himself, "go on." He knew she couldn't hear him, but he wanted to hear the rest of the story.

She took a sip of her water. "Very well. It was then that a war broke out. The king asked for all the sons who were able to fight. This left out the son with the broken leg. While all the other sons were taken away, the old man got to keep his son. The villagers came to him once more, congratulating him on keeping his son. 'What great luck! How blessed you are!' they all said to him. The old farmer simply smiled at his friends. 'We shall see,' he simply said."

"Go on," the woman urged.

The one telling the tale chuckled slightly. "That is the end of the tale. The story has no ending. It is only a tale about how you don't know how life will turn out. Sometimes bad things happen, and good things can happen from them."

A woman scoffed as she sat back. "That was a dumb story. They need endings."

"Not all stories have endings. Sometimes we don't know what happens after the story is done."

"What do you think will happen next?"

The woman shrugged. "If I had to guess, something happens in the war, like a daughter takes a horse and runs away. But she comes back with a husband who is a war hero."

"Why does the daughter run away?"

"Because I believe in romance." The woman laughed.

Someone cleared their throat, and Amir turned around to see Lysander looking up at him. "Sire," he ground out in a low voice. "You are to be tending to the gardens, not listening to the women tell stories."

Amir gave a sheepish smile to him.

"Lysander, is anything wrong?" the storyteller asked.

Amir wanted to turn around and see her, but he figured Lysander wouldn't like that. "Nothing," he smiled at them, "go back to your stories." He began to push Amir towards the private gardens.

She giggled. "Very well."

Amir started to look towards the women, but by then, the storyteller had turned back to the others. He groaned as he started to walk on his own. "All right, Lysander, I am going."

"Sire, I don't mean to physically push you, but I do have to make it like you're a guard and you aren't supposed to be here."

"No one knows what I look like."

Lysander groaned. "Many of them do. So please, tend to your flowers, then go home."

"This is my home, Lysander."

Lysander's face grew red. "I misspoke; go back on your journey. You told me not to let you come back home, because you didn't want to be fawned over like the late king. I am trying my best to do as my king commanded."

"I am your king." Amir snickered.

"No, right now, you're a guard at the palace."

Amir was still snickering as he walked towards his private gate. "Come in, Lysander, I need to talk to you privately."

Lysander nodded, following the king in the fenced off area. To say a fenced area was an understatement. The private gardens of the king were in a glass dome greenhouse. It was vastly large despite the look from the outside. The king had gathered flora and fauna from all over to fill his private garden.

Amir smiled as he looked at his garden. It was green, lush, and starting to turn wild from not pruning. He shook his head, as he picked up his shears from the side and began at the rose bush next to him. They were desert roses, and they needed to be treated with care. Lysander stood very still behind him.

"Lysander," he said calmly as he snipped a piece off. "Who were the ladies who passed the exam?"

"There were several."

"Tell me their names."

"Very well, my lord." He pulled out a small scroll from his pocket. "Zahra, Samira, Yasmin, Noor, Jamilah, Fatima, and Estella."

"Are they all from the same place?"

"No, my lord."

"Hmm." Amir snipped another vine that was turning black. "What is each woman like?"

"Some of them are very sweet to the staff. Some are uneducated in writing and reading, despite the lessons you had given to them."

"And?"

"And, my lord?"

"What else? There is something you want to say."

Lysander took a deep breath. "I do not want to show favoritism to anyone, but there is one that shines above the rest."

Amir paused, cutting another stem. He turned around while still on his knees and raised an eyebrow at him. "Oh? Lysander likes one of them?"

"Not in a romantic way."

"Just you taking a shine to anyone is something to be praised."

"My lord, I like a great many people."

Amir chuckled as he went back to his bush. "Who is she? Royal?"

"No, my lord."

"Tell me about her, but do not tell me her name yet."

"She is respectful, my lord. She treats those around her with kindness, and though she isn't of royal blood, she carries herself as if she were a queen."

Amir rolled his eyes. "So she is arrogant."

"No," Lysander said quickly. "She is..." He trailed off.

"Say it," Amir commanded as he moved onto another bush.

"She reminds me of the second queen," he said softly.

Amir stopped moving. He was so still, you might think he wasn't breathing. After a hard swallow, he resumed his work. "What makes you say that?"

"She uses the servants' names when speaking to them. She listens to them. She doesn't do everything on her own, but if she can, she will retrieve something. She is not creating waves between the women, but trying to make friends with them, especially in her room."

"Very interesting," he said finally when Lysander finished. "She has the material of a true queen."

"Yes, my lord." Lysander bowed his head.

Amir wanted to know who she was. He wanted to see what kind of woman she was; one that would figure out his chess puzzle while also having Lysander take a shine to her. It couldn't be just her being kind, or that she reminded him of Amir's mother. There had to be something else. However, he knew that he couldn't show favoritism immediately. The chess challenge wasn't even for the queen challenge—it was for finding the woman who told him to play instead of drinking away his problems.

Finally, he rose from the ground. "Lysander, I hope you will do everything in your power to make sure the correct woman is to become queen, regardless of your feelings, or mine. The future queen must be someone with all the morals of a ruler."

Lysander nodded in understanding. It was the women's job to outshine the other, to stand out on their own, to ensure that they were truly a star in the night sky.

CHAPTER 10

The Hand We're Dealt

I T HAPPENED THAT ESTELLA was the only one left in the classroom. Some of the other ladies gave up after a few weeks. Estella knew how to read by now, and write well enough for real paper, not just the wax tablet. Lysander usually would sit there with her, writing something in his little book, while she was busy with something. She figured it had to do with his actual duty as the king's head servant.

"Ask what you want," he said as he continued to write in his book, not looking up.

"How did you become a eunuch?" she finally asked.

He looked up from his book, raising his eyebrow at her. "You're asking a personal question."

She nodded. "I know, but I am curious since you are more fair-skinned. You have a high position of power and are close to all the women in the palace."

"*Close* is not what I would call it. I am able to see to their needs easily."

"Are there needs in their beds?"

"More personal questions." He closed his book, looking her in the eyes now.

"I'm sorry, Lysander." She lowered her head.

He sighed. "My lady, you are the first person to ever ask me about myself."

"Really?" Shock graced her face.

"I'll tell you about myself, so get comfortable." He sat up straight, looking at her. "I grew up in Elysiumara. I was a young boy, and honestly, I loved being who I was. It wasn't a crime to be with anyone. One day my village was raided. We were being killed, being..." he paused, "things happened, and eventually we were sold to different parts of the world."

"Did you have a family?"

"I had a lot of family, but none of them survived the raids. A soldier had taken a liking to me, and happily, I was just sold."

She wanted to hug him, but dared not move from her seat. "Happily?"

He smiled at her, seeing the pain written in her eyes. "It's okay, my lady. I have had years to come to terms with the memory of my family."

"How did you get here?"

"Well, when I was sold, they classified me in the sodomy group for what I was. It wasn't long before they castrated me." He paused, giving an apologetic smile. "I'm sorry, this is a little graphic now."

She shook her head. "Please, go on." In her culture, boys were snipped of their foreskin in infancy. Women were usually the ones who cleaned the bodies for burial, as well.

"I was castrated, not as extreme as I heard some from the East are, but nonetheless, a part of me was taken by force. It was a painful and extreme process I wouldn't recommend to others." He took a deep breath. "After I was healed, I went from place to place, my slavers wondering if they could find a proper buyer for me. Finally, I came to this kingdom; the king's father had purchased me for the second queen."

Estella saw the sadness in his eyes.

He swallowed. "I was quickly given to the prince, who is now our king. Prince Amir was raised away from all the other royal children, which led him to treat his servants with more kindness."

"There have been laws in the last few years which have been put into place," Estella said.

Lysander nodded. "Yes, there were many laws about slavery with the previous king, but our great King Amir has been doing his best to change the laws so that slaves are no longer accepted."

"I remember my aunt telling me about that. They took a similar path to another culture; seven years of servitude, then you're free."

Lysander nodded. "The king is met with a lot of opposition, and though he is king, one cannot force laws without consequences. His father had different views."

"Surely, there are very few people left from the previous king's advisors. Surely King Amir got rid of them as I suppose he relieved all the mistresses from his father's time."

"Once the king died, our King Amir took all the women and threw them out, sending them to nunneries for the remainder of their lives. Most of the staff remained unless there was a threat. Then it was up to the now former queen to take charge of the servants. Since I was already a personal servant to the king, she could not touch me. I honestly don't think she liked me very much."

"Did you not like the previous queen?"

"Though Queen Tabitha was from good breeding and a royal family, she did nothing for the palace that any servant worth their salt couldn't do."

Estella noticed he didn't answer, but allowed him to finish.

"The king and queen had no lavish parties, mainly because the king was always gone for one war or another. Six years, the king and queen never conceived, making talk begin to swirl. I know my king heard some of the rumors, which didn't help her case when she pulled her last stunt."

"What did she do?"

"The king was high on the spirits, and thought it would be nice to see his wife. I am not sure if it was the alcohol or the comments from some of the men, but whatever the reason, he thought of seeing her." He paused. "Tell me Estella, with what I have told you so far, what would you do?"

"What do you mean?"

"Would you go see the king in the middle of the party? After a week of hosting and entertaining the public, or would you tell him you are busy?"

She put her finger to her lips, thinking. "Without knowing the consequences, I would have probably seen him."

"Why is that?"

"It would have given me a break from the public. And knowing what little I know of the king, having never met him, it probably wouldn't be for long. I don't think anything inappropriate would have happened to me. So why not go see him, smile at all his friends, talk to them for a bit, then go back to the party? It would be a nice breather from people watching your every move."

Lysander nodded. "That is a good answer." He smiled. "But more people would be watching you with the king."

Her face winced. "Oh." Estella looked down into her hands as she rubbed the back of her nail with her thumb.

"What is the matter, my lady?"

"I was wondering about what is to become of me? I will not be fit for anything else. I am being trained to be a queen, but should I fail to be a queen, then what is to become of me? I will not be allowed back to my home, so will I be thrown into a nunnery? Forced to live out the rest of my days praying to the creator for guidance?"

Lysander's eyes softened at her. "What if you were to become queen? What would you do then?"

Estella shook her head. "I don't know the answer to that either." Her eyes met Lysander's. "I do know though, if I were to become queen, I would want some of the women to be free. King Amir allows slaves to be free, so he should free the women he has enslaved, as well."

Lysander gave a genuine smile to Estella. Just then, there was a knock at the door. "Enter," Lysander said.

"Lysander," a guard said, "there is one from room four that wishes to continue to learn."

His eyebrows rose. "Oh? Send them in." He turned his attention back to Estella for a moment before looking back at the guard. "Can you please escort Estella back to her room?"

Estella smiled, putting away her things quickly. "Thank you, Lysander," she said softly. As she walked out, a small young woman with dark complexion and a beautiful warm sepia walked in. Her long hair was braided, draped over one shoulder, the ends meeting where her hips were. Estella thought she looked quite young, but then again, Estella was older than most of the women within marrying age.

"Ah, Aisha, I thought it was you." Estella heard Lysander exclaim as the door closed behind her.

CHAPTER 11

A Game of Kings

FIVE MONTHS AND ELEVEN DAYS SINCE THE PARTY

AMIR WAS BITTER THAT he had to leave his plants, but he knew it was important for his kingdom. He looked out into the vast sea, seeing the Kingdom of Zerzura off the shores. It wasn't one of his countries, but they were considered allies. They also happened to be an ally with his former wife's kingdom.

Zerzura was a seafaring nation, and several months ago, the king had sent a letter to Amir while he was in the middle of his divorce. Apparently, Zerzura was planning to cut off all trading with Zephyria. It was a timely letter, one that Amir had to see to personally.

One of the sailors shouted about coming up to the dock. Once able to walk onto the deck, he saw it was a bunch of stuffed shirts, or rather known as the Zerzura King's advisors. They were all darker than he was; the dark umber of their skin glowed under the sea's sky.

"Hello, King of Zephyria, may you have a long reign."

He nodded to them. "Please, rise. I must see your king."

Amir looked to the mountains. In the face of it was a castle carved that showed craftsmanship and the age of the kingdom, even from the distance of the sea. There were no carriages or horses in the town of Zerzura, so walking was the only option. As Amir walked through the town, he noticed how similar his own kingdom was to Zerzura. The only real difference was that there were more fish and sea creatures in different stalls.

"I see his majesty is admiring our fish market."

Amir nodded as he kept looking around. "Zerzura is a seaside kingdom, it makes sense there are plenty of different fishes."

"Yes, quite different from your sand and deserts." The man smiled.

Amir ignored the snide in his voice as he looked at the people; some of them ignoring him, others looking at him curiously. They probably heard the rumors about him, and though he didn't pillage kingdoms of his alliances, he could understand why they were hesitant.

It didn't take much longer for them to reach the castle and go into the greeting room. The man who had made the snide remark earlier ran into the room first, closing the doors behind him. Amir raised an eyebrow at Hamid who was behind him. Hamid simply shook his head.

After a minute, the doors opened, the advisor smirking. "He will see you now."

Amir furrowed his brows a bit before he entered. The room was large and extremely spacious. There was little in there except the massive dining table with an abundant amount of food on it. There at the head, was the king; large and dressed in a rich purple. He had a rich mahogany skin color. He had a piece of white meat in his hand, never looking up from his plate.

"Hello, Oba." Amir gave a customary bow.

"Hmm," the king replied before biting into the meat.

Amir rolled his eyes. "Oba, I am not some common man, I am the King of Zephyria."

King Oba stopped eating, looking up from his lashes. "For now." He chuckled.

Amir narrowed his eyes. "What does that mean?"

King Oba put down his food, smirking. "I hear you threw back your wife to her family." His voice was deep, rich with resonance that vibrated through the room. If Amir had to use a word to describe it best, it would be thunderous.

Amir gave a shrug. "I should have known that you would hear the rumors."

King Oba shook his head. "No, what the rumors say is that she had another lover and you found out." He gestured with his clean hand to take a seat.

Amir took a seat, a servant placing a plate full of food in front of him and some wine. Amir waved the servant off before handing his drink to Hamid to try. "Those are false."

"No." He smirked as he took another bite of his food. "I wouldn't think you would care if you found her with another lover."

Amir rolled his eyes. "I don't think someone would find her warm enough to be a lover to her. However, I didn't come to discuss her today."

"When will I meet the new wife?"

"I haven't even met her yet."

King Oba furrowed his brow. "What do you mean? Surely you would not divorce your wife to not have another one to take her place?"

"There is a contest in my kingdom to see who will be the next queen. I haven't exactly been there to see any of the women. I am waiting till the ball."

"The ball?"

"Yes, a ball for all the men to wear masks, and the women have to be themselves," he waved his hand nonchalantly, "or on their best behavior. I want to make sure they are who they present themselves as."

King Oba scratched his chin, nodding. "You like to play a dangerous game. What if they are disappointed in meeting you?"

Amir chuckled. "Then I don't want them as queen."

"Reasonable." He smiled, taking a small pinch of some fufu on his plate. "Do you think you will find her?"

"There are several women I want to meet. They passed one test I had my servant set up for them."

"What was the challenge?"

"Chess," Amir said casually.

King Oba let out a loud boisterous laugh. "Chess? You have some interesting fetishes."

Amir chuckled. "No, I wanted to see—"

"My lord," the impish advisor interrupted. Amir's eye twitched a bit. There was no respect from this man. "There are things you need to discuss."

King Oba didn't look any more pleased than Amir with the sudden interruptions. "Ah, yes. King Amir, I know there are a lot of problems regarding you needing to make sure you still have friends, but as I said in my letter months ago, we are going to dissolve our trade with Zephyria."

"Why?" Amir's eyebrows drew together.

"We don't feel it is fair," King Oba said nonchalantly, looking at different foods at the other end of the table. "There is talk that you think we just pluck the hairs off our goats and charge you a high price."

"I do not have all my figures with me, but I guarantee it is fair."

King Oba waved his hand. "No, you are not confident, you don't know your own figures, and right now, you are looking for a bride. You will be busy, and we have decided to stop all trade."

Amir didn't like it. Zerzura was a big trading post for fishes as well as the famous wool from their mountain goats.

"I'm sure you understand." King Oba grinned. Amir glanced at the advisor and noticed the sly smile on his face. He wondered who was actually running the country.

Amir gave a soft sigh. "In that case, am I no longer welcomed as a guest from my old friend?"

The advisor opened his mouth, but was cut off by the king. "Of course, my friend! I want to see how your chess game has improved to make it a challenge for your future wife."

Amir gave his best genuine smile. "Thank you so much, Oba. You truly are a great friend."

The advisor grimaced as he walked away to the corner from whence he came from. Amir glanced at Hamid, who had a red neck. Clearly, he was mad about how his king was treated. Amir gave a nod to Hamid, before smiling at Oba.

"When would you like to play?"

King Oba clapped his hands so loud it sounded as if thunder was in the room. "Right now! Someone bring a chess board with the pieces!"

"Oba, we still have to discuss our trade situation."

"Ack," he waved him off, "later. Right now, let us be entertained. Be a guest in my home for now, Amir. I have not seen you in a great many years."

"We should talk about the trade; it would be a large shift for both our countries."

"How about this: I will not dissolve the trade until you are married, yes?"

Amir's weight shifted in his seat, then he gave a single nod.

"*Xerhu*!" he said with excitement. "Let us play!"

It wasn't long before a small table was set up with the chess board on it. King Oba insisted on playing the black one, even though it has somewhat of a disadvantage.

"Black is king!"

Amir chuckled. Even though they were both dark in skin, King Oba was darker by quite a few shades. "The king is the one who wins."

"And black will win!" His voice boomed through the halls, his spirits high.

"My game has improved greatly." Amir moved his first piece.

"Why is that? For the new queen?" King Oba moved a black pawn.

"Actually," Amir moved his other piece to parry Oba's black pawn, "a woman told me to not drink, and to take up the game of chess instead."

King Oba's eyebrows shot up. "Who is she?"

Amir smirked. "I have no idea. I was drunk, and my servant said they found me with a curtain over my head. I just remember her telling me to play chess."

"Is she one of the women who passed the test?"

"I hope so," Amir said as he moved another piece.

"If she isn't," King Oba moved a piece, and Amir overtook it, "*zykar*!" he cursed.

"I hope she is, so I can find her."

"What will you do if you find her, and she does not care for you?"

"If she entered the contest, surely that means she wants to be queen."

"From some of the rumors, I heard not all of them were willing." Oba moved another piece, this time putting his king in likely danger.

Amir looked hard at the board. "How did you hear that?"

"I have many ears in places I trade."

"Well, if that is true, there is nothing to be done now. She is considered part of the palace."

"Hmm." His friend pondered as he made another move.

Amir moved his piece to defend. "What's wrong?"

"I worry about you, my friend. What if you don't get what you are looking for?"

"What if I get everything I am looking for?"

"What kind of queen are you wanting?" Oba moved his queen out.

"A good queen." Amir moved his other pawn near Oba's queen.

"You said she will become part of the palace, I thought you got rid of slavery in your kingdom."

Amir looked up from under his lashes at the king. Oba was leaning on his hand, his index finger pressed into his cheek. Amir knew that his friend was being genuine in his question, but it still rubbed him the wrong way.

Oba took the pawn. "This contest, did you think about what would happen to everyone afterwards?"

Amir did, but he didn't have a definite answer. He sat there and thought about the question. He thought of dark, stormy hair, a soft voice, gentle spirit, and—

"Who is it that you think of?" Oba looked seriously at Amir.

"I thought of my mother, someone who was a good queen, and loved by all."

"All but your father."

Amir's eyes went dark. "Poor choice of words."

Oba softly chuckled as he moved another piece. They continued to play in silence; the only sound was the pieces moving across the board.

"Check," Oba said in a low voice.

Amir blinked a few times, and saw the board. He had been playing in a state of mind where he didn't notice his game. He took the only opening he had. Oba countered the move, declaring check once more. Amir still had a pawn, but he noticed the game was over. No matter what he did, Oba would eventually throw him in a corner and checkmate. He is playing with him.

"Give up, my friend?"

Amir smiled, knocking over his king. "A king knows when to spare what lives are left."

"You sacrificed your queen earlier," Oba shook his head, "that was a poor choice."

"How so? I was able to take most of your board before that happened."

"But a king without his queen is nothing. Queens can rule without us, but a king always needs his queen." Oba gave a sad smile to Amir. "I will retire for the night, my friend. Please, enjoy your time here, but know that I think you should go back to your queen." He paused, bowing before standing up straight. "Whoever she may be."

CHAPTER 12

A Pearl in a Sea of Gold

A YEAR SINCE THE PARTY

IT TOOK MONTHS OF oils, massages, and perfume to be poured on Estella. She was sure she was going to sneeze out a flower with how much they had placed on her. Lysander had told her everyone had to endure months of this.

It was made abundantly clear that most of the women had come from well-off families in her own room, as most of them stopped coming to the lessons of writing and reading. Estella wasn't sure about the other rooms besides the one girl. All the women were quickly taught how to dance; one by one, the women stopped attending the classes. Estella had been the last one to exit the class, after the dance master had informed her she had nothing else to teach.

It was then, the other lessons began; poetry, painting, sewing, special story-telling dances, music, even calligraphy, were taught to those who wanted to learn. These were special skills, ones that Lysander said would help in impressing the king. In saying so, it enticed the women to take their lessons seriously. Estella had decided to take up weaving and needlework. It was the closest to her own people, and she wanted to stay close to them, even in the gilded cage.

"What do you think we are going to be doing?" a woman with red hair sneered. Estella hadn't seen her before, and figured she must be from one of the other rooms.

Another woman yawned. "Maybe they will make us do those boring things again."

Another woman groaned loudly. "If I have to hear another word from that man-servant about how we all should be taking this seriously, I'll throw my drink at him."

A small amount of snickering and cackling emerged. Estella gave a cautious smile as she looked at everyone.

"Speaking of which," the red-haired girl looked at Estella, "aren't you the one still taking writing lessons from him?"

Panic rose in Estella, but she did her best not to show it. "I still need practice on a lot of things."

"Are you slow?" one woman asked.

"Or dumb?" a girl who looked no older than sixteen asked.

Estella gave a polite smile. "I just think I should be well-practiced since I would have never gotten anything like this where I came from."

A few of the women nodded in understanding before turning back to each other. It wasn't a few moments later, until Lysander walked in, a letter in his hand. All of the women sat up straight. A letter only could come from the king, so they expected this to be the grand reveal. It had been a year of them being here, whispers of the king showing up and vanishing. News of him traveling the world, and seeing his ex-wife swirled the palace walls. Even Estella leaned in a bit.

Lysander cleared his throat. "Now, the king has set to return."

A chatter of voices filled the courtyard, people squealing they could finally meet the king.

"Ladies!" Lysander yelled out. "We are here to compete, but in two days' time, we will have the ball I know many of you have been setting out for. The king has promised to have a ball where all the men are masked, and the women must show off themselves. It is imperative that you behave yourself. You never know who is in the room, including which is the king."

"I know what the king looks like." One woman smiled. "I saw him when he came home several years ago."

Lysander shook his head. "I'm sorry to say but the king is going to disguise himself, as well. Many of the men in the ballroom will be there as spies for the king, so be aware they will write reports on you." He gave a weak smile. "So in accordance to our laws, we will allow you all to go through the riches of the king and gather what it would take to make you beautiful before the eyes of the king."

Screams, clapping, and so much noise erupted that Lysander visibly winced. Estella covered her ears and backed up a little. Women stood up, congratulated each other, and hugged one another as if the king himself had chosen them to be queen. In between the loud chatter and screaming, Estella heard several of the women say that this was the best day.

"Ladies!" Lysander yelled. "We will get to who goes each round first. Will Zahra, Samira, Yasmin, Noor, Jamilah, Fatima, and Estella come first?"

A hush fell over the women as the ones named walked out. Estella really had hoped that she wouldn't have been called first, but here she was. Each of the other women were smug as they looked down at the women they passed. Estella prayed they would ignore her. She caught a glimpse, no such luck. If looks could kill, she would be dead ten times over. Lysander led them down a hallway.

With each step that echoed against the stone walls, it felt like Estella was on her way to her doom. She didn't have a good feeling about all the women when she would come back.

"Don't worry." Lysander spoke up as if he read her mind. "You will be escorted back to your rooms, and anyone who comes into the room will already have chosen their own pieces. I don't want any fighting to happen," Lysander muttered, but Estella didn't hear it, being all the way in the back.

Finally, they reach an unassuming door—wooden with no special locks on it. She might have walked past it without thinking. Lysander opened the door, ushering all the women into the room. Once inside, she realized why it was unassuming. Inside were five guards guarding a steel door. The real wealth was in the guarded door. She thought about how the king was smart. Having a door visible to everyone with all these guards would raise awareness. The unassuming door isn't the one chosen first. Estella wondered if it was the old king's choice or the current's.

Lysander walked up to the men. "It is time for the women to choose."

The man in front was tawny skin-colored, large, and had muscles bulging everywhere. She knew her uncle Zeke was very strong, but she wondered if her uncle could take down this man.

"Touch nothing but two items. If you take more than two, you will be hanged like a dog."

One of the women gasped as her hands went to her throat.

Lysander waved his hand. "Just two items, ladies, and please—these men *do* know what is in here. So don't think that you can sneak anything out."

The steel door opened, allowing the women to pour into the vast room. Behind them, Lysander and the large man followed them in. His arms were crossed as he scowled at all the women. Immediately, the women went running in each direction, and squealing about deciding on which ones to choose.

"Does a pair of earrings count as one?" one of the women asked.

"What about the pair of bracelets?" another one cried out.

The man said nothing as he stood there at the door. Estella looked around gingerly, thinking about what the king would probably like. Being a man who gardened, she didn't think he would love gold and diamonds. Then again, she could be wrong.

She walked over to the guard and smiled up at him. "What is your name?"

The man blinked a few times before looking down, as he was much taller than her. "I am called Arash."

"Hello, Arash." She looked behind her and then back to him. "Tell me, what do you think the king would like?"

He stared at her with wide eyes before he looked at Lysander, who just nodded.

"Just answer her," he said.

"Um," he swallowed, "the king doesn't come in here often. Just to ensure everything is here."

"Is there anything he likes to look at?"

"His flowers," he said plainly.

Estella gave a soft sigh. "I was afraid of that."

Just then two of the women came running up. "Are these okay?" Fatima showed off a necklace and a crown.

The other woman, Jamilah, giggled. "Assuming you're queen already?" She looked at Arash. "Are these okay?" Jamilah held up a necklace in blue and gold and a pair of earrings that matched it.

"Yes." Arash nodded.

Lysander motioned for the women. "Come on, I'll have you escorted back to your room." The three of them left the treasure room, leaving Estella and four others.

Estella resumed going back to look for a piece of jewelry that possibly would be pretty enough. After a few minutes of digging in several piles while crouched down, she found a hair comb that was adorned with white pearls. It was luminous, and it was beautiful.

"Here, my lady," Arash said in a low voice as he handed her a cloth.

She stood up straight and opened it. There were a pair of dropped pearl earrings that matched the comb. She grinned at it, then looked up at him. "Thank you, Arash."

"It was the late second queen's earrings," he paused, "so care for them well."

She nodded. "As if they were my own mother's."

"Ah, you finally decided on some pieces," Lysander said as he walked up to them.

"Sort of," she smiled, "I found something I like."

Lysander looked at the items she had. "They suit you well."

"Thank you."

"Come, let's get you back to the room." He looked at the other women. "Are you ladies about done? The others are complaining."

The remaining four came running. "Yes!" they all said in a sort of unison.

"Good, let us all go back." Lysander sighed, knowing he had several more rounds of this with all the other women who were waiting their turn. He had to let them go in order of who he deemed worthy to go first.

CHAPTER 13

Sneaking Out

"Hmm, hmm, hm," his mother hummed as she stroked his hair. Amir wasn't asleep, but he tried his best to pretend to be.

"Azizi," she said softly.

"Hmm, Mama?" he asked in his best sleepy voice.

"What kind of king will you be, habibi?"

He looked up from her lap, worry in his eyes, as he saw tears brimming hers. "Mama?"

She stroked her thumb on his cheek. "What kind of king will you be? A tyrant? A cruel one? A kind one?"

"What kind do you want me to be, Mama?"

She took a deep breath, looking away for a brief second. "I want you to be a good king, one who will love his people, and be just."

"Like Baba?"

She swallowed hard. "No." She smiled. "Azizi, I want you to be better than Baba."

He smiled at her. "Then I will give you a palace to live peacefully in."

She gave a chuckle, a tear escaping and rolling down her face. "Yes, Azizi, one we can grow flowers in."

He hugged her tightly.

Amir woke up in a bed of sweat, his chest rising and falling quickly. He rubbed his eyes, realizing it was a dream.

"Why?" he asked to no one in particular.

A soft knock came on the door. "Your majesty?"

"I'm fine!" he barked out before clearing his voice. "I'm fine, Lysander, just hot."

"We can send in someone to fan you, if you wish."

"No," he ground out. "I wish to be left alone."

"As you wish."

Then there was silence.

Amir sat up, looking at the window as the slightest breeze blew through the sheer curtains that hung high. Slowly, he made his way to it, opening up the doors fully and pulling back the curtains, letting the cold night air wash over him. Just as he was going to turn back in, he noticed a figure creeping around his garden. Instantly in a rage, he grabbed some clothes and slid down the palace wall as he always had done.

It didn't take long for him to reach his gardens. He had made sure they were close enough to get to, but far away enough to admire. Quietly, he crept behind the figure. From the shape, it appeared to be a woman. She was wearing a dark cape, probably to try to keep out of sight. With as much stealth as a cat, he was behind her in a moment, placing a careful hand over her mouth, immobilizing her with his other hand. She attempted to let out a scream, but his hand was fast.

"Don't," he warned. He did his best to deepen his voice in an attempt to disguise himself. She smelled sweet, and to be honest, he liked it. It was a subtle oil, not overpowering his nose. He felt the curves of her body against his. She was plumper than his ex-wife. Which actually was a point towards this woman.

She muffled something.

"I'll release you if you don't scream." He tried to look at her over her hood, but it was rather difficult. All he saw was dark hair.

She nodded.

He slowly released her mouth, and even then, his hand hovered close by in case she needed to be silenced again.

"Release me," she snapped, trying to sound like she had authority.

"No." He chuckled.

"You are touching the king's property," she hissed.

"Hm," he mused. "If I remember correctly, the king's property isn't supposed to leave their rooms without a chaperone. So forgive me for not really believing you."

"It's true." She straightened, but she was still shorter than him by a good margin. He could easily rest his head on hers.

"Then why are you out here alone?" He was annoyed. The women knew they weren't supposed to be alone, but what if... "Are you out here looking for a secret lover?"

"No," she groaned. He could swear he could hear her rolling her eyes.

"No?"

"No," she repeated, the woman now annoyed. "I am just trying to..." Her voice trailed off.

"Trying to what?" Her scent was making him relax a little, but then he stiffened. If he allowed it, he could fall asleep to it. "Are you trying to kill the king?"

"*What*?" Fear immediately filled her voice. "Why would you say that out loud?" she hissed. "Are you trying to get both of us into the dungeon?"

"Technically, I am asking a question to the person who is sneaking around. So, it would just be you who gets thrown into the dungeon." He gave a half-chuckle.

She fidgeted in his arms. "I'm not trying to die."

"You're sneaking around with a dark cloak in the middle of the night. You're lucky it was me, and not someone else."

"What does that mean? Who are you?"

He chuckled. He couldn't remember having this kind of conversation with a female before. "If you're not sneaking around for a lover or to assassinate the king, where are you going?"

"Does that mean you're letting me go?" There was hope in her voice.

"Depends on how you answer my question."

"I was looking for some flowers," she said finally.

"Flowers?"

"Yes, I was told the king is quite a hobbyist botanist. I thought instead of jewels, I would find some flowers he didn't grow and use them as my jewelry."

"What if he grew everything?"

She blew out a defeated breath. "Then I am marked by misfortune."

He laughed low. "Why?"

"Because I don't think the king would like it if I picked a flower he grew." Her body was relaxing now under his grip.

"I think the king would be happy if someone wanted to wear his flowers."

"How do you know? Aren't they all precious to him?"

He gave a shrug, not sure if she felt the movement. "Flowers die, it's better they die on a beautiful woman than die on the vine."

"Most flowers don't come from vines," she quickly responded.

"Oh?" He knew that, but it didn't roll off the tongue to say bush instead of vine.

"Yes," she said quickly. "Which ones do you think would cause the least amount of offense tomorrow?"

"What is tomorrow?"

"The mask ball," she replied, confused. "Don't you know?"

"It's my first night back on duty." He wasn't exactly lying. He was finally able to relax after all the work that had piled up from the divorce.

"Oh, well the mask ball is for all the men to attend under disguise and mingle with the ladies. It's for the king's fancy." She waved her head a little since her arms were still encased by him.

"I see." Amir didn't know how he felt about her saying things like that, but it was nice to see how people saw him, even if they didn't know it was the king they were talking to.

"So which flowers do you think would cause the least offense?" She looked around.

"Probably the ones from over there?" He pointed with his free hand to a small bush of newly bloomed desert rose. The tree wasn't big enough, and he knew he was going to have to prune them soon.

She let out a gasp. "Are you mad? Those are clearly special."

"They are just desert roses."

"Exactly," she hissed.

He pointed to the trellis that was on the other side of them. "How about the jasmine then." The jasmine was crawling up all over the wall, becoming a large monster. Amir knew he had neglected it and the plant had decided to run wild.

She hummed. "I suppose he won't miss a few of those."

He rolled his eyes. "There are hundreds of them, I don't think he would notice."

"He'll notice I'm wearing a flower instead of jewelry," she hissed.

He chuckled. "So? Wouldn't that work in your favor?"

Suddenly, she got quiet and still. "I don't want to be noticed too much. I don't want to be a mistress, but also, I don't like how I, and many other, ended up here."

His smile faded. "I see." He didn't though, really. The women were living a life of luxury at his expense, and she was standing here saying she didn't want it.

"However..." she said.

He perked up. "However?"

"I feel like he is different. After all, he is choosing anyone, no matter their birth." She gave a small snicker. "Perhaps he doesn't like this any more than we do."

He smiled. "Maybe he likes it less."

"Maybe he is ugly," she joked.

He rolled his eyes. "And fat, like a plump, old sultan."

She laughed, wiggling free before walking to the jasmine. "He could be a great many things," she took a few tender flowers, "just as I can be." She turned back to him, smiling brightly.

Though Amir was hidden in the shadow, there was no way to miss her, the way the moon hit her face, her bright green eyes sparkling as she cradled the jasmine in her palms. The clear way the light glowed around her hair, as if it was a halo.

"Thank you," she said, but when she looked back up from her flowers, he was gone. She did a few turns, looking around to see if he was anywhere but to no avail. She gave a small shrug before pulling her hood over her face once more, and slipped back inside.

Someone cleared their throat. "Your majesty," Lysander said in a cross voice.

Amir chuckled, turning around to see Lysander with a straight back and a regal posture. He knew he was in trouble then.

"Yes?"

"Why are you in the garden and not in bed? Or at least, with an escort?"

He raised an eyebrow at him. "Why are the ladies able to roam freely?"

"Ladies?" Panic rose in his voice as he looked around quickly. "Who?"

Amir raised his hands in defense. "Calm down, they went back to their room." He started to walk towards his bedroom. "But you might want to think about putting more guards around their chambers. I wouldn't want some of them to sneak off and try to kill me." He paused. "Or worse, try to seduce me in bed."

"Yes, since your room is very easy to access," Lysander said under his breath.

"Only to me."

"Sire, I don't mean to sound cruel, but I think if you let the guards stay around your room like they are supposed to—"

"They could stop me from sneaking around my own castle?" he cut him off.

"You don't need to sneak off, you're the king. You have free reign everywhere."

"Not as me, just as the king. I sometimes miss being ignored," he said wistfully.

"My king, I must insist on more guards around you. There are rumors."

"There are always rumors. Just make sure I stay alive."

"That is rather difficult to do when you sneak around," Lysander said more pointed.

Amir let out a laugh. "I'll try to behave, Lysander, but really, you are starting to sound like a mother hen."

"Mother hens will kill anything that intends to do harm to their chicks. I don't see how this is an insult."

They finally reached the bedroom where several guards were standing with the doors open.

"Is it secure?" Lysander asked them.

They nodded.

"Good." He turned to Amir. "May you have a wonderful sleep, your majesty. I have ordered you some tea in case you wish to have some after your impromptu midnight walk."

Amir smirked. "Thanks Lysander, but remember, I don't need guards. The women do." He closed the door and fell into bed, remembering the woman's face as the moonlight hit it. The sparkle in her green eyes, showing their sincerity.

"I wonder how she will be at the ball," he said to himself as he drifted off to sleep.

CHAPTER 14

To be a Queen

LYSANDER SMOOTHED THE FOLDS of her dress, examining every inch of it. "Okay young one." He smiled.

"Lysander, you can't be much older than me." She smiled.

"No, I'm wiser, therefore I'm older."

Estella giggled. "Very well."

They were in a grand room with the other women from all the rooms and their mothers. Several of them glanced at Estella and snickered. She wished she, too, could have had her aunt with her, helping her prepare, but she was not so fortunate. She was, however, lucky enough to have Lysander.

"Having some servant help her," one girl said.

"She really does want to be a nun," another one said in a loud voice.

"At least there's one person we will beat." A third one cackled.

Estella steeled herself, not letting them see that their words had an effect on her. "Continue, Lysander."

A cackle was heard from across the room after she said his name.

Lysander seemed unfazed by it as he continued to fuss with the hem of her dress. She was wearing a simple lavender gown, adorned with delicate lace and embroidery, and long sleeves with lace flowers over it. Her dark curls cascaded down her shoulders, framing her face in a cloud of ebony beauty. Lysander's fingers gently brushed against the fabric, smoothing out any imperfections.

"Lysander, why this color?" she whispered to him as she looked around the room. The women were wearing gold, royal blues, deep purples and maroons. All in all, it looked like the rainbow was in the room. Estella was the only one in a lighter color.

"Because his majesty loves soft colors," he whispered. "He doesn't like gold dresses. One time Queen Tabitha wore golden embellishments on her dress—it wasn't even the whole dress." He waved on. "But he yelled at her, saying if he wanted her to be dressed in gold, he would have bought a statue of her in gold."

"Why does he hate it so much?"

"Gold is something you dominate, not love," he said with pride.

"Is that line from you?" She smiled.

"Certainly not," he snorted. "My lord and master said that."

"It doesn't rhyme." She chuckled.

Lysander's smile vanished, looking rather serious. "Don't tell him that."

Estella nodded. "Yes, sir."

He placed a hand on his chest. "Oh, I have never been called that by a woman before."

"Not even the female servants?" she asked.

"Oh, that doesn't count. That is work."

Estella laughed. "I think it counts still."

"No," he said plainly, fixing the last bit of the dress.

"I thought Yenta from the sewing room fixed all the pieces on me already."

"She did, but I have to make sure this is completed." He stopped and looked up at her. "This is your introduction to the king. I want everything to be perfect."

She gave a single nod, the corners of her mouth forming into a smile. Over the course of the year and getting close to Lysander, she realized how much of a stickler for perfection he was. It wasn't that he didn't trust the other servants, he just believed in making sure everything was as it was supposed to. Probably how he became the highest-ranking servant.

"There." He smiled, standing up straight. "I have other things to ensure, but please don't ruin your dress in the meantime," he warned before leaving her alone.

Estella took a step down from the platform, taking a look around at the women who were fixing their hair differently than she. Some had their hair up in intricate braids with gold ribbon. Some had their hair up high, curls upon curls piled high. They were drastically different from how Estella had her hair done. Her soft curls fell down her body, lightly dusted with some pearls ground up. Two small braids from the side of her were pulled back, with the comb she chose holding them in place

"Joy." Cassia smiled as she walked up at her. "You look beautiful."

"Estella," she corrected coolly.

"Right," Cassia winced, "you said that the last time I saw you."

She smiled at her old friend. "I'm well, how are you?" Estella noticed that Cassia was wearing a heavy satin yellow dress. There were very little jewels on it, probably because her mother had to pay for some of the fabric. She also took notice of the golden arm bands and large golden broach she was wearing.

"My mother is driving me nuts with her nagging." She gave a sheepish smile.

"I see." Estella didn't understand. She hadn't seen her family in a long time.

Cassia probably felt the awkwardness of the conversation. "I'm sorry."

"I'm fine." She gave her old friend a warm smile like she was taught. The one that hid her true feelings.

"I'm glad." She smiled. "I better get back to get ready. It's happening finally tonight."

Estella nodded. "Of course, go ahead." She motioned for her to rejoin her mother.

"She wanted her daughter to look like gold without the gold," Lysander commented in a whisper as he came back.

"Interesting choice." Estella smiled at Lysander. "I want to help her like you helped me."

"Do it when you become queen, not before."

"Why?" she questioned for the first time.

"You need to secure your place."

Estella nodded. She knew she had to become queen before she helped anyone else. But it didn't feel right.

"Are you ready for the night?"

"I think so." She smiled nervously.

"Remember, there are many noble men in there tonight. The king instructed everyone to be as natural as possible—but beware. Your natural is to be polished, poised, and above all, you are regal," Lysander warned.

"And the men will be wearing masks to conceal themselves, to report on us later," she remembered.

"The only ones who are not wearing masks are the guards. Do not dance with them."

"Okay, but how will I know the king?"

"I unfortunately cannot reveal what my master is going to be wearing, that would be cheating."

"And helping me wasn't?" she said quickly.

"See?" he hissed. "None of that quick talk."

Estella bit back a giggle, giving a gentle nod.

"Helping you is part of my job. Helping all of them. I have been helping the other potential brides, but we allowed the mothers to help and that made things easier on me to focus on you."

Estella took his hands in hers. "Thank you, Lysander." She smiled before giving him a small peck on the cheek.

He quickly smiled. "It's a good thing you don't have the red stain on your lips yet. I might have been put in danger."

She laughed. "You are a eunuch, there is no danger with us."

He patted her hand. "I have never been as happy to have met someone as you, my lady Estella. I wish you the best of luck."

Estella took a deep breath, then turned to her corner where she kept her makeup. Some of the women had become fast friends and shared everything, from clothes, to makeup, and of course, gossip. However, there was a distinct distance they had kept from Estella.

Estella picked up a clay disk with a red stain on the inside, dropping a single drop of rose oil inside. With a small mirror, she brushed her red lip stain on. The stain turned to a bright, pomegranate red on her lips, drying instantly.

"Excuse me." It was Noor. She was a plump woman who seemed to be just enjoying her life at the palace rather than competing to become queen.

Estella smiled. "Hello, Noor, how may I help you?"

A small bead of sweat rolled down her face. "I seemed to have broken my stain, may I borrow yours?"

Estella looked at the women chuckling in the corner, seeing a small piece of pottery being picked up by a servant. She turned her attention back to Noor, giving a gentle smile. "Of course."

Noor took the pot, giving a half-bow, then ran over to her entourage. Estella wasn't sure if it was on purpose, some plan, or just Noor genuinely knowing Estella would share.

She looked over at the corner of her area, seeing the small jasmine blooms she had picked the night before. Her cheeks turning a rosy color. "I wonder if *all* the guards will be there."

CHAPTER 15

Waltz With the Unknown

WOMEN OCCUPIED EVERY CORNER of the ballroom, the sounds of them filling the air. Every woman from every room was here for the occasion. It was mentioned that there were over a hundred women who entered the palace for a chance to become queen.

Estella watched as the women mingled and conversed amongst themselves. They were all dressed in vibrant colors and adorned with precious jewels, each one vying for the attention of the noble suitors who would soon arrive. She felt a twinge of nervousness in her stomach, but she knew she couldn't let it show. Tonight was her chance to prove herself worthy of becoming queen.

The doors opened, and the first noble suitor brought a hushed excitement to the room. All eyes turned to the grand entrance where a tall man with dark hair and piercing brown eyes stood. He was dressed in a fine silk suit that accentuated his broad shoulders and chiseled features. The women couldn't help but fawn over his appearance. Even if he was wearing a mask that covered most of his face, he was quite handsome.

The women parted ways for him, allowing him to walk into the room. He stopped every so often at different women, greeting them. The other women muttered some *good evenings* as they all stared at him. They all contended for his attention, fluttering their eyes, fanning themselves, each hoping to catch his eye. The eagerness on their faces were evident. Estella figured this man was not the king.

"Good evening," she greeted him gracefully with a smile and curtsy.

"Hello." The man smiled, looking at each of them. "I would introduce myself, but it is against the rules." He chuckled.

The girls all laughed at his joke. As they engaged in small talk, Estella observed the man closely. She could sense that he had an air of confidence about him, but it was also clear that he was not here for love, rather for power and wealth. She quickly made her way around him, realizing that he was definitely *not* the king.

As the night went on, more and more suitors entered the ballroom. Each one seemed to be more charming and wealthy than the last. But to Estella, they all blended into one another.

She watched as the other women flirted and laughed with the suitors, trying to make a lasting impression. And yet, she couldn't bring herself to do the same. It all felt so fake and forced. When talked to, she gave all the correct responses, and walked with several of them who asked. But nothing lasted long. They soon found other women who fawned over them.

In between conversations, Estella snuck away to the balcony for some fresh air. As she leaned against the railing, she gazed out at the moonlit garden below. It was a stark contrast to the extravagance inside the palace.

Her thoughts were interrupted by a soft voice behind her.

"May I join you?"

Estella turned around to find a man standing there, his dark mask hiding just his eyes.

"Of course," she replied politely.

As he stepped closer, she could see that he was quite handsome with dark hair and deep brown eyes.

"I don't believe we've met," he said with a smile.

"I'm Estella," she introduced herself with a small curtsy.

The man smiled at her, giving a low bow. "Estella, after the stars?"

She chuckled. "It was so the stars may always watch over me."

"Can the stars watch you?" he asked, looking up.

"My family believes that we are always watched over." She smiled.

"Interesting thought." He looked at her.

Estella also took a quick glance at him, noticing his basic suit made of cotton and the deep blue hue with a fit that hung awkwardly at the edges. She couldn't help but internally roll her eyes at how Lysander had constantly lectured her on types of fabric and proper fit for clothing. It may have been useless knowledge for a girl from a poor village, but as queen, it was essential according to him.

As she gazed into his eyes, she noticed the absence of a regal spark or commanding presence. The weight on her shoulders lifted as she realized he was just an ordinary man, not the all-powerful king she had yet to meet.

"I know you can't tell me your name, but would you like to dance?" It wasn't socially acceptable for a woman to ask a man to dance, but Estella appreciated the fact that he didn't bring up money or her potential as a future queen during their conversation as the others had.

The man rubbed his beard for a moment, then nodded. "Surely." He extended his hand to her, guiding her to the dance floor.

"Tell me about yourself, since I can't tell you about myself." He twirled her.

Estella's lips curved upwards as she recalled the rule that prohibited her from mentioning her past, but encouraged her to share her dreams. "If I am not selected as queen, I hope to still make an impact within the palace and contribute in some way." She had rehearsed this response countless times until it flowed effortlessly from her lips.

"That is quite ambitious," he commented with a smile. He spun her around on the dance floor, his grin slowly transforming into a mischievous smirk. The music swirled around them, filling the air with lively melodies. "What else do you have in mind?" he inquired playfully, his eyes sparkling with excitement.

Estella's smile wavered as she asked, "I'm not understanding, what else you mean?"

"Tell me about your family."

"Uh..." She forced a smile, trying to hide her nerves. No one had asked any follow up questions. They usually did end up talking about the palace and how many rooms it had, etc.

He danced with her, guiding her to face him. "Come now, you must have something else to tell me."

"I am an orphan," she said finally.

"An orphan? That is a new one."

"*A new one*? There are lots of orphans, even outside the palace walls," she chided.

He chuckled. "Yes, there are always orphans, but I meant from the women here. Most of them come from doting parents who dress them up."

Estella nodded, spinning away from him. "Yes, I am aware."

"So what happened to your parents?"

"The plague," she said in a low voice.

He spun her in a graceful circle, her skirt billowing out like a blooming flower. As she came back into his embrace, he pulled her close, his arm wrapping around her waist. She could feel the heat of his body and the strength of his hold, making her heart flutter with anticipation.

"Was it near here?" he asked in a low voice.

"No." She leaned back as directed by the dance.

"So you moved here to be queen because you're an orphan?"

She gave a low chuckle, extending her arms out. "No, I moved here some time ago before the king decided to throw this contest."

"So you want to be queen," he said, more matter-of-fact than questioning.

"I want to be," she started, twirling in a circle, "happy," she whispered at the end of the dance. Everyone clapped as the dance ended. Chatter grew and Estella gave a curtsy, signaling she was done dancing with him.

"Thank you," she smiled at him. "You dance wonderfully."

"As do you." He smiled softly at her. "I hope to meet you again, Estella."

She chuckled. "After this night, who knows?" She shrugged a little before she walked off to the edge of the ballroom.

Within five minutes of her stepping off the dance floor, someone grabbed her arm and quickly pulled her behind some curtains.

"Estella!" Lysander hissed. "Did I not tell you to behave?" His whispering was heavily more on the hissing side.

"I am behaving." She blinked a couple of times at him.

"Like a cat that stole the cream."

Estella rolled her eyes. "Lysander, I am behaving myself. All I did was dance with someone."

"Yes, *everyone* saw who you danced with. It was the first man you danced with all night. For someone who does not want to be noticed, you know how to make everyone notice you."

She gave him a half-smile. "I may have asked him to dance."

Lysander's hand went to his forehead, rubbing it slightly. "Of all the..." He took a deep breath. "Estella, you can't ask just *anyone* to dance."

"I was bored of the stupid conversations I was having with some of those men and wanted some fun. Did you know most of the men who have given me their time have only talked about money or this castle?"

"Estella, you can't get bored of the conversations. If you become queen, it will be your life." He paused. "As for the conversation, the men were instructed to keep them simple to not give away identities."

"How boring," she muttered.

"Regardless of how dull it may seem, always keep in mind that the goal is to make you queen," he stated firmly. "As queen, you will hold the second-highest position of power under the king."

She took a deep breath and said, "I understand, Lysander, but I didn't see any harm with the man I danced with."

"Hopefully that difference didn't cost you the crown," he said in a small voice.

She placed her hand on his cheek, her thumb rubbing it softly. "I'll behave from now on."

He gently placed his hand on hers, offering a reassuring smile. "Please take care, my lady," he said softly before letting her go back into the ball.

CHAPTER 16

Dance of Our Own

THERE WERE GROANS, AND a dismal mood set upon all the ladies as they scrambled to find new, exciting outfits that might please the king. Apparently, the king didn't see everyone who he fancied, and wanted another night to see them again. Or so they were told by a disheveled Lysander this morning.

"He is so demanding," one girl said.

"Honestly, I hope he isn't like this when I marry him," another girl said.

"*If* you marry him." One girl cackled as the rest of them joined in.

Cassia walked up to Estella, now in a deep purple dress. "Estella, do you think we will see the king tonight?"

She gave a shrug. "Who knows, maybe we will be swept up by some prince in a neighboring kingdom," she teased.

Cassia grinned. "It would be nice, but we both know we are to remain here."

She nodded. "Yes, and hopefully one of us will marry the king."

Cassia leaned in and whispered, "You really should be wearing something more flashy, Estella. My mother heard some of the servants say he likes flashy girls."

Estella looked down at her dress. It was a pale blue dress with long, tulle sleeves that made them look like wings when she walked. There was nothing flashy or glittery on her dress. Lysander had, of course, chosen the dress. Her hair was also in a similar fashion as last night—long, full curls cascading down her back.

"Thank you for your advice." She smiled sweetly at her.

"Of course." She smiled before bouncing back to her mother.

It wasn't long before they were all in the ballroom once more. Estella glided through the room, saying hello to several women from the other rooms, making small talk about their dresses and watching to see if she could see who the king was. She figured he would be wearing something simple but elegant. Some of the men were dressed in just as lavish items as some of the women.

The first night, she hadn't looked too closely at the decorations, but tonight, she could see all the curtains that were draped in a whimsical fashion from the ceiling, and the lanterns that seemed to be hanging from the ceiling by nothing. She knew there had to be some sort of trick to it, but she simply enjoyed the magic of it. The white columns around the edges were draped in a rusty red sheer curtain that moved anytime a woman danced too close to them. She started to take in the small geometric designs that adorned the walls and ceilings.

"Estella," a male voice said behind her.

She turned around to see the man from last night. A smile graced her face as she gave a curtsy. "Hello, sir."

"You look beautiful tonight, but plain in comparison to the other women."

Her body froze momentarily, before she gave him a well-practiced smile. "Sir, I am just a humble woman."

His eyes narrowed ever so slightly for a split second before he glanced at her hair. "No flower tonight?"

She blinked a few times. "Sir?"

"You had a jasmine flower in your hair yesterday. Why not tonight?"

"Oh," she gave a nervous smile to him, "I put it in water, and didn't want to disturb it again." She opened her mouth to say that she didn't want to risk drawing more attention to herself again, but thought better of it.

"Well," he smiled, extending his hand to her, "would you care to dance?"

"Of course." She gracefully took his hand, and they made their way to the dance floor.

This particular dance was slower, one with twirls, bows, and lots of hand holding. He asked, "How are you tonight?"

"I'm well," she simply replied.

"I am pleased to hear this. However, I am not sure how I feel about the king making us come to this thing twice in a row," he said with a sigh.

"I think marriage is a serious matter, and he is allowed all the time he wants to find his bride."

He smiled as he snaked his arm around her tighter. "You're not as feisty today as you were yesterday."

"I was told to behave," she admitted as she twirled.

"Behave?" He smirked, pulling her back to him. "I don't think you should behave. It's not as becoming of you."

"Unfortunately for you, it doesn't matter what you think. I need to behave for the king." She spun out into a twirl.

His eyes lit up. "What if the king is nearby and he hears you say that?"

"I would hope he would be busy at this moment," she teased, looking around.

"With what?"

She gave a shrug. "Wine, women, gambling? Take your pick. I'm sure he has many things he enjoys besides watching all of us make fools of ourselves."

"Aren't you afraid?" He leaned in close.

She leaned back. "No, why should I be?"

"What if I am an adviser to the king and told him you said those things?"

She looked over his clothes. The ill-fitted suit that clearly was a hand-me-down; the mask looked to be about the newest thing on his person. "I don't see how you would be so high ranked as to have the king's ear and still dress in the same suit as yesterday."

"Touché." He chuckled, standing up straight.

He spun her around as he looked at the room, whispering in her ear. "Let's play a game while we dance then."

"What game?" She gave him a wry smile.

"Who do you think has the king's ear?" His breath tickled the nape of her neck before he spun her out.

"Not who is the king?" She chuckled, raising an eyebrow at him.

"No," he shook his head, bringing her back to him, "too easy. I want to see if you can guess who has the king's ear based on the way they look."

"Do you actually know?" She cocked her head to the side.

He gave a shrug.

"Is there a prize?" She eyed him suspiciously.

"How about I tell you a secret if you guess it right?"

"How do I know this secret is worth it?"

He gave another shrug. "You'll just have to trust me."

After a moment of thinking, she agreed. "All right, choose who I examine."

He took her in his arms, and they both spun around the space. "The man in the blue suit and the *gaudy* headdress."

"Talking to the redhead?" she asked.

"Yes, what do you think of him?"

"I think he handles the money, all the treasure the king has."

"Oh?" he asked, giving her a bow, same as all the other men in the dance.

"Yes, I think he is in love with money, but doesn't want to use it. The *gaudy* headdress you speak of has fake jewels in it."

"How do you know that from all the way over here, and while he is dancing nonetheless?" He spun her around once more.

"I saw him earlier, and noticed up close how the gems were fake."

He gave her a curious look. "You can tell if they are fake or not by glancing at them?"

She gave a small shrug as she gave a dramatic dance pose. "Not truly. The women in the palace were taught how to spot some of the obvious fake gems, natural elements of the world. However, I am unable to see the difference between fake gold and real."

He gave a small tsk. "And here I thought you were perfect."

She chuckled, moving around the room with him. "Next."

"The man who is talking to the blonde, wearing the dark green."

"He isn't anywhere near the king."

"What makes you say that?"

"He made a slip yesterday about how he is a lower page. I was talking with him after I danced with you. He simply made a comment about having to wake up early before his master."

"Oh? I must say I'm quite impressed with your memory."

"It comes in handy." She smiled, letting her dress swish around her.

"All right," his smile grew with each moment, "the man in the yellow."

"The one who is alone? He is captain of the guard, and is not really attending this party, but working rather."

"How do you know?" His eyes went to the man. He was taller than most of the others, and his head was on a swivel.

"The way he watches all the exits and surveys the room." *And he used to visit Uncle Zeke from time to time*, she thought, but didn't dare speak.

"Anything else?" He looked back at her, the corners of his mouth turning into a smirk.

"Any woman who has talked to him received a cold shoulder from him, in addition to him never taking his eyes off the entrances."

"I guess that does show that he is working." He chuckled.

"Anyone else?" Her green eyes were glowing under the light.

"Yes." He nodded to the left of them, to the man from yesterday with the brown eyes and dark hair, now wearing a purple suit. The women were surrounding him, his smile radiant, like moths to the flame. "Him."

They swayed in place, Estella looking at him much longer than they had with the others. "He has the king's ear," she said in a serious tone.

"How do you know?" His own tone became serious as he led her away from the man in purple.

"Yesterday, when he came up to me, I felt like he was more confident than the other males."

"Is he the king?"

"No." She shook her head, then looked at him once more. "He isn't looking for love. He is looking for a good time tonight, though. The only time these men will be able to flirt with so many women dedicated to the king, without losing their lives."

"You seem to have a low opinion of the king," he said thoughtfully.

She shook her head. "No, not at all. I think he is a kind king. He is generous with his lands and cares for his people earnestly."

"Then what upsets you about the king?"

"The mistresses," she admitted, her tone steeled. "I know it is tradition to have many mistresses in case you can't conceive a child or a male heir, but he is throwing this contest for a reason, isn't he? Surely, he must want to find someone to love, not just obey him." She paused. "Unless this is just a faster way to find all the women in the proper placement for their roles. But surely that can't be it since he didn't have a mistress with his previous wife."

He gave a gentle smile to her as the dance ended. "You're a very interesting woman, Estella."

"Thank you." She smiled at him, curtsying, leaving him on the dance floor. "Enjoy the rest of your night, sir."

CHAPTER 17

A King's Choice

LYSANDER BIT BACK A comment as he stood there in salute. Zeke was there next to him, looking as stoic as ever. If Lysander didn't know better, he would say Zeke was bored. Amir smiled as he moved pieces of the chess board around. He wasn't playing this time, but placed the queen at one end, and moved all the other pieces as if they were crowding her.

"Speak," Amir said in a deadpanned voice.

No one made a noise.

"Lysander!" he snapped, looking up from under his lashes. "Speak."

"My lord," he whined softly, biting his lower lip.

"Say what is on your mind."

"What are you doing?"

"I am setting up what I think is a good placement for the next phase in this *contest,*" Amir said *contest* as if it was bitter in his mouth.

"And what is that?" Lysander looked nervous.

Amir smirked. "I want to see exactly what I can do to push these ladies into madness."

Lysander silently groaned, as his shoulders sagged a bit. His eyes tightened and he hung his head.

"What do you want to say, Zeke?"

"Nothing, my lord."

"Come now." His smirk grew as he moved a pawn closer to the queen. "You must have something to say."

"I have nothing to say about this, my lord."

"I am sure you do, but for today, I will drop it."

Lysander looked hard at Zeke, and noticed the slight relief escaping him. Nothing that the king would probably notice, but Lysander could see that Zeke did not want to answer that question.

"There." Amir stared at the board. The queen was on one side, in the middle of the edge. Three squares diagonally was a small white pawn. Two more squares away behind the pawn were two rooks and a bishop. Slowly, it was all the larger pieces of the chess closer to the queen, and after all the larger pieces were used, was a straight line of pawns. As if they were at the start line, unmoved.

"My lord?" Lysander asked.

"Well!" The door burst open and Darius smiled as if he had won a gambling game. "Did you decide on a queen yet? I have a few suggestions."

Amir leaned back in his chair, resting his chin on his hand. "Oh? And tell me, Darius, who do you think is worthy for a queen?"

"I have several who I think would be great!" Darius sat down from across Amir.

"Who?" Amir looked very intensely at Darius.

"Oh, one of them is from a very well-bred Zephyrian family. She is educated in music, and her father is wealthy, so we know she isn't after the title."

"Oh?" Amir's eyebrows shot up, a soft smile tugging at the edge of his lips.

"Yes!" Darius smiled broadly. "I believe she would be a great match."

"Who is she?"

"Her name is Kelli."

"I see." Amir nodded. He remembered Kelli. She threw a drink on a servant for not filling the cup all the way, then laughed. Her cackling at the wet servant made him decide against her. "Anyone else?"

"Oh yes!" Darius looked up and thought for a moment. "There was another woman, she isn't pure Zephyrian, but she is from good breeding. You could tell by the way she held herself. She didn't stumble on her etiquette, and to be fair, I think she would be a submissive wife."

"Who is she?"

"Leila, if memory serves me correctly." The brown in Darius's eyes shone.

"To my understanding, you want me to marry her because she would be submissive?"

"Yes." Darius nodded.

Amir remembered Leila from the first night after he had finished dancing with Estella. She had come up, asking him to dance, which didn't bother him. But he soon found out why she wanted to dance with him. All she could talk about was how plain Estella was, how stupid she was by still having lessons in writing. Nothing good came out of her mouth about Estella. He got the feeling that she was jealous, trying to make Estella seem bad. Amir wasn't into having his future queen talk badly about someone with such vigor.

"How did you come to think she was submissive?"

"She answered any question I had for her without delay."

Amir nodded. After a moment of silence and watching his friend, now picking out the dirt from under his nails with a small knife, Amir asked, "Who is it that you did not like?"

Darius was caught off guard. "Oh..." He looked pensive. "I think that one girl who wasn't wearing any jewelry. She is easily the most beautiful of all of them, but she looked coldly at me. She didn't know who I was, I could be the *king*!" He said *king* as if it was to happen soon. "But she looked through me as if I wasn't the king, and she should just pay me common courtesy."

Amir smirked. "Perhaps she knew you weren't the king."

"I was well dressed; many of them thought I was the king," he huffed. "At the very least, she should think I have a high position."

"You do," Amir said plainly.

"Then why only give me common courtesy?"

Amir shrugged, sitting up straight finally. "Maybe she knew she couldn't get through the hordes of women who thought you to be me."

Darius pouted a bit. "I didn't have hordes."

Amir chuckled. "I'm pretty sure I saw you with every woman at least once."

"I have to do a thorough check." Darius laughed, finally noticing the chess board. "What is this? This doesn't look like a normal chess game."

"It's not," Amir said casually. "It is my visual way to know what I am going to do henceforth."

"So you know who is going to be queen?"

Amir shrugged nonchalantly. "In a way, I have a few favorites."

Darius looked cautiously at the board. "Who is the pawn closest to the queen?"

"My favorite."

"And her name is?" Darius waved his hand as if trying to pull out the information from Amir manually.

"I can't tell you, my friend." He grinned. "But I hope after the series of tests, she will prove to be the best."

"What are you going to do? Have a beauty contest?"

Amir shook his head, grimacing. "No."

"Then what?"

"They must entertain me," he said with a smirk.

CHAPTER 18

Ink in the Waters

A HORN BLASTED THROUGH the palace, making everyone walk out of the rooms and into the courtyard. Lysander stood there at the front of it.

"Attention," he started, "there is an announcement from the king."

"Is it another ball?" one girl whined loudly.

Lysander gave her a sideways glare. "No," he said in a bitter tone before pulling out a piece of parchment.

"What is going on then?" another girl asked, her voice clearly annoyed.

"The king was taken by several of you, therefore, invitations to spend a night with the king will be sent out to those personally."

"Spend a night?" one shrieked. "Before marriage?"

"Not that kind of night," Lysander hissed. "It will be a night of you entertaining the king with your talents, your wits, and most of all, your dignity."

"What happens to the rest of us?"

"The king has not informed me on anything, so far. I do know that the king has set his sights on a few of you. There will be several tests you will know nothing about in between each individual meeting, so always be on your best behavior." He gave a glance to Estella, whose cheeks burned slightly.

"Is he going to meet with us if we pass these tests?" a nervous woman asked.

"I don't know." Lysander was now getting very annoyed, evident by the clip in his voice.

"So you want us to just sit there and do nothing?"

"The king is the only one who knows what he is doing," Lysander chided. "So please return to your rooms. The letters will be sent out to the lucky women in due time."

There was chatter between the women as they began to head back to their rooms.

"Also," Lysander's voice dropped, sounding very serious and commanding, "I hope there will be no sabotaging of any kind."

There was complete silence.

He continued. "Remember, the servants, though invisible to you, can hear all. I will be keeping tabs on who does what. Conduct yourself in a queenly manner at all times."

A small murmur was heard through the women.

"Dismissed." He waved his hand before leaving.

As the women dispersed, returning to their rooms with a mixture of curiosity and trepidation, Lysander retreated to a secluded chamber within the palace. It was a dimly lit room adorned with ancient tapestries. He closed the heavy doors behind him and sighed deeply, running his fingers through his slick hair.

Lost in his thoughts, he failed to hear the soft footsteps approaching from behind. Startled, Lysander turned around to find a figure cloaked in shadows standing before him. It was the king, wearing a light tunic.

"What's wrong, Lysander?" he asked, laughing in a hearty manner.

"Sir," he said softly, feeling his heart beating wildly in his chest, "I came to collect the letter. You told me you had it ready."

Amir pointed to the desk that sat in the corner of the room. It was somewhat messy with papers stacked high on one end, and a small envelope in the middle with the king's seal on it.

Lysander bowed. "Thank you, sir." He collected the parchment, making a mental note about the desk later. "My lord, I will send someone up in a few hours to help you get ready for tonight."

"Why?" Amir's arms crossed over his chest, his eyes narrowed ever so slightly.

"Because you can't keep wearing Zeke's old uniforms!" Lysander shrieked.

Amir chuckled, waving off his servant as he sat down in a chair. "I'm the king, I am pretty sure I can do what I want."

Lysander resisted the urge to glare at the king. "My lord, I insist that you allow me to send someone to help you get ready for the date you have set for tonight."

Amir groaned. "I don't need help, but if it will make you feel better Lysander, I will dress for the occasion."

"Sire," he said as calmly as he could, "you realize that *you* set this up, correct?"

Amir nodded.

Lysander silently sighed. "Then I will take my leave now." He bowed and left.

"Farewell, Lysander." Amir smirked, waving off his man-servant. Amir knew that Lysander was reeling on the inside, wanting everything to be perfect for him, but Amir also enjoyed torturing him. Out of the corner of his eyes, he saw the chess board from the other night. He walked over to it and picked up one of the knight pieces, moving it closer to the pawn that sat so close to the queen piece.

"Let it begin," he said coolly.

As Lysander made his way to the designated wing where the eligible women were staying, he couldn't help but feel a sense of nervousness.

"Lysander," a male's voice called out.

He stopped and saw it was Hamid, one of the guards. "Yes, Hamid?"

"I was wondering which room you are going to. I was told I had to protect the one visiting the king tonight."

Lysander thought hard for a moment. He didn't remember being told about this. However, lots of times, there were miscommunications happening, and with how secretive the king has been with this endeavor, it was possible Amir had set this up without telling him.

"All right, follow me. You will have to stand outside the room until I come to collect her for tonight."

Hamid smiled and nodded. "Correct."

Lysander strode through the luxurious corridors of the palace, the strong sound of Hamid's boots stepping with each of Lysander's was noticeable. He didn't know Hamid very well, but he did think he was quite handsome for someone so young. Suddenly, Lysander got a sense of dread, realizing he was now twice his age as when he first started working in the palace.

"Are you all right, Lysander?" Hamid asked timidly.

Lysander waved him off. "Yes," he said with dismay in his voice. "I'm realizing that I have been here a long time."

Hamid blinked a few times. "As a eunuch?

Lysander sighed loudly. "That, too, but never mind."

Happily, they made it to the chosen room. Hamid stood off to the side, guarding the room. There were already two guards per room, so Hamid was an extra. Lysander entered the room, and it fell silent. All eyes turned towards him. They waited anxiously for Lysander to reveal who among them had been chosen for tonight's rendezvous.

Slowly, he walked to one of the women. She was in a deep blue saree that was made from very expensive material. He gave a small bow before handing her the letter. The friends around her squealed with delight. Her eyes lit up as she took the letter from Lysander.

"Fatima," he said sternly.

"Me?" she asked almost inaudibly.

Lysander nodded. "Yes."

The women squealed once more as they surrounded her. Some of the other women stayed in their areas, and glared.

"Congratulations, Fatima," Estella said, truly happy someone was chosen from the room.

"Thank you," she called out. "What do I wear?"

"Nothing," one girl joked.

"Might make her queen on the spot." Her other friend laughed.

Lysander cleared his throat. "I would recommend that you wear something simple and elegant."

"No," one of the women snapped. "She needs to be shining the best. She is first to be invited. She *needs* to stand out."

Lysander gave a bow. "Of course, madam." He wanted to say that isn't what the king likes, but he gave his suggestion and that was all there was to it. "I will come back later to receive you. A guard outside the room is your personal guard for the night, so I suggest you don't do anything foolish."

The woman nodded. "Of course."

"Then, I shall take my leave."

CHAPTER 19

Entertaining the King

"MY KING," LYSANDER BOWED to Amir, "the woman is ready for the arrangement."

Amir placed his quill down in the ink well, blotting the ink before closing the book. He gave a soft sigh, standing, looking at Lysander. He adjusted his sash.

"Tell me, Lysander," he paused. "Do you think she is worthy to be the next queen?"

"It is not for me to judge, my king," he replied, still bowed.

"Would you like to serve her until death?" he asked, seeing that Lysander was unmoving. "Speak plainly, Lysander, I know you have an opinion."

"I think there is a reason you chose her that I do not understand. But I wouldn't mind serving your choice."

"Tsk," he sighed again, "nice speech from someone who didn't want to go on record for not liking my choice."

A smile tugged at the edges of his mouth, but the king did not see it.

"All right, where are we meeting again?"

"My lord, she is in the dining hall."

"How is she dressed?"

Lysander finally stood up straight. "You will notice her the moment you see her, my king."

He rolled his eyes, groaning. "That means she is dripping in gold."

Lysander smiled wide to him, "I am ready to follow you, my lord, when you are ready."

"Wipe that smirk off your face, Lysander," Amir chuckled, "I am going to regret this. Make sure there is plenty of wine for me."

Shock graced Lysander's face for a moment. "Sire?"

Amir pinched the bridge of his nose. "That's right, I told you to not serve me more than a couple of glasses."

Lysander nodded timidly.

"Why do I feel as if she will bore me?" he groaned.

"Maybe she will be smart and love to talk to your majesty about things that are interesting to you, my lord," Lysander said, hopeful.

Amir shook his head as they walked out of the room. Amir was aware that he could end the contest in just a few words, but he also had to be sure that he wasn't dismissing anyone simply because he had a favorite.

As he strolled towards the grand dining hall, his eyes wandered over the ornate details of his palace. White, intricately carved pillars that lined the hallway, adorned with shimmering gold and jeweled accents. Reminding Amir that his father had gaudy taste and insisted on showing his immense wealth. If it didn't take more money to remove the golden items, he would have done so. Amir's restlessness grew as they got closer to the dining hall.

Lysander opened the door, allowing Amir to walk in. There in the middle of the grand dining room was a woman in a turmeric-colored dress, with golden threads sewn into it. The years of practicing his facial muscles came in handy at this moment. She was beautiful, for a golden idol: her raven hair up in the current fashion, small curls framing her face, her alabaster skin, and her ruby red lips. Her bright blue eye makeup made her blue eyes seem larger.

"Your majesty." She bowed low to the ground. Amir felt a flicker of surprise at the genuine warmth in her voice. It was a stark contrast to the usual simpering flattery he received from noblewomen seeking his favor.

She has been taught well by Lysander, he thought to himself.

He remembered why he chose Fatima first. It was at the first ball when he spoke to her; though she believed him a servant, she still accepted his invitation to a dance. Not without giving a small snicker when he initially asked. Amir was sure she laughed because she didn't think he was serious.

"Hello, Fatima." He walked over to her and gracefully took her hand, gently kissing it.

"Your majesty," she blushed, fluttering her eyes.

He motioned to the table, waiting for the servant to pull out her chair. She sat down before him and he silently smiled to himself. He knew Lysander was watching the whole ordeal, and was not happy that she sat first. Amir actually didn't care who sat first, but it wasn't the custom in Zephyria for him to sit first. Fatima, however, was not from Zephyria.

In a moment of desperation to salvage the evening, Amir decided to shift tactics. He leaned back in his chair and against his arm, studying the woman before him.

"Tell me," he began, his voice carrying a note of genuine interest, "what is it that truly ignites your passion? What is it that makes your heart sing, beyond the realm of silk and jewels?"

The woman paused, taken aback by his unexpected question. She blinked a few times, before giving her most coy smile. "My lord? I'm not sure I understand the question."

He leaned in closer to her, smirking. "What do you love?"

"Fashion." She blinked, leaning back from him. "It is important for the queen to know all that is fashionable so that we may set the trend for those below us."

Below us. He internally sighed and leaned back once again. "I see. Lysander, you may start serving the food now."

Lysander nodded, and the food immediately whirled out. Course after course, they sat in mostly silence with Amir asking a few questions and the woman responding. The problem Amir truly had was that he had higher hopes for this one. She wanted her fashion to come from the people of Zephyria themselves rather than from foreign lands. However, she also thought highly enough about herself to show up in the most glittered gold outfit; Amir was sure that the story of his ex-wife circled all the rooms for the last year.

"How were your travels, my lord?" she asked as she placed her fork.

"They were," he looked at the wine and knew no more was coming, "fruitful."

"Oh, I am glad for that." She smiled.

"This has been a lovely dinner," Amir said sweetly.

Fatima's cheeks blushed, she looked away, coy. "It is you who is lovely, my lord."

"Yes, thank you, er, um..." He furrowed his brows at her.

"Fatima," Lysander offered.

"Yes." He grinned. "Thank you, Fatima."

Her facial expressions were not as well-practiced. He saw the disappointment settle in as she realized he had forgotten her name. In truth, Amir knew it. But he wanted to see how well she could muster her facial expressions. A good queen is always going to have someone who will say something cruel and she must never let them have the upper hand.

Amir got up while she remained sitting, watching him. Amir internally rolled his eyes; she really should have stood up as well. As he entered the hallway, Lysander hot on his heels, he let out a heavy sigh. "Lysander, are you to tell me that you allowed her to wear that in front of me?"

"Allowed?" Lysander asked, his face contorting with a look of confusion, offended.

"She was like a golden idol," Amir said exasperated.

"I had given my suggestion on something more simple, less grand. I was met with resistance, and therefore, let it be."

Amir rubbed his forehead, groaning. "I thought she would have been better."

"Does that mean you wish to never see her again, my king?"

Amir nodded. "Yes, please see to that."

"Very well, my lord."

Before he started to head back, Amir turned to Lysander. "Find a way for me to see the one I danced with."

"Your majesty?" he asked, confused.

"Lysander," he gave him a stoic glare, "find a way for me to see the girl I danced with. I know you know who it is."

"You want to have a date with her, my lord?"

"Not the dinner date kind," he paused, "not yet, anyway."

Lysander gave a single nod, his voice timid. "Very well, my lord. I will find a way for you to see her."

The next morning, as the sun rose above the horizon, casting a golden glow over the palace grounds, Amir found himself sitting on a low branch in the shadow of a grand oak tree, waiting anxiously.

"Estella," Lysander said as he pulled her to the lawn. "You need to know how to tend to some plants."

"Why?" She laughed casually. "I thought the king does that himself."

"He does." Lysander was having a hard time trying to convince her to come into the main garden. "The king cares about the earth."

She eyed him up and down. "Really?" She scoffed. "After he sets it ablaze with the wars?"

He waved her off. "That's different."

"Is this penance for burning half the world?" She looked around at the lawn area. It was mainly grass and some hedges. "I don't think there is anything here for me to do."

"Of course there is." Lysander looked around, seeing that the garden really was well taken care of. The gardeners knew that their king was around, and therefore, they manicured it. "Estella, I told you, you need some sort of knowledge of plants."

She smiled sweetly at him, patting his cheek. "Very well, Lysander. But I already have some knowledge from talking with the gardener the other day."

"When?"

She shrugged. "It was after the first dance." She saw the look of horror on Lysander's face. "I took an escort, don't worry."

"Too late," he snapped.

She chuckled. "Well, the main gardener, he told me that the small clipping I took of the jasmine, somehow I had picked it just right where I can grow another jasmine plant."

"Interesting."

"Why? Do you think the king is going to ask me about it if I do see him?" Slight panic settled within her.

"No," Lysander simply said before sighing. "Now wait here while I go get one of the gardeners."

Estella chuckled for a moment before turning to one of the plants that had purple leaves. She crouched down next to the plant, her fingers gently grazing the velvety leaves. As she examined the intricacies of the plant, Estella was left breathless. The deep hue of the leaves seemed to shimmer in the blinding light. Her fingers brushed against the velvety surface further. She got lost in staring at the small veins that the plant had on its leaves, the coolness under her fingertips, despite the heat of the day.

Lost in her thoughts, Estella didn't notice the approach of the gardener until he cleared his throat politely. Startled, she stood up straight, smoothing out her skirt as she faced him. Her cheeks flushed with embarrassment as if she had been caught doing something naughty. The man before her donned a cream-colored tunic, stained with patches of dirt. His face was partially hidden by the woven straw hat, the tip pointing towards the sky. His face and hands were covered with some smears of dirt as well.

"Hello," she said nervously.

"Do you like the plant?" Amir asked in a gruff voice.

"I think it's beautiful, but I don't know anything about the plant. Just what I have been told by the head gardener."

"Ah, so you're honest." He smiled. "Do you plan to become a gardener when you become queen?"

"*When*?" she asked confused, before chuckling slightly. This laugh was not one of mocking, but of genuine delight. "Good sir, I think you are mistaken. The queen has yet to be chosen."

He leaned down and pulled out something from the ground before casting it aside. "So you don't believe you are worthy to be queen?"

"I think," she crouched down, seeing he was pulling up some weeds, and began to mimic him, "that the king will make his choice once he has examined all the candidates."

"Very diplomatic," he said in a more scruffy voice.

"Do you need something to drink?" she asked, concern laced in her voice. "I wouldn't want you to get sick from the sun."

"No." He coughed a bit, still making his voice gruff. "I am fine, my lady." He looked up at her, and there was a slight panic on her face. "Fear not, my lady."

"I should get you some tea at least." She ran off before Amir could stop her.

Amir stood up straight, giving into a slight stretch from hunching over. "Lysander," he called.

Lysander came out from the side. "Yes, my lord?"

"Get ready for my next date, I am going to go bathe."

"Are you done here, my lord?"

"Yes, see that she makes it back to the room safely."

"Did you find everything you needed from this meeting, my lord?" he asked, bowing.

"Some of it." He nodded, wiping the dirt from his face before disappearing.

When Estella came back with some tea, she looked around frantically. "Lysander, where is the gardener?"

"He was called away for the king."

She looked down at the cup of tea, her shoulders sagging, "Oh, I'm sorry I missed him."

"The king?" Lysander asked.

"No," she shook her head, laughing, "the gardener. He was in need of something to drink."

Lysander smiled, taking the cup of tea. "How about I drink it for him? I am also in need of something to drink."

Estella's eyes lit up, smiling as he drank the tea. "Thank you, Lysander."

CHAPTER 20

Another Round of Baths

O VER THE COURSE OF several more days and several more letters from the king, Estella began to feel a twinge of sorrow. It wasn't quite jealousy, and it definitely wasn't envy, but it would have been nice to be formally rejected by the king instead of waiting for a letter that never would come. Her mood was also affected by the fact that Lysander had become increasingly busy with all the letter business. She had always known that their friendship was contingent upon her becoming queen, but she saw him as a wonderful friend.

One good thing that did come out of the king and his letters was that the doors were opened. They were free to roam at their will without escorts as long as they stayed within the inner palace. The guards within were either hand-picked by her Uncle Zeke or the king according to Lysander, so they were the most honorable ones.

Estella enjoyed taking walks around the gardens and the inner courtyard where the fountain lay. She had gotten accustomed to telling stories to the ladies there. Today was no different as she walked the perimeter.

"My lady!" a male voice called out.

She looked around her to see a young man with a clean, shaved face bounding towards her. His arm was raised and waving at her with extreme vigor.

"Hamid." She smiled as she placed her hands in front of him, showing him she could not embrace him as was the rule for the ladies in contest for being the queen.

He stopped a foot away from her, smiling large. "I was told you were here, but I hadn't seen you the entire time. I also heard you changed your name to Estella."

She nodded. "I have been here the whole time."

He rubbed the back of his neck. "It's a shame. If I had made a declaration for your hand before the party, you wouldn't be in this mess."

She gave a forced smile to him that looked as natural as she could manage. It was common knowledge amongst the Ātash people that her Aunt Mari and Uncle Zeke had refused his proposal of marriage. Her aunt had said they were *old* and needed her to care for them in the years to come. Never mind that Uncle Zeke was in his best health, and Aunt Mari was as spry as a young chicken.

"Anyway," apparently Hamid was still talking while Estella was lost in thought, "I'm glad to see you before the king has his way with you."

"Excuse me?" Her brows furrowed.

"You'll be a mistress, or something."

She eyed him. "Why do you say that?"

"I heard from one of the other women who likes to talk badly about people. She said you will never get chosen, even though you are prettier than her." He paused. "That's my observation, not hers. That you're prettier than her." He winked at Estella, chuckling. "But she kept saying you dress so plain, and you had a flower for your jewelry on the night of the ball."

"Didn't you go?" Strange, since she was sure everyone near the king had to attend.

He shook his head, his smile fading. "Nah, I had outdoor duties with your uncle."

"Patrol?" she asked.

He nodded. "Yeah, I forget how much you know sometimes."

She shrugged. "I just remember things."

They stared at each other for a moment until a large clang happened behind Hamid, which made them both look at the commotion. It was a soldier who had knocked over a few spears.

"Hey," he said in a low voice, "do you want to practice like we used to as kids?" He had a gleeful look in his eyes.

"Hamid," she said in a low voice, "even if I was allowed to practice, I wouldn't. And you say as kids as if it was when we were five. It was only two years ago before you joined the king's army."

"Guard," he corrected. Estella could have sworn she saw something in his eyes for a moment, but Hamid quickly smiled at her.

"Yes," she nodded, "guard. Well, I better get back. Have a wonderful training, Hamid."

He nodded at her. "Thank you, Estella." He ran back to the other men, telling them something that made them look over at Estella.

Without wanting to draw attention to herself, she quickly retreated back to her room. Once she was there in her corner, she relaxed a little. Hamid always made her nervous, especially when she first met him—mainly because of his commanding presence. When her uncle told her that he joined the king's guard, she was shocked, as well as relieved, since he had always said he wanted to be someone important in town. She figured he would be a merchant, since he was learning that trade from his father or perhaps one of the elders. This would not be possible now that he had joined the king's guard. The Ātash people had strict rules about a lot of things.

After a few minutes of taking a few deep breaths, Estella returned to a calm state. It was then that the doors slammed open. Everyone turned their attention to the doors, seeing Lysander standing there. He had a letter in his hand. All the women who had yet to get a letter slowly stood up, some of them making their way towards him. Lysander's eyes scanned the room, before they landed on Estella. There was a grim expression on his face.

"Estella, your letter."

A hushed murmur rippled through the room. Estella extended her hand and took the letter.

"Am I to open it?"

Lysander nodded. "Yes."

She opened the letter, and saw the words.

> *Estella,*
> *Please be so kind to meet me in the gardens for our meeting. I request*
> *that you set up something that will please me.*
> *King Amir*

Estella's forehead crinkled a bit. "Do you know where?"

Lysander nodded. "I am to take you personally."

"Oh," she smiled at her friend, "then I shall get ready, however I am not sure about the rest of this letter." She didn't hear about any of the other ladies having to get ready for their date by setting it up. Was she actually the one who was going on the date or was he setting her up for head maid?

Lysander shook his head. "You have until the sun sets to figure that part out. I am not to help you in any way but getting you to the garden."

"I need a dress," she quickly said with more authority than she had ever given him before.

Lysander's face told her that he wasn't expecting that from her. He blinked a few times before a smile tugged at the corners of his mouth and he nodded. "Of course, my lady." He gestured to the doors. "Follow me."

They quickly left, as all the women watched as they hurried down the corridors. When they entered the grand wardrobe room, Estella was immediately surrounded by an array of colorful dresses in the arms of several maids. Each one fluttered around her, presenting various options and discussing which colors would suit her best.

"Quiet down," Lysander demanded in a stern voice. All the maids gave a slight glare to him before taking a few steps away from Estella. Lysander looked at each dress and accessory in the arms of the maids, carefully touching the fabric, looking at the beading. Estella thought he reminded her of her Aunt Mari in the market. She had to touch every fruit and nut before she bought anything.

"This one," he declared, holding up the elegant gown for Estella to see. "The color will complement your eyes and make you stand out amidst the lush greenery of the gardens."

Estella's eyes took in the lush green fabric that draped over his arms. It was made of a thick, heavy fabric that felt completely soft to the touch. There were small golden designs woven into the edges, but it was very minimal. "I thought we went for simple."

The maids and Lysander blinked at her. Lysander cleared his throat. "This is simple. There is minimal beading and little lace on it."

"Plus, it will be warm enough for the outdoors," the plump maid said.

"But not warm enough to make you sweat," another servant added.

Estella approached the dress, taking great care to look at it. She let the fabric brush her fingertips as she stared at it. "Tell me," she started, before looking at Lysander under her lashes, "did you pick the clothes for the previous queen?"

A small smirk tugged at the corners of his lips. "I always made a suggestion to the previous queen, but she always stated she knew best."

Estella looked at the other maids who were still holding their dress choices. "Do you trust Lysander's choices?"

Several looked at each other, unsure what to say.

She pointed to the maid on the far end; she looked to be the youngest of the bunch. She was holding a blush pink dress that had loose, flowy fabric. "You," she said with authority, "what made you choose your dress?"

The girl stammered, "Um..." she swallowed hard, "my lady, I thought it would complement your olive skin and give you a nice breeze on this warm night. Plus, the king..." She looked around herself nervously, but the other maids made no attempt to rescue her. "He loves flowers. I thought you w-would look like a flower."

Estella smiled at the young girl. "Thank you for your choice." She looked back at the green velvet of Lysander's choice. "Do you like Lysander's choice?"

The girl nodded. "Yes, it's a good choice. You will not stand out like the others did, but still look regal, like a queen."

Estella nodded. "I agree." She looked at Lysander, her smile warm to him. "Thank you, my friend."

Lysander bowed at the waist to her. "For the future queen."

Estella laughed. "I have to get through this dinner first. I don't even know what to do as entertainment."

"A story?" he suggested.

"What story?"

"You must have plenty from your people."

Estella bit her lip nervously. "None I think the king would be interested in."

Lysander cocked his head to the side. "How would you know?"

Estella let out a half-hearted laugh. "You're right, I don't know."

Lysander smiled at her. "Let's get you ready."

Estella gave a shrug. "Only a few hours isn't enough time for me to get ready."

"I think that was by design." Lysander gave a more sheepish smile to her.

She laughed. "I did have all these months to get ready."

A small snicker came from the maids. Estella looked at them in her good humor, but they silenced themselves the moment she looked in their direction.

"Oh, please don't," she pleaded. "I wish to enjoy this moment longer."

Lysander waved his hand in dismissal. "Come now, we need to get you ready."

"What about the entertainment? I thought you weren't to help me?"

"Do you need help?"

She nodded at him.

"Then ask, my lady."

"Lysander, will you see to everything being prepared while I bathe? Set out things that will please the king, his favorite food," she gave a sheepish smile, "and some of mine, as well?"

"Naan?" he asked.

She nodded. "Yes please."

"Anything else?"

"No," she shook her head, "that is all, my friend."

Lysander bowed, leaving her to the mercy of the maids.

It wasn't long before Estella was whisked away, placed into a rose bath, and made to soak in it. One of the maids started with washing her hair, combing through all the knots and loose hair that had built up. Estella had grown to love the way her hair was combed in the baths. During the time of preparation, everyone was given the same treatment. While some didn't enjoy it as much as others, Estella fully enjoyed it. The way they oiled her hair, the way they rubbed the ointments into her skin until she glowed.

Some of the maids helped her out of the water, drying her off with lush linens. They led her to a soft, cushioned chair, letting her damp hair drape over her shoulders. The maid in charge of her hair combed it, drying it with some of the linens as she went.

Another maid rubbed more lotions into her skin as she relished in this moment. If Estella wasn't chosen, she would lose all this. From what had she heard, the mistresses and those not favored with the king are meant to be barely above servants. Estella opened her eyes, looking up at the frescoes painted on the ceiling. They depicted continuing patterns of squares and triangles. The blues and golden colors showed the riches of the king. A small frown formed on her lips. If she were to be queen, she would lose much, as well. It might do well to pretend to be dimwitted and be a mistress he never touches. She could live her life pure and....

Estella shook out the thought. She had to believe she was here for a reason. She had to become the queen, if for no other reason than to speak with her family freely.

"My lady?" The woman drying her hair gave her a curious look.

Estella smiled at her, then she caught a glimpse of herself in the mirror. There was a thin light green ribbon woven into small braids in her hair. Her eyes glanced at her face, seeing the soft glow on her olive skin, and her bright green eyes.

A single clap snapped Estella out of her trance as she looked over, seeing Lysander standing there in a very clean, white, and rich outfit. He looked like he belonged next to the king, rather than behind the curtain. His eyes trailed over her as she sat there. Estella stood up, and folded her hands in front of her.

"Am I presentable?"

A soft, almost sad smile graced Lysander's face. "Very much so."

She returned the smile; they both knew so much rode on this evening. She had to do everything right, but she also had to be herself. There was a fine line she must walk. And even if she became queen, she had a different, new set of rules she was to follow. She would never be alone again. It was a bittersweet moment.

"Don't be so sad, Lysander. Trust that I remember everything and do everything correctly." She tried to make it sound casual.

Lysander walked up to her. "Then," Lysander took her by the shoulders, "I hope this is not the last time we can speak freely to one another." He gave her a formal bow before standing up straight.

CHAPTER 21

The Garden

ESTELLA HAD ARRIVED BEFORE the king. According to Lysander, this was normal. The king isn't the one to be kept waiting. Estella didn't think it was right for anyone to be kept waiting, but that was how she was raised. She was seated where the rugs and blankets adorned the ground, and a small table was set on top. Behind her was a sheep-skinned tarp filled with some fruits, nuts, and small smoked meats. Estella didn't touch anything.

There was no one in the garden, but she knew better than to do anything. Estella took this time to touch the garden with her eyes. She noticed that though they were in the king's personal garden, it really just looked like a large greenhouse. There were large roses that scaled the walls, making them into a thick barrier, one Estella had no desire to touch. Then there was some stonework placed in various places, with geometric shapes and bright colors.

It was then that Estella heard the doors open. She sat straighter as a line of guards, servants, and maids made their way into the garden. Parts of Estella were relieved that her uncle Zeke was not going to be there. One could find it awkward to have a parent standing over as the king woos them. Or, more accurately, Estella attempting to woo the king.

At long last, the king walked in. He wore a white, simple tunic, no headdress, and his beard was shorter than most men's, but it was clean. His tawny complexion had been kissed by days in the sun. In the light of the torches, his brown eyes looked golden. He gave her a smile that made him look like a raven with a shiny new object.

"At long last." He continued to smirk as he sat down in front of her.

Estella gave a gracious smile to him as she averted her eyes. "I am honored to be here, my king."

His smile faltered a bit. "You don't sound honored, you sound like a well-practiced book."

"And you look like a raven with a new shiny object," she said absentmindedly.

He chuckled. "I like that."

"I am flattered you find it amusing." She could hear Lysander groaning, even though he was nowhere in sight.

"I like it because it was not like a book. I am sure Lysander is shaking his head somewhere."

Estella glanced as slyly as she could. "I wouldn't know. I try my best to behave."

Amir laughed once more. "Like you did at the ball?"

Estella blinked a few times, her eyes still averted from him.

"Estella?" he asked.

Slowly, Estella began to recognize the voice. With a gasp, she looked up, horror written in her eyes and all over her face.

Amir let out a loud laugh, throwing his head back. "Took you a minute."

Her mouth began to gape open.

Amir's eyes trailed over her face, smiling large. "Definitely not like a book." His voice was soft, his eyes were warm, and the smell of earth radiated off of him.

"What does that mean?" she quickly rushed out the words in a breath.

"Most of the women I had entertain me were either strictly like the book *What it Means to be a Queen*, or they believed they were entitled, as if they were queen already."

"So I am for your entertainment only?" Her chest heaved as she tried to keep a calm and even voice.

"Not in the way you think."

"Then what way?" she ground out.

Amir looked around before looking back at her. "Be careful, Lysander is going to throw a fit."

Estella said nothing as her mouth was left open. She wanted to say something in the worst way, but she also had to remember that the king was only going to be generous with her sharp tongue as long as he was amused.

Amir picked up a small grape, eating it. "But to answer your question, I like your response. You were trained well by Lysander, but have a way of saying something not so queen-like."

"Forgive my rudeness, your majesty." Estella tried not to make it sound forced.

He raised an eyebrow at her. "Do you intend to be this way should we get married?"

"Forgive me, my king, but I do intend to behave in all manners—no matter where fate lays me."

"Hm." He took a date this time and chewed on it before taking a sip from his cup that was handed to him by one of the servants. The smile had faded from his face, replaced with a pensive look.

They sat in silence for several minutes, before the king broke it.

"Why is it that you intend to be like this instead of how you were at the ball?"

"Forgive me, my king, but I did not know it was you. I didn't believe I would have been chosen for the position of queen."

Amir looked over to the right of him, behind the curtain. "I don't believe Lysander did either."

"Sire?"

He waved her off. "To tell you the truth, Estella, I rather enjoyed you on the nights of the balls."

"Why is that?"

"Because you treated me with respect, even though you thought I wasn't the king. I did enjoy your rather sharp tongue and wit, but it was your kindness that I loved. Not just towards me, but anyone you graced. I watched you both nights and saw how anyone you interacted with was treated the same as I was. A young man with untailored clothes, tattered, and yet," he paused, giving her a genuine smile, "you treated me with such kindness."

Estella blinked a few times at him. "I didn't think I did anything different."

"You didn't," he continued to smile as he leaned on his arm on the table, "you simply were yourself."

She sat there stunned, her mouth agape.

Amir raised his eyebrow to her. "Are you going to eat?"

She nodded, tearing off a piece of meat, carefully chewing it.

"You don't have to be so nervous around me." He sounded a bit concerned; his eyes had worry written in them. "So, tell me more about yourself."

"What would you like to know?" she asked absentmindedly.

"What kind of books do you enjoy?" He took some smoked meat.

Estella hesitated for a moment. "I love *One Thousand and One Nights*. The adventure, the love between the two, but I love the mystery the most."

"Mystery?"

"Whether he was going to kill her or not."

He gave her a wicked grin. "Are you wanting me to kill you tonight?"

She let out a small gasp, her eyes widening. "Kill me?"

"Mhm." He nodded, though there was a glint in his eyes. "It's about a king who is scorned, then kills a new woman every night."

"But one," she said with a straight face.

"Yes, but one." His smirk turned into a smile.

"Then he has a romantic life with his wife."

"All in the efforts so he doesn't kill her," he corrects.

"Yes," she nodded, "it is in the effort to save her life, but they learn to love each other."

"Are you sure they love each other?"

"Of course," she said, matter-of-fact.

"What makes you so sure? After all, he loved her story, not her to begin with."

"Are you usually this cruel with your thinking?"

"Cruel?" He chuckled. "I think I just see the world as it is."

Estella said nothing as she took some more food. She finished her piece, then looked him in the eyes.

"What about you, your majesty? What is your favorite book?"

"I rarely have time for books."

She nodded, taking the last bite of her cheese. "Conquering does take a lot of time away from pleasurable things."

Amir's eyebrows shot up, a smirk spreading across his face. "Is that a jab?"

She gave a fake smile. "No."

"Do you have a habit of lying?"

"I am not lying. I was raised better."

Amir chuckled, shaking his head. "That one was a jab."

Estella said nothing as she licked her lip.

"Tell me Estella, do you not want to be queen?"

"Excuse me?"

"You are being most unlikable. And I can't tell you how many comments I have heard about how you will never be queen."

Estella's face fell. She wasn't about to cry, but her heart deflated. So he really brought her here to poke fun at her, after all.

"Forgive me, your majesty." She lowered her head as best as she could while sitting with a table in front of her. Her forehead all but touched the table. "I meant no disrespect."

He leaned on his arm, looking at her, waiting to see if she was ever going to lift her head up. After what felt like forever, he finally pulled her chin up. "Estella." His voice was soft.

"Yes?" she asked, almost inaudible.

"Play with me."

She blinked a few times, thinking she must have misheard him, before following his eyes to where there was a small table set up. Amir took her hand, leading her to the chess board. He settled her down in front of the white side and took his seat at the black.

Estella looked strangely at the chess board, almost as if she had never seen one before.

"Don't play chess?"

"Not well." She gave a weak smile to him.

"Then how about we place wagers on this game." He gave a sweet smile to her.

She arched her eyebrow to him. "Gambling has never made one smart or unregretful."

Amir chuckled. "It will not be money, but," he thought for a moment, "how about every time you check me, you can ask any question you want."

Her look didn't lessen. "And if you win, or get me in check?"

He gave another heartfelt chuckle, "I will ask a request from you."

She gave him a dark look from under her lashes. "Within reason, my lord. After all, we are not yet married."

The corners of his smile tugged into a smirk. "Yes," he gave a single nod, "within reason."

"Then I accept."

He motioned to her side. "I will let you have the advantage, with white."

"How sweet," she said as she adjusted all the pieces, "to think that I would need the advantage." She looked at him from under her lashes once more. Amir liked how long they were, how the green of her eyes stood out from the darkness of her lashes.

She moved her fourth pawn from the right forward two spots. Amir parried with his own pawn. Estella moved her right-side horse to the left of the L.

"So, how is it living in the palace?" Amir asked, moving his knight to defend his pawn.

"I thought questions were only to be asked once someone was in check?" Estella moved her bishop out.

"I said your questions were to be asked. I simply want a request when I check you." He moved his pawn that was in the line of the bishop up one space. "So tell me, what is it like being in the palace?"

Estella shook her head as she moved her bishop forward. "There are worse pretty cages."

"Cages?" he asked, confused, looking up at her, only to see her concentrated on the board.

"Yes." She gave a slightly mocking smile before settling into a more understanding one. "A horse may be allowed to roam in a field, but does that field not have a fence around it? It is still caged even if they are allowed to roam, eat to their heart's content, and sunbathe. A cage is still a cage." Estella looked up at him, smiling broadly. "Check."

Amir blinked a few times before he chuckled at the board. "You got me."

"Don't flatter me, you allowed me to have this check."

He said nothing as he smiled at her.

"Do you enjoy the contest, or is it simply tradition for you?"

"For my bride?"

She nodded.

He leaned back in his chair. "I am following some traditions, but a lot of the tasks have been for my own amusement."

"I see. Thank you, my lord." She redirected her attention to the board.

Amir took the bishop with the king to get rid of the threat. Estella moved a pawn, having the king take out his other pawn to create a fortress around his king that was forced out into the open.

"Do you see a path to victory?" he asked as he watched her move her bishop out.

"To that, if you are referring to the chess game, I see that the king is toying with me." Amir moved his king to the right. A move that wasn't normal to do, as the king was not in danger. "Tsk," she hissed. "If you are referring to the contest of brides, I would say I was also being toyed with by the king." She smiled as she took the pawn that sat in his way once more. "Check."

"What is your question?"

"Do you miss your ex-wife?"

"Interesting question. You know I could have you killed for such a question?"

"I would hope that the king is a man of his word and answers my question before killing me."

"Is living in a cage so bad that you wish to die?"

"Is your honor worth so little as to not answer the question placed forward as part of the wagers in the game you proposed?"

Amir took a deep breath before moving his queen forward, taking the bishop. "I thought I missed her at times, but then I realized it wasn't her, or even the idea of her. I found myself missing my man-servant more than anything. The previous queen was someone I once knew, but it wasn't as if I was in love with her."

Estella opened her mouth to ask another question, but said nothing. She moved her pieces, taking the pawn, only then to have the king take her knight with his own knight. Estella moved her pawn on the left side forward, only to be taken by his queen.

"Check." He smirked.

"What is your request, my lord?"

"I'll wait." He smiled.

"Very well." She moved her queen in the way of his check.

"Bad move," he said before he took her queen, "checkmate."

She shook her head. "Check."

"No," he laughed, "it's mate."

"No." She smiled before moving her other knight and taking his queen. She smirked as she looked up from under her lashes at him. "It appears as if we both have lost our queens."

Amir smirked, shaking his head. "It appears so." He took one of his pawns out. Estella reached out to move a piece, but Amir took hold of her hand. "Walk with me" he said in a low voice.

CHAPTER 22

Stories in the Garden

AMIR KNEW HE COULD eventually win the game, but he wanted to leave it there, where they were on equal footing. He led her down a pathway that was lined with the pink desert roses. He got so caught up in looking at his plants, he didn't hear her.

"What?" he asked. Not how he wanted the night to go, daydreaming away from her.

"Which one is your favorite?" she asked as she looked around.

"A secret one," he answered.

She gave him a coy smile. "Oh? Why so secretive?"

"Because it's my weakness."

A glint appeared in her eyes. "So if I were to pluck that plant, what would happen to you? Would it be like those foreign stories where the weakness is their downfall?"

He gave a shrug. "Does your family have any of those stories?"

Her smirk turned into a genuine smile. "Yes."

"Tell me."

"Well," she folded her hands in front of her, "there once was a man who was the strongest of men. He was blessed by his creator. He was told he would remain strong as long as his hair was never cut. So he stayed true, never to cut his hair."

"Is that it?" he asked, confused.

She giggled. "No. He falls in love with a woman. She was beautiful, but she wasn't from the same clan as him, so his parents forbade him from marrying her. He ignores them, and at his wedding feast, he gives a riddle to his guests."

"What was the riddle?"

"Out of the eater, something to eat; out of the strong, something sweet."

"Eater," he muttered, "sweet?"

Estella smiled as she looked at him. "Give up?"

"No," he smirked, "give me a moment."

As they continued to walk through the garden, the sweet smell of the flowers began to waft around her. Estella saw a lot of white jasmine and other flowers that were blooming that reminded her of the stars. Their gentle steps made little sound as they continued down the path.

He groaned after several minutes. "All right, I give up."

She chuckled. "The answer is a lion and honey. I'm sorry, I tricked you. There is no knowing the answer without the story before it."

He narrowed his eyes at her a bit. "What story?"

"Well, he killed a lion with his bare hands, and later, bees made their home in the skull. Honey, in the skull of the lion, which would have eaten him, but instead, he ate the honey."

"Hm," he gave her a suspicious look, "that was tricky."

"Yes," she nodded, "that was the point. On his wedding feast, the man made a wager of this riddle. The bride knew the answer only after she told him if he loved her, he would tell her. But then the men at the feast pressured her to tell them the answer. When they answered the riddle, the man was thrown into a rage and ended up killing everyone."

"That's harsh."

"Well," she sighed, "it's not the end of the story."

"What else happened?"

"His wife was given to another; he kills her, his father-in-law, and several thousand men with the jaw of a donkey."

Amir let out a laugh, holding his stomach. "Of all the weapons."

Estella chuckled. "It is a rather strange thing, but he killed over a thousand men with it."

"Impressive," he was still laughing, "for the donkey jaw."

"It wasn't long before he met another woman, but this woman was *bad*." She paused. "She was bribed to find the source of his strength. Remember he had been burned by one woman before, so he gives wrong answers three times. Finally, the woman grows angry with him, and makes him reveal the real reason for his strength."

"The man has a problem with women."

Estella nodded, pursing her lips together for a moment. "Yes, he does. Well, once he went to sleep, she cut off all his hair. His blessing left him and he became weak. The men who bribed her took him, gouged out his eyes, and made him a slave."

"Is that it?"

"Mostly." She nodded.

"Mostly?"

"As his hair grew, he cried out to his creator, and in one last effort, he brought down all the evil people, killing them as well as himself."

Silence hung in the air as he looked at her. It was almost as if he was studying her, but at the same time, intrigued.

"And you want me to reveal *my* weakness?" He smirked, his eyes alight with delight.

Estella chuckled. "Yes, I wish to pluck out your eyes and make you a slave."

He shook his head, giving a tsk. "I'm sorry, but I won't be doing that."

She laughed with him, having stopped in the middle of the garden. He stared at her, the way her hair was soft, the way she looked to be actually enjoying herself, the way—

"Your majesty?" She cocked her head to the side.

"Uh," he swallowed hard, "my mother loved plants." He knew it wasn't the smoothest transition. "So I naturally took an interest in them."

"That's sweet." Amir didn't like how she said that. It was almost like an automatic response. She must have seen it in his face. "I like that you took an interest in what your mother loved. After all, many skills are lost due to the child never showing a desire in the same thing as their parents."

"Gardening isn't a skill," he said a little more bitterly than he intended.

Estella let out a genuine laugh. "Gardening is indeed a skill. One that I do not have."

He eyed her with suspicion. "What do you mean?"

"I am able to water plants, and even weed them. Perhaps I know the right fruit to pick in the correct season, but I have none of the talents it takes to create this." She motioned at all the plants around them. A wicked smile showed on her face. "I'm sure you could tell me which plants play nice with each other."

A smirk formed on his lips. "You mean which plants are harmonious?"

She took a few steps away from him, looking at other plants. "Is that what you call it?"

"Yes." He nodded, watching her.

"Interesting." She gingerly ran her fingers over a bush of roses. "I would think that plants could be next to each other no matter what."

"Uh," he gave a chuckle in dismay. "No. Saffron cannot be planted next to garlic. They both compete for their place, but garlic is more aggressive, so it will stunt the saffron."

"Plants are aggressive?" Her eyes widened.

"Of course." He smiled at her.

"Is that why women are called plants?" Her shocked look shifted to a smirk.

"I never thought of it like that."

"Sweet-smelling beauties but sometimes," she looked at him from under her lashes, "there are things that can stunt your growth."

Amir was stunned on what to say; he just stared at her. The way the moon hit her hair, the look she gave him from under her lashes—she was beautiful, but not just the way she looked.

"Estella," he said in a low whisper.

"Yes?" Her green eyes were like a field of grass.

"Marry me."

She blinked and suddenly stood up straight. "I'm sorry?"

"Marry me," he said more aggressively as he closed the gap between them.

"Your highness..." she muttered.

"I know." He wrapped his arms around her waist.

She swallowed hard as she leaned back in his arms. "Your highness," she said in a breathless tone.

He smirked as he drew closer to her, pulling her chin closer to him. "You haven't answered me."

His thumb ran over her bottom lip. Estella knew she had to answer him. She knew she had to say yes. He was the king; she couldn't refuse to kiss him. His scent of the earth mixed with her perfume, creating a heavenly smell. Ever so slowly, Estella leaned in.

CRASH!

Both of them looked over and saw that one of the servants had accidentally knocked over a tray of food. Estella glanced at the king from the corner of her eye, noticing how he looked a little annoyed. His grip on her loosened, allowing her to step out of his embrace.

His expression softened as he looked at her. "Estella, I will expect an answer soon. I will not wait more than till the new moon."

She lowered her eyes. "Of course, my king."

He bowed his head. "I will leave first. Lysander will take you back to your room." With that, he was gone.

Estella stood there, flabbergasted as she watched him disappear. Lysander came out of the shadows and waved a hand in front of her face.

"Are you okay, my lady?"

She shook her head. "I wanted to kiss him."

Lysander gave an aghast expression as he stuttered, "I'm sorry?"

"The king was going to kiss me." She lightly touched her lips. "He was so close, I could almost taste him, but I wanted—"

"You just said you wanted to kiss him."

"I did," she played with her lower lip with her teeth, "but I want to know he actually wants me."

"What?" He gave a grimace to her. "In my country, people made love in temples and out in the open baths." He paused. "Is it because of your religion that you didn't kiss him?"

She gave a huff. "Nothing about being from my people says I can't kiss the one I'm engaged to, and I am sure the king would have kissed me if I said yes to his proposal. However," she bit her lower lip, "I wanted something more for why he chose me."

"When will you say yes?" Lysander asked, his frown now deepening.

"What is his schedule like?"

Lysander put his finger to his lips, looking to the sky as he thought. "Hmm, I believe tomorrow he is training with the soldiers, and the day after tomorrow, he is going over the documents for the kingdom."

She nodded, looking at her hands. "Then I will answer him when he is going over the documents." She took in a deep breath. "Lysander, we have a full day to get ready."

His brows furrowed. "What do you mean *get ready*? You're not scheduled to meet with him."

"I'm going to surprise him," she said definitively.

Lysander's eyebrows shot up and his eyes widened; it looked as if they were going to pop out of his head. "No," he said in a low whisper as he shook his head. "Don't."

"Why not? He said I could answer him, and I will answer him."

"Not even the previous queen was allowed to visit him without being asked to visit. This is punishable by death."

"It is death if I don't marry him."

"Estella," he took hold of her hand, "don't. He is likely to be in a foul mood and kill you."

"I doubt that, but if I don't become queen, then I might as well be dead."

"Why didn't you just say yes when he asked?" he whined.

She waved him off. "He said he will receive my answer before the new moon, so I will have all of tomorrow to get ready while he is busy with the troops. Then I will go to him, and answer him." She bit her lower lip. She sounded more confident than she felt.

Lysander's face went into his hands, as his voice fell into a groan. "Very well, my lady."

CHAPTER 23

Answers and Assassinations

I T WAS MIDDAY, AND Estella couldn't stop ringing her hands together. She was in her plain outfit, staring up at the sky, hoping to see some bright stars in the sky. The last twenty-four hours had been nerve-wracking, but today was the day. She was going to tell the king her answer. It was, of course, yes.

"Please," she begged. It didn't escape her that she could have just said yes immediately and avoided all of this, but here she was, taking the longer path. "Please," she pleaded again.

"The great creator doesn't answer all the time."

Estella turned, seeing her uncle Zeke in his official uniform today, clean pressed, his sword at his side, and his helmet on his head. "You're going to guard the king today." It wasn't a question.

He nodded silently.

"I'm..." She didn't know how to finish the sentence, twiddling with her fingers more.

"I know," he gave a grim smile, "Lysander told me."

"He doesn't know, does he?" She shook her head, hope in her voice.

Zeke shook his head. "No, Farih."

Estella wanted to cry at the name he had used for her; to run into his arms, hug him, and cry against his chest, but all they could do was stand apart. There, the silence hung between them before he began to turn back.

"Do you have to go?"

He nodded. "Yes."

Tears welled up. "Okay."

"May the creator of the Ātash People bless you, my child." With that, Zeke was gone.

She looked back up to the sky, with the sun shining high. She would soon be in a room with her uncle Zeke, the king, and several servants. How was she supposed to try to speak to the king with all eyes on her, waiting for any kind of mistake?

"Estella?" Lysander came out from behind her. "Are you ready to get into your dress?"

She nodded. "Yes, it is time."

Now was the time. It was an hour later from when Lysander came to fetch her to get into her dress. She smoothed the front of her dress as she walked up to the large golden doors. They reached up to the high ceilings and the doors looked quite heavy. Estella gave the guards as gentle a smile as she could muster. Each guard stood off to the side of the doors, but as Estella grew closer, it was evident on their face that she was not to be there. Estella steeled her resolve as she took one final deep breath, then stood up straight.

"Open the doors," she commanded.

Without hesitating, the guards obeyed. *Suppose they knew who was to be in charge soon.*

Estella walked into the long corridor in her white dress. It had a long train on it, and the dress was loose, looking like the delicate petal of a calla lily. The dupatta that was draped on her shoulder was made of a sheer fabric and embellished with white pearls. She held her head high as she walked. Each step seemed to echo in the halls; the faces of everyone were stunned, aghast, and some even truly horrified. Estella was not to let them know she was nervous.

She got half way through the hall before she saw Amir closely. He was sitting behind a large mahogany desk piled high with papers and books. He looked like the keeper of records. Amir had a scowl on his face before he paused, looking up. Their eyes clashed together; Estella's felt as if hers told her nervousness, and his were unreadable. She took in every facet of color in his deep brown eyes. Estella stopped walking, waiting with bated breath.

It was then that a small boy, no older than seventeen, popped his head out from behind one of the piles of papers. His auburn skin was pale, a kind of gray color—one could only guess from the lack of sun. He had sunken eyes with black circles under them. He was skinny and wore a white tunic. Estella didn't see her uncle, but knew he was there.

After waiting for what felt like an eternity, Amir smiled at Estella. "What do I owe this honor?" There was humor in his voice.

Estella let out a small breath that she didn't even know she was holding. Giving a low bow, she said, "I came to deliver an answer to you, my king."

"Oh?" Getting up from his desk, he walked around to the front and began to lean against it. "I'm sorry, but you'll have to come closer. I can't hear you from all the way over there."

Estella willed her legs to move. Parts of her were worried that if she took another step, she might fall down. But she, as gracefully as she could muster, walked closer and stopped at the bottom of the steps, which led right to the king's desk.

"Estella, up here." He motioned with his finger for her to come closer.

"My king," she bowed her head, her voice lower than normal, "I am unable to stand at the same level as you." Now she was mocking him.

He narrowed his eyes, yet the smile on his face was still broad. "Why?"

"Because a queen does not make themselves greater than their king."

A puzzled look graced the king's features before the words began to sink in. "Did you say *queen*?"

She smiled, then looked up at him from under her lashes. "Yes." Her voice now husky, ever so slightly.

Amir took the steps two at a time as he made his way down to her. In one swift movement, he captured her in his arms, twirling her around. *Yes, the dress did in fact get a little swept around the king's feet.* "Let's celebrate for we shall have a new Queen of Zephyria!" he announced.

A loud cheer erupted from the room.

"We will have to have a small one," she said when he finally placed her back onto the ground.

"So three days?" he asked with a raised eyebrow.

"With the whole kingdom?" Her eyes widened.

"Of course, maybe more days if people from other countries show up."

"It's an engagement," she insisted.

"To a king." He laughed.

"I understand that." She gave a nervous chuckle. "How about we have a small celebration, perhaps go to the garden and eat some cake?"

He gave an interested look. "I like that, but we still need the party."

She rolled her eyes.

BANG!

Everyone turned their attention to a man who was running in with a dark cloak over his head. In his hand, he held a curved sword high in the air as he screamed, charging towards Amir and Estella.

"Your reign will end!" he screamed out.

Amir shielded Estella as the man continued to run towards them.

Before he got close, the man was tossed to the ground. The man now laid on his stomach, foaming at the mouth, the sword no longer in his hand, with Zeke's foot on his back with a sword to the man's neck.

"If the future queen were not here, you would be dead," Zeke said in a dark tone.

The man flailed some more. "Unhand me!" he spat. "I will carry out my mission! Your reign will end, Amir!"

Zeke's sword pressed into his skin. "Do not move if you value your life," he said softly to the man.

"You are just a dog, a commoner, one who must be wiped from the country, and make it pure once more," the man sneered.

Zeke's eye twitched as he looked at the man, saying nothing. Other guards started to come to Zeke's aid, grabbing the man's arms and legs. He was lifted up, the men carting him out.

Zeke bent at the knee to the king. "Forgive me, your highness, for being late. I am afraid that in my advanced years, I am getting slow."

Amir laughed. "Advanced age? Zeke, you were still faster than all the other guards and the captain of the guard combined. I will forgive you for being slow, as you call it."

It was then that Darius walked into the room, his eyes watching as the man who was cursing was being carried off by several guards. He then turned his attention back to Amir, giving a smile.

"What happened here?"

"I don't remember inviting you." Amir narrowed his eyes at his friend.

"I am the advisor." He waved a dismissive hand. "I heard you were doing paperwork and thought I would give a hand." He glanced at Zeke, looking rather confused to see him.

"Farid is more than capable of doing it without me, but I like knowing where everything is going."

"He is just a boy." Darius made wild movements with his hands. "Surely I am more capable than him."

Amir frowned. "Farid is a genius with numbers and writing. No one is better than him."

Darius shrugged it off, looking back at where the man once was. "What happened just now though?"

"Someone tried to assassinate the king," Zeke answered.

"Weren't you *not* supposed to be here today?" Darius asked.

"I was reassigned," he quickly answered.

"Hmm," he said before looking back at Amir, then his eyes crashed with Estella's. "What do we have here?"

Amir smiled as he turned to show Estella. "Darius, please meet the new future queen, Estella."

His eyes widened. "You chose someone?"

"I did." He smiled. "I did have plans to celebrate, but now I am thinking it is not wise to open up the gates at the moment."

"Understandable." Darius nodded, crossing his arms.

"So I will have you set up a parade in the streets to celebrate Zeke for saving the future queen and their king."

"You want me," Darius's arms dropped and his mouth hung open, "to plan something?"

"Yes." He smiled. "That way, you can be put to use *while* not bothering Farid, and then Zeke will get the recognition he deserves."

"My king," Zeke bowed low, "may I please have some time to check everything before this parade? I won't be able to enjoy anything unless I am sure you are safe."

"Granted." Amir smiled. "In the meantime, Darius can plan the parade."

"With song and dance?" Estella chimed in.

"Yes!" Amir agreed enthusiastically. "Make sure there is plenty of food, dance, and songs for Zeke." He paused. "Also, make sure it is appropriate for him and his people to eat."

"Of course." Darius grinned. "Anything for you."

"Farid, please make sure the announcement of our engagement is ready to send out to everyone."

"Right away, your highness," the small voice in the back said with more vigor than Estella thought he had.

"So," he smiled as he walked with Estella, "about that cake."

"I'll have Lysander see to the cake right away."

"What does it have in it?"

"Pomegranates, rose water, and pistachios."

"Perfect."

CHAPTER 24

Of Rings and Rage

THE CAKE NEVER DID end up happening. When Lysander was summoned, he came, but only to drag the king back to other duties that he was ignoring. Apparently doing paperwork was his way of getting out of doing something else. Estella was stuck because she wasn't given the queen's corridors yet, and she wasn't sure she should go back into the prep room or the room with all the other women.

"Estella," Hamid walked up to her, "I was told to escort you."

She blinked a few times. "I don't think you're allowed in the area."

"You're going to the queen's quarters, of course I'm allowed to go there."

Estella didn't know how to answer this. She wasn't sure it was true, but Lysander hadn't told her what was the proper protocol yet. She nervously gave a nod. "All right."

"Don't worry." He gave a relaxing smile to her. He didn't move in front of her, but stayed beside her.

She knew this wasn't right. "Aren't you supposed to be behind me?"

"We are old friends."

"But no one knows that."

"Cassia does."

She stiffened at the mention of Cassia's name. It was someone she thought of often, but hardly saw. Cassia was also someone who knew her real name. Someone who could put her family in danger.

"Yes, but you are to stand behind me," she said firmly.

He blinked a few times at her, not moving. When she saw he wasn't walking, she started towards the queen's corridors. Lysander had showed the women where the queen's rooms were once. She had some knowledge of where they were.

"Estella," he said in a low voice.

"Yes?"

"Are you really going to marry the king?"

"Of course."

"Why?" He sounded annoyed. "He's not one of us."

"Clearly I have found favor with him; there is a reason I must be here."

He made some sort of noise, but Estella didn't catch it. She debated whether or not she should drop it. "What was that?"

"Nothing," he muttered.

She looked forward and continued down the hallways. The sound of people walking by and the small echoes of their steps against the cobblestones. The walk felt like hours as they walked in silence. Just as they were reaching the queen's chambers, she heard a loud sound of footsteps to the left.

Estella looked over to see a large group of women making their way to them.

"Hamid." Her voice was hard.

Without another word, he stepped in front of her, bracing for the onslaught.

"Estella!" one of the women shrieked. "How dare you steal the king!"

"I thought you were dumb, but you were really plotting against us."

"Just as I thought, she is not one for sisterhood."

"We should take another test to see who is really fit to be queen."

Estella's eyes widened as she heard the bombard of statements hurled at her. There was very little she could say to them. Hamid braced himself as the women got closer, getting louder.

"My ladies, you might want to return to your chambers," he said in a stern voice.

Estella took a deep breath, placed her hands in front of her dress, and stepped forward. The women stopped moving as they watched her.

"My ladies," she said as coolly as she could muster. "We all knew this was going to happen. If any one of you had become queen, this group would be here. There was always going to be one winner."

"A winner, but there are rumors that the king won't take a mistress." Vashti folded her arms.

Estella glanced at her. "I have no idea what the king has intended to do with anyone. I was aware that the king did not have any mistresses with his prior wife."

"So you will encourage him to have a mistress?" another woman asked from the back.

"Would you?" she asked back.

A hush fell over the women. Estella looked at all of them, then gave a small sigh.

"I will not promise to encourage the mistress business." Some grumbles were made. "However, I will try to find a place for everyone."

"Not all of us wanted to be here. How is it that we can go back to our families?"

"I was not here by choice either," Estella steeled herself, "but we are all property of the king. We have to be released by him in some way. I will try to fight for you." She paused. "Does that satisfy you all?"

"For now," Zahra said in a snappy tone, but it didn't surprise Estella.

Estella bowed her head to the women. "Thank you for listening to me." She stood up straight. "Now if you will excuse me, I must return to my room." She turned, leaving them behind her. Hamid waited for a moment, then walked after her.

"Is she having an affair with the guard?" one woman asked.

"Hardly," Cassia said.

The women looked over at her, eyes widened.

"Tell," Zahra said as if she was a snake trying to hypnotize its victim.

Cassia realized what she did as she looked at all the hungry eyes on her. "Um," she swallowed, "her family had rejected his proposal when she was in the village."

"So she could like him?"

"Like star-crossed lovers?"

Cassia winced. "I don't think she ever liked him."

Suddenly, they all deflated. "That's boring."

"Wait," Vashti raised an eyebrow at her, "what else do you know?"

Cassia looked at everyone, realizing she could say something damning if she wanted to.

"You handled that well." Hamid smiled.

"It is my job to calm the people. The queen is the heart of the king, therefore I am to keep the hearts of the people."

"So to make fake promises?" The way he said *fake promises* had a bitter undertone.

"Never," she said, matter-of-fact. "I was not raised to make promises that I won't keep. I will talk to the king about the women. See what he wants to do."

"Because he is to be your husband?"

She stopped walking, then looked at him. "The king was considered my husband the moment I accepted. It is the same in our culture."

"The Ātash People no longer see you as theirs." He looked at her head. "You were cast aside when you took that off." Hamid bowed at the waist, then left without another word.

Estella took hold of a piece of her hair, letting it twist under her fingertips. She knew Aunt Mari did it to protect her, but she also didn't know if Hamid's words were correct. Her heart hurt and she wanted to see her family, to hold them, to weep with them. But she was given no comfort as she walked into her new bed chambers.

CHAPTER 25

On a Magic Carpet Ride

THE SOUND OF SOMETHING hitting the pane of glass made Estella jump while sitting at her vanity. Cautiously, she went to examine it, seeing that it was a small, smooth, gray pebble. Just as she was wondering how it hit her door at this late in the evening, a dark figure leapt onto her balcony. Just as she opened her mouth to let out a scream, the figure's hand muffled her.

"Shh," the man said in a low tone.

"Your highness," she hissed, pulling his hand away from her mouth. "What do you think you are doing here?" she asked breathlessly.

"Seeing you?" He pulled his mask down, flashing a smile at her. He was wearing a plain black outfit with a mask that covered his mouth.

"You look like a prowler." She crossed her arms, looking him over. "I have every right to scream for the guards."

"Will you?" He smirked.

"I will think about it." She turned to go back into the room.

He caught her wrist, pulling her back. "Don't leave, Estella."

"Sire," she looked at where his hand was touching her. "If someone were to see us, they would kill me and think you impatient."

"Perhaps I am." He shrugged, pulling her closer to him. "But no one is going to kill you. I didn't when you barged into the room today, and I'm sure everyone was expecting it."

"You did think about it," she gasped, her voice getting a little higher. To be honest, she sounded a little like Lysander.

"And?" He chuckled.

"And nothing. I am behaving, as should you."

"Why?"

She squirmed. "Just because you are the king, it doesn't mean I won't run away from you," she warned.

Amir let out a soft laugh as he let her go. "All right, Estella, tell me what do I have to do in order to stay by your side for the night?"

The thought of him staying by her side was tempting. No one around them to make her feel nervous or spread gossip. "Don't you have someone looking for you?" She raised an eyebrow at him, stepping just outside his reach.

He gave a nonchalant shrug. "Maybe, but I am the king. I can do what I want."

"You're incorrigible." A slight smile tugged at the corners of her mouth.

Both of them stared at one another, taking in the cool night air, and...the smell of meat cooking? Estella got a wonderful idea, licking her lips. "All right, King Amir. Say I tell you what I want, will you fulfill it?"

The king replied with a cautious look on his face, but his curiosity was piqued. "What might that be?"

A mischievous smile played on Estella's lips as she leaned in closer, her voice barely above a whisper. "You'll have to prove yourself worthy of my trust and devotion."

The king furrowed his brow, his eyes narrowing in contemplation. "How would I go about doing that?"

"Let's go sneaking into the village." She giggled.

He raised an eyebrow at her. "The village? Why there?"

"I heard that there was a festival down in the village." She also knew it was the last day of the Feast of Lots.

"The Feast of Lots?" He eyed her more suspiciously. "Are you sure you want to go there?"

She shrugged. "I guess."

Amir looked out at the distance. "How would we get out there?"

"A magic carpet?" She chuckled.

"Sneaking out of the palace with me alone to a festival that isn't technically Zephyrian isn't misbehaving?" He raised an eyebrow at her.

Estella gave a sigh, dismissing him with a wave. "Oh well, then you might as well forget it, my lord. I only thought it might be fun to see, since it would be different as king and queen." She gave another wistful sigh, turning back towards her room.

Amir shook his head. "Oh my, Estella, you really are something."

"How?" Her brows furrowed as she turned back slightly to him. "My lord, if we announce we want to go to the village, how do you think Lysander will reply?"

He chuckled. "Not well."

She gave a coy smile, shrugging. "Then shall we go?"

Amir simply nodded.

She bounced slightly between each foot before taking a deep breath, "Stay here, my lord, *and* do not peek."

"Peek?"

Estella ran into her room, and closed the door and curtain before coming back out a few minutes later. She was dressed in a dark, long tunic with a salvar (baggy pants that tie at the ankle). The rusari she wore was a deep indigo, which spoke rich, but she was happy to see it back on her head. She lightly touched it, ensuring it was to stay on all night.

"Ready?"

"Ready."

Amir looked at her under the moonlight, and his heart fluttered in his chest. "Let's go, my queen."

"Estella right now," she paused, "Amir."

He pulled her close by the waist. "Maybe I should be in a mask always; you are less formal."

"Don't get comfortable with it." She rolled her eyes at him as she grinned from ear to ear.

"Wait." He adjusted her rusari to cover her face a little. "Can't have people seeing us," he said before pulling her mask back up. He grabbed the rope that was dangling down the side of the balcony and gave it to her. "Are you able to go down on your own or do you need me to help you?"

"A strong man like you?" She faked a swoon. "I might faint if you hold me all the way down the building."

"Can't have that." He chuckled, letting her go reluctantly.

Estella had never climbed down the side of a building. She was a rather good girl when she lived in the village, but she quickly found that climbing down the building was easy to do. She did have to be cautious about burns from the rope. As she reached the bottom, she looked up, seeing Amir glide down with ease.

"How will I get back up? I don't have the strength to climb that."

Amir landed on the ground with a soft thud. "I can carry you." His smile was borderline smirking.

"No, I think it would be safer to just go in the front."

He shook his head. "You might as well shout out for Lysander right now if we do that."

Estella bit her lower lip, looking back up the wall she had just shimmied down. She let out a small groan. "I guess we will figure that out when we get to it. Come on," she said as she started to walk towards the gate.

He caught her wrist and pulled her to him. "Really now, you tell me *let's go* and then try to walk right out the front gate?"

"Well," she tried not to look him in the eyes, "where are we supposed to go?"

"To the tree." He motioned to the other side of the wall. There stood a large mango tree that had to be a few hundred years old.

"Oh," she gasped.

"I know, it's a little scary-looking, but once we are over there, it will be easy to get to the village."

She raised an eyebrow at him. "Why do I feel like this isn't your first time?"

He shrugged, leaning in closer to her mouth. Amir's cologne filled her nose, a refreshing mix of mint and musk that made her inhale deeply. As he wrapped his arms around her, she could feel the heat radiating from his body, enveloping her in a comforting embrace. He paused breaths away from her lips, just as he had when he proposed.

Amir cleared his throat, releasing her. "I better stop, or I won't be able to." He took her hand and started towards the mango tree.

Happily, the cover of darkness concealed that Estella was heavily blushing. When they reached the mango tree, Estella couldn't see the magnitude of it, though she knew there was an end to it, but standing underneath it, she couldn't see it.

"How will we get back?"

"There is a rope." He smiled, taking a few steps onto the tree. "Let's go." He extended his hand to her.

She took hold of his hand, stepping where he stepped and grabbing where he told her to grab. She wasn't so thoughtless to think she was safe to do it alone without his guidance. When they reached above the wall, there was a worn rope curled up.

"Is that safe?"

He nodded. "Yeah, it gets replaced often enough for me to know how much tension I can have on it before it snaps."

She raised an eyebrow at him. "So it *is* often."

"Not as often since I am the king, but I did used to do this when I was a boy."

"Why?" she asked as he threw down the rope over the wall, tugging the rope that was attached to the tree branch.

"My stepmother didn't care for me," he said as he swung over, climbing down the rope.

"Oh," she remembered Lysander saying that he was the second wife's son. Estella figured it didn't come with great perks.

Amir landed on the ground with a soft thud and extended his arms. "Jump, I'll catch you."

She shook her head. "No."

"Come on," he smiled, "I promise I'll catch you."

"I could hurt you."

"Doubtful." He shook his head. "Come on. Grab the rope, climb a little down, then let go."

Estella hesitated for a moment, contemplating the risk. However, with Amir's reassuring smile and outstretched arms, she decided to trust him. Taking a deep breath, she reached for the rope and began to descend slowly.

As Estella descended, each grip on the rope became more confident. Her heart pounded with a mix of fear and adrenaline, but she refused to let it consume her. She knew that Amir was waiting patiently for her below, ready to catch her if needed.

Finally, when she felt ready to let go of the rope, Estella released her grip and leaped into the air. The wind rushed past her face as she plummeted downward, but before panic could set in, strong arms wrapped around her, catching her in a secure embrace.

Amir's laughter filled the air as he held her tightly. "See? I told you I would catch you," he said with a mixture of amusement and relief.

Estella couldn't help but laugh as well, trying to place her feet on the ground.

"Did I give you the impression that I was going to let you go once I caught you?" He smirked devilishly.

She wiggled in his arm, trying to free herself. "Amir, this isn't proper."

"So? I'm not the king here."

"Still," she hissed.

He chuckled, letting her down. "All right, I'll let you down, but I'm not letting you go." His hand found hers quickly.

Estella began to protest, but then some guards started to walk towards them.

"Come on, Estella." He pulled her down an alleyway and made his way to the end.

Once the coast was clear, Amir turned to Estella with a mischievous glint in his eyes. "Well, that was exhilarating, wasn't it?"

Estella couldn't help but smile at his infectious energy. "I must say, your highness, you do have a knack for getting us into rather adventurous situations."

He grinned back at her. "I've learned that playing it safe all the time is no way to live life. You have to take risks and make the most of every moment."

She eyed him up and down. "You're the king, you're not supposed to take risks."

He hushed her. "I'm Amir right now, and you're Estella. We are just enjoying the cool air and the party."

"You seem to like parties."

"I like a good time when I relax."

"Sounds like you're trying to fill a void."

He shrugged. "Perhaps."

As they wound their way through the streets, the sounds of laughter and music grew louder. It was at the edge of Zephyria that there was a massive fire, with people dancing around it, and singing.

"Wow." Amir looked around, the soft glow of the fire making his eyes shine.

"The fire is meant to show the struggle of the people."

"I didn't know there were people in the kingdom who worshiped fire."

Estella giggled. "They aren't worshiping the fire. The fire represents a story in the clan that is passed down."

"Why a fire?" He looked at her curiously.

Panic started to rise, realizing she was saying too much, but she couldn't stop now. "A fire spoke to them and told them they would be delivered to a promised land."

"So a fire is important to them?"

"It is meant to represent the fire in them, the spirit that lives in them in times of hardship."

Amir nodded, looking at the way the women danced and the men banged on the drums. They were dressed in light-colored clothes, the women wearing head cloths and carrying some plants in their hands as they danced.

"It's beautiful," he whispered.

"It is." She smiled, looking at him.

"Have you ever danced by a fire before?" he asked, his eyes sparkling with mischief.

Estella hesitated for a moment before shaking her head. "No, I can't say that I have."

Amir's smile widened as he extended his hand towards her. "Would you like to give it a try?"

Her heart raced at the thought of dancing with him, but she couldn't resist the pull of his outstretched hand. With a small nod, she placed her hand in his and let him lead her towards the flickering flames.

The heat from the fire warmed their skin as they joined the swirling mass of dancers. Estella stumbled at first, trying to match the rhythm of the dancers.

"Amir." She laughed as he pulled her into his arms.

"You danced at the ball effortlessly, but here you can't?"

"I didn't learn this dance." She laughed, trying to keep up with the steps.

"Ah," he pulled her closer to him, "then we will just have to make up the way you dance."

"And have their creator smite me?"

"I think if you just dance with your heart, you will be fine." He twirled her around, swaying to the music.

Their movements became more fluid and synchronized as they danced around the fire, lost in the hypnotic rhythm of the drums. The flickering flames casted a warm glow on their faces, highlighting their smiles and the sparkle in their eyes. As they twirled and swayed together, the soft fabric of their clothes brushing against each other, a warm sense of closeness enveloped them. With each step and turn, their bodies seemed to merge into one fluid entity. It was a moment frozen in time, where nothing else existed except for the two of them, lost in the beauty and connection of dance.

The onlookers cheered and clapped, their voices blending with the beat of the drums. The night seemed to stretch on endlessly, filled with laughter, music, and the crackling of the fire.

As the dance came to an end, Amir held Estella close, his gaze locking with hers. In that shared moment of silence, unspoken words passed between them.

Amir leaned in, inches away from Estella, and then a roar of laughter erupted. He pulled back, looking around, seeing everyone looking at them.

"Ah, my good sir, you must go home if you look at her like that."

"Yes," he said as he laughed, "I will need to go home with her."

"Hamil, we don't know if they are married," a woman cried out, hitting the man on the arm.

"He obviously wants to kiss her, of course they are married." The man, Hamil, flayed his arms as if making a bigger point. "Why else would he look at her like that?"

"He's immoral," an old woman muttered.

"No, he loves his wife," a young girl who sat next to the old woman swooned.

Amir laughed, looking at Estella, who was visibly embarrassed.

"Then why the mask?" the old woman asked.

"Maybe they are converting to us?"

"Then we need to see their faces."

"I think they are the king and queen!" someone shouted.

"Ack, no king or queen would be caught here. And do you see guards any-where?"

"No, but why else hide themselves?"

"I think they are circus performers, and they came to join us for the evening."

Amir grabbed Estella's hand. "Come on," he whispered in her ear. "Let's go before they find out we *are* the king and queen."

She nodded quickly as she was dragged away. Amir had pulled her off towards the castle but stopped short when they reached the outer castle. Slowly, and in the shadows, he pulled her towards the tall tower. It was fairly dark, so Estella was hoping nothing would jump out at them or crumble underneath them.

They finally reached the door of the tower, and Amir ushered her inside.

"Your highness," she hissed. "This is *really* inappropriate."

"Relax," he chuckled, "we are going upstairs for the view."

"I can't see anything."

"Just be careful about where you step."

Estella felt around with her foot as she took each step carefully. Slowly, she started to feel more comfortable walking up the winding stairs. It smelled of old, stale air.

"What is this?"

"It used to be a guard tower, but now it's just ruins." Estella noticed that the sound of his voice had a clip to it when he said *ruins*.

As they made it higher in the tower, the lighter it became. Estella could clearly see the steps and even glanced back at Amir a few times. He caught her gaze every time, and smiled. After several minutes which felt longer, they reached the top. It was a solid stone floor; the air was clear and the arches had no glass. They were open and evenly spaced, going all the way around.

"It's beautiful."

"It's dirty, but it has an amazing view," he said as he gently took her hand, leading her to the edge.

From the edge, you could see the wild gardens below, and the peace and serenity it seemed to bring with it, was beautiful. Estella looked further, seeing the glowing lights of the inner palace. The cleanliness and sturdiness of it showed its might.

"What are you thinking?" he asked as he stared at her face.

"That the city of Zephyria is more like you than I realized."

He gave a puzzled look. "What do you mean?"

"The strong fortress of the inner palace and the wildness of the outer palace. Both make you."

Amir had no expression on his face for a moment, then gave a gentle smile. "I like that."

She turned around and looked at the town. "And behind you are your people. Those who have gathered here for one reason or another."

"Like those at the Feast of Lots?" He chuckled.

"Yes." She blushed as she suppressed a giggle. "Even they are allowed to celebrate their own traditions without true fear from you. That shows how kind of a king you are."

"I'm not sure about kind," he said as he looked at the town. "Darius wants me to regulate more of the other people who come here, but I see no problem as long as they don't disobey my laws."

"Your laws are fair, and have been for the seven years you have been king."

He looked at her, his smile growing.

"Have you always been one for sneaking out of the palace to look at your kingdom?" she asked.

He shrugged. "No."

"Don't you think this is a good way for you to get invaded and possibly raided by constantly sneaking out?"

"No," he simply replied. "I know the timing like the back of my hand. It's never the same from day to day. And the guards are careful with the amount of shift changes."

"You seem very sure of this."

"Of course, because I am the king."

"That doesn't make you the almighty creator." She laughed, then instantly regretted it. She hoped her face didn't show it though.

"When I was a kid, I was kind of shunned from the inner palace. My father was off to war all the time, so I learned how to fend for myself the best way I could. I learned all the routes of the guards, the amount they had each day. It took me a few years not to get caught every time, but I finally managed it."

"Is that why you have this old outfit?"

He looked down for a second, then back up at her. "I bought this in the market one day when I was exploring."

Estella laughed as she examined it on closer inspection. "It looks like it was well-loved."

"Well, I have worn it several times."

"So you admit it, sneaking out all the time."

"Not as much, I told you," he said, exasperated.

Estella giggled before looking out once more at the lights in the desert from the festival. She wondered if her uncle and aunt were there. She didn't see them but it was a large party. Estella knew she shouldn't be out alone, but it was nice to have Amir without pretenses and someone watching them constantly.

Amir gave a soft sigh, as if he was reading her mind. "I better get you back before someone comes to check on you."

Estella nodded. "Yes, we don't want there to be questions."

"I'm the king, I wouldn't be harmed, but I wouldn't want your reputation tarnished for no reason."

She eyed him, before relaxing into a smile. "Thank you."

Amir carefully walked her back to her room, scaling up the wall first, and helping her along the way. He would have liked to go after her, and though she was wearing pants, he didn't see how that was appropriate. Finally, they reached the top, with Amir pulling her onto her balcony.

"Safe and sound."

"Mostly." She smiled as she pulled a stick out of her hair and brushed a web off his shoulder.

"This was nice, Estella."

"I had a lot of fun." She began to walk towards her room. Estella stood in the doorway for a moment before she turned to face Amir, her eyes filled with gratitude and wonder.

"Thank you," she whispered, her voice barely above a breath.

Amir simply smiled, a glimmer of pride in his eyes. He turned around, going over the balcony on the shadowed part.

"Wait," she whispered loudly as she ran towards the railing where he was.

He looked up into her green eyes. "Yes, Estella?"

Her chest rose and fell quickly before she leaned down, holding onto the railing and giving a kiss on his cheek. Not one that was like kissing one's grandmother. Without another word, she ran inside, her cheek flushed and the door closed tight. The soft sound of the lock echoed slightly.

Amir smirked as he stayed there a moment longer, staring at where she once was, before he continued to scale down the wall.

CHAPTER 26

Zeke's Gambit

ZEKE CLEARED HIS THROAT, breaking the silence. "Do you truly think they will accept her as their queen, Lysander?"

Lysander leaned against the wall, his face etched with weariness. "It won't be easy, Zeke. These women have spent the last year vying for the king's affection, hoping to secure their positions as mistresses. With Estella's sudden rise to power, they are bound to question her worthiness."

"Yet the king chose her," Zeke said solemnly. "He saw something in her that he didn't find in them."

Lysander nodded, his eyes distant. "Estella possesses a strength and intelligence uncommon in these royal halls."

"I will thank you both not to discuss my queen when I'm being forced to do other things," Amir said as he dried his hair, the wet strands still dripping onto his bare chest.

Zeke bowed humbly. "Forgive me, your majesty."

Amir looked at Lysander who was leaning against the wall still. "I do believe you are taking advantage of me, Lysander."

He quickly stood up. "No, of course not, your majesty."

Amir sighed heavily. "Stand up straight, Zeke, I don't wish to play the king right now."

"Planning to sneak out once more?" Zeke asked as he stood up straight.

Amir let out a loud laugh as he threw back his head. "Only you, Zeke!"

"Who left?" Lysander exclaimed, looking back and forth between Amir and Zeke. "Your majesty, did you escape?" His voice went into a higher squeak.

Amir said nothing, only smirked as he walked away.

"Your majesty!" Lysander shrieked. "You could have been killed."

"Hardly," he said as he threw his voice.

"Your majesty," Lysander whined.

"Calm down, I simply went on a date with my new wife."

"A date?" Lysander looked at Zeke who had a grim expression on his face.

"Yes." Amir chuckled. "How did you see, Zeke? I was sure to be discreet."

"I'm sorry, my lord, but it is my job to see where you go."

"You see too much." Amir walked out, giving a grimaced look.

"It is my job." He bowed again.

"Stop bowing." He waved him off. "How much did you see?"

"I followed you the whole time, my lord." He stood up straight.

"Goodness," he smirked, "so you saw everything."

"Everything?" Lysander's voice squeaked to almost inaudible sound.

"Lysander," Zeke chided. "There was nothing happening that was not right before the creator."

"The creator of the Ātash People must be interesting," he said in disbelief.

Zeke said nothing.

Lysander's hand went to his forehead. "I will never grow old. I will just die from all the stress."

"What stress?" Amir chuckled as he finished getting dressed.

"The kind you place on me. How will I be able to keep you safe, and the queen, for that matter, if you two are sneaking out?"

"It was *one* date." Amir smirked. "For now."

Lysander's face went white, and Amir let out another laugh.

"Lysander, if you're done turning white and throwing a fit, can you arrange my dinner with my new wife?"

Lysander took in a deep breath. "Zeke, please go gather the queen, and meet in the great hall."

Zeke nodded as he headed to the queen's room. As he walked, a voice came from behind some curtains.

"Zeke," the voice snapped. It was meant to be disguised, but he still knew who it was.

"What?" He saw no point in being formal.

"You better not stand in the way, just because the king gave you some party."

Zeke's jaw tightened. "I do not seek favoritism from the king, I simply do my job."

"I heard an interesting thing about your niece."

Anger grew in Zeke, but he remained calm in his voice. "My niece?"

"Yes, the one who is going to be queen. All the women are talking about it now. Simply dreadful if the next attack was on her."

"She is safe from you, and all others who intend to do her harm."

"Is she?" The voice was like a snake, charming and deceitful.

"I will protect her at all costs."

"What if she is the cause of the king's fate?"

Zeke said nothing as he looked at the curtain; he knew he could reach in and kill the person, but it wouldn't help Joy. If this person knows her real origin, then it won't be long before everyone knows it.

The voice gave a malicious chuckle. "Nothing to say?"

"Excuse me, I have to see to the queen."

"Remember, don't get in the way."

Zeke's hand balled into a fist as he walked away. Without much effort, Zeke reached the queen's rooms. He paused right before he knocked on the door. He was nervous, swallowing hard before he cleared his throat, giving a hearty knock.

A few moments passed, then a maid came to the door. Her eyes scanned over Zeke.

"Yes?"

"The king requests the queen to join him for dinner."

The maid nodded, then closed the door. Zeke stood at attention, waiting for the queen to emerge. After only a few minutes, the future queen emerged from the room, dressed in a dark green velvet saree with light embellishments on the edges. Her hair was in an intricate bun with a silver comb holding it together. Her lips were painted, and Zeke thought how she looked like his sister, her mother.

"Are you ready, Zeke?" she asked, smiling at him.

He nodded, waiting for her to walk ahead.

Estella took five steps ahead, as was proper for her to do as queen. Zeke had spent his adult life here, working in the palace, seeing lady after lady. None of them compared to Estella. She was a genuine queen, as was the second wife.

"I heard you had the parade already, Zeke."

"Yes, your majesty."

"How was it? I'm sorry I wasn't able to attend." She was not to meet the public until she was queen.

"It was delightful. My wife was very proud of me."

She said nothing for a moment. Then finally, "How is your family, Zeke?"

The question took him by surprise. "My wife had taken ill for some time when our niece left to get married."

Estella faltered a bit. No one would have noticed it, but Zeke knew her all too well.

"I'm sorry to hear about that," she said with grace.

"Thank you, ma'am. I believe she will recover in time for the wedding."

"Really?" There was a lighter tone to her voice.

"Yes," he nodded, "she is a henna artist. Our niece used to collect the leaves for her when she lived with us."

She smiled. "I would be honored if she would adorn me on the henna night."

"I will speak with her about it."

"Thank you." She turned her head slightly and smiled at him.

They had arrived at the grand hall in little time. Zeke had taken his place by the door, his hand on the handle, waiting for her to command to open it.

Their eyes locked for a moment. "You may announce me now."

He nodded. "Of course." He opened the door. "Presenting, the future Queen of Zephyria, Estella."

Estella began to walk in.

"Congratulations," Zeke said in a low voice as she walked in. "May the creator of the Ātash People bless your marriage."

It took all of Estella's will not to cry as she approached the table.

CHAPTER 27

An Innocent Request

ESTELLA HAD ARRIVED BEFORE the king, which was the custom in Zephyria. However, for the Ātash people, it was rude to make anyone wait. Especially if you asked for the other party to join you. There was a small table with two settings. A male servant had pulled out one chair for her. Estella had remembered the lesson on sitting; she was to sit, and wait. Once the king arrived, she was to stand.

It didn't take long before Amir showed up. He was finally in a well-fitted suit, fit for a king: an indigo blue jacket and pants with golden trim. His beard, though full, was well-groomed and clearly had been trimmed recently. As for his hair, it was styled in a slicked back manner, not a single hair out of place. If Estella didn't know he was king before, she would now.

Amir walked in the room as if all eyes were supposed to be on him. They were, but his air of confidence was unmatched. Each step was with power, not grace as *she* had been taught to walk in her lessons.

Very few of his strides were taken in order for Amir to reach Estella. It was there, she gave a low bow, her knees bent.

He made a sort of grumbling noise. "Why are you so low?"

"Excuse me?" She looked up at him, confused.

"You're my queen, you're never supposed to be that low. Your head is the only thing that should bow."

Estella slowly rose, then bowed her head to him.

He relaxed into a smile. "Much better."

Amir sat first, with Estella shortly after him. Lysander rushed out from the side, giving a single clap. Tray after tray, a servant brought out silver platters, settling them down on another table that was away from them; this one was long, meant to hold the plates of food. A single course was made for the king and queen, given to the tester first, of course.

"So," Amir's smile grew as he looked at her, "tell me more about the *great* Estella."

She suppressed a giggle as she took in the smell of the food. "There isn't much you don't already know."

He shrugged. "I suppose."

"How about you tell me about yourself, my lord."

"Me?" His brows furrowed. "Why me?"

She gave her own shrug. "There are a great many rumors about you."

"Hmm." He took a few dates and began to chew them slowly.

She smirked before taking a piece of the naan into her mouth. "Why are you so dark-skinned, despite being the king? Zephyrians are known to be lighter in complexion, despite still being brown." She looked him over carefully, letting her eyes soak up as much as she could. "It is sun-kissed."

He looked at his skin before looking back up at her, his own smile turning into a smirk. "I believe a good king goes to war with his men. It is not right to send men to die for a king who will not serve his own men."

"So you serve them?"

"I lead them."

"And that makes you sun-kissed?" She arched her brow.

He nodded. "Yes." He looked over her face. "Why are your eyes green, even though it is not common?"

"I don't come from here, remember?"

He nodded. "Yes, but anywhere outside my kingdom that you could have traveled is also not plagued with green eyes. In fact, I would say that they are quite rare."

She smiled. "My mother had them. My aunt said she was blessed with the earth to keep the family grounded. It was passed down to me somehow."

"Did you keep your family grounded?"

She didn't let the emotion show on her face. "I did," she nodded, "as best as I could."

"Then perhaps you were blessed," he paused, "by..." he trailed off. "What is that saying?" He looked around the room, until he spotted Zeke. "Zeke." He motioned him to come.

Zeke walked towards the king, bowing low. "Yes, my lord?"

"What is it that your people say when a blessing is given?"

"May the creator of the Ātash People bless you."

"Yes," he smiled, turning back to Estella, "perhaps the creator of the Ātash People blessed you?"

She gave a warm smile, hoping it didn't look pained, "Thank you, Zeke."

Zeke gave a humble bow, with no emotion on his face as he went back to his post.

Amir chuckled as he motioned for the next course. Lysander had lamb prepared for them in jelly made from the plants the king had come home with. The rice served was golden and rich with herbs. More naan came out, given that it was Estella's favorite. Lysander had prepared berry juice instead of wine for the evening.

"Do you enjoy being king?"

"I enjoy that *I* am king."

Estella wanted to roll her eyes, but thought better. Instead, she took a bite of another naan that was placed on her plate.

"Do you think you will enjoy being queen?"

"I think," she paused, looking up, "that this is a beautiful room."

He looked around, both eyebrows raised, as if he was seeing the room for the first time. "The paintings on the ceilings are beautiful."

"They are," she beamed as she stared up.

Amir looked at Estella, a gentle smile on his lips. "Very beautiful."

It didn't dawn on Estella that he was talking about her, but it still made her cheeks blush as she looked away from him and down at her plate. Gently, she took a sip of her goblet, before softly clearing her throat.

"Tell me," Estella smiled as she took a bite of the lamb, "what do you intend to do with the women you had compete for your hand and crown?"

Amir stopped mid-bite, his eyes looking up at her from under his lashes. Slowly, he moved his food back down and sat up straight. "Why are you asking that now?"

"I was curious." Her eyes never left her plate.

"Did the women come up to you?"

She wanted to bite her lower lip, but dared not. "Yes," she said breathlessly, "but it is a question that has been on my mind since the beginning."

He leaned back in his chair, resting on his hand. "What do you think I should do with them?" The smile had now faded from his face.

Her gaze crashed into his. "Sire?"

He had a dark look in his eyes. "Are you wanting me to take a mistress?"

"No," she said quickly.

"Then what?" His voice was getting darker with each question.

"I was simply asking if you were going to release them to their families or allow me to have some of them as my ladies-in-waiting." Her words were flowing out faster.

"A harem?" he asked with a very dark look in his eyes.

"No!" She was panicking now as she shook her head. "There is a misunder-standing. I don't want—"

"To what?" he snapped. "The previous queen accused me of having affairs often." He swallowed; it was painful for him to speak of Tabitha. "Though I didn't love her, I was loyal." He sat up straight now, his eyes bore into her. "You wish to have me with another so you can be queen without me touching you?"

Estella could see this wasn't going the way she wanted. "My lord," she pleaded, "I simply wanted to know if I could deal with the contestants in my own way."

Amir stood up, his chair sliding back from him. The room was silent. Amir's chest rose and fell as his eyes bore into her.

"Do not," he said through his teeth, "do anything with the other women contestants. I will deal with them in my own way." He glanced at her from under his lashes. "You will be queen, and you will do as I command."

Estella sat up straight, all nervousness leaving her body as she stared at Amir, his once golden eyes a dark color. She thrusted her chin in the air. "I will obey, my lord, but I assure you, my question was to ensure that *I* would be the only one in the king's bed. I do not wish to share, and," she rose from her seat, "I will not be talked down to as if I am a servant to be commanded. I am to be your queen, and you have already made up your mind to keep me. However, you will not speak to me in such a manner." She bowed her head. "I will leave you, my lord, for you need time to yourself."

Estella, with her back straight, walked out of the dining room, alone.

CHAPTER 28

Henna and Whispered Blessings

THE KING AND THE future queen did not see each other after that dinner. It had been several weeks since the dinner, leading the two to plan the wedding, the guest lists, the food choices, all separately. Using the servants, Lysander, Farid, and even some guards to carry messages between each other. Stubbornness and pride stood between them.

Estella, because she wanted the king to think about what she said, especially in regards to the other women in the palace. Amir, because he was still mad. He didn't know if it was at himself, or Estella, or even Tabitha.

For years, Tabitha had made it clear that he was taking common women into his bed. After all, he is the king, he must have women falling over themselves to reach his bed. Even if it was true, he never went to another woman. Tabitha refused to allow Amir near her because he was unclean from the "whores" as she called them.

Years of her verbally refusing him and calling him names, Amir hadn't recovered from it.

"Why not just get another bride?" Darius asked as he ate some of the grapes on the plate. "I heard how she talked back to you. And then that business of her entering the throne room without being called for." He shook his head. "Find a new one."

"I don't want a new one," he muttered, staring at the queen chess piece in his hand.

"Why not just have a bunch of mistresses then?"

"I don't want—" Amir didn't finish the sentence. He didn't want his children to have the same fate as he grew up with. That his mother was subjected to. He told his mother he would be better than his father.

He stared at Darius, his friend sitting there, chewing on grapes. Darius's loud chewing was getting on Amir's nerves.

"Get out," Amir snapped. All the servants quickly made their way to the door. Darius didn't move. "Get out, Darius," he said with more force.

"I am your friend," he lazily stood up, "I am here for comfort. After all, you are getting married tomorrow."

"I know." He chewed on his cheek before he stopped, furrowing his brows. "By the way, why are you here?"

"Hmm?" He looked confused, then he relaxed into a sort of amused look. "Oh yes." He took another grape before walking over to Amir. "There have been rumors of some people at the borders of our kingdom."

"What rumors?"

"Some people who are not from this land are setting up camp at the edge of the border."

"Do we know who they are?"

"Not yet," he said nonchalantly, eating another grape. "But," his mouth was full of grapes as he continued, "we know it's not a small camp of people. They could mean war."

Amir gave a pensive look. "As long as they don't cross the borders, it will be fine. However, send some troops discreetly there, perhaps a few towns away. I don't want the other side to think we are setting up for a war."

Darius nodded. As he started towards the door, he patted Amir's shoulder. "You could call it off," he said with a smile. "You have enough women in the palace."

"I *will* get married tomorrow to Estella," Amir said with conviction.

Estella wanted to scream, wanted to shout. "How?"

"I will always help you, my queen," Lysander said before walking over to the door, opening it. There, standing in a mauve outfit, with an apron draped over her arm, was her Aunt Mari. The years of her being gone had taken their toll on her. More grays in her hair and a few more lines around her eyes. But Estella thought she still looked radiant.

"Hello," she said as gracefully as she could as tears threatened to fall.

Her aunt smiled at her. "Hello." She did a low bow. Estella's tears fell; she couldn't stand to have her aunt bow so low to her.

"Don't." She reached out, but Lysander shook his head, "Please, you may set up anywhere you need."

"You know the process, please ensure that you are ready. No more water after you use the latrine. No more food until you are dry." She was stern just as she had been before Estella had left.

Estella nodded. "Okay. Where should I sit?"

"Over there," she said, pointing to one of the wooden chairs it seems Lysander had set up beforehand.

Estella walked over to it, but as she was about to sit, Aunt Mari let out a shriek.

"Change clothes," she snapped.

Estella let out a giggle. Besides Lysander, no one had yelled at her that way.

"You know what to wear," she warned.

Estella quickly changed into some lighter wear, a cloth dress. The sleeves stopped at her elbows. By the time she came back, Mari had set up her bowl of henna, and had her apron on and a stick in her hand.

The process took hours, and though Estella loved all the time they spent together, it was bittersweet.

"How many friends did you make?" her aunt asked.

"It wasn't an easy thing to do, but I made a few loyal ones, like Lysander."

"He is the king's servant. What about the women?"

Estella gave a guilty smile. "That is harder."

"No one?" She looked up from under her lashes.

"Well, Cassia is here."

"That girl isn't to be trusted."

"Why?" she asked, concern written on her face.

Her aunt waved her off. "Ack, she is just one of those who is shifty."

"Auntie," she warned.

"Mari," she corrected.

She took in a deep breath. "Mari, you are letting the fact that she isn't from the Ātash People be the reason that you don't like her."

"No," she shook her head as she applied more on her feet, "that is not it at all. She is," she paused, "the kind who will try to get ahead."

She groaned. "You're just overthinking it."

Mari gave a shrug. "Since we are here," she looked up for a moment, "do we need to have the talk about," she cleared her throat, "the secret of life?"

Estella's eyes widened, and she dared not move since her aunt was applying henna to her skin.

"The secret to life?"

"Yes." Her aunt nodded. "Now, the king will be experienced, he had another wife before you. Don't let that scare you."

"*You're* scaring me, Auntie," she said nervously.

"Well, when the man's zayin enters the woman's cus, it is painful."

Estella felt as if this conversation was painful.

"Don't worry," she patted her knee, "it becomes quite pleasurable later."

"Please stop, Auntie," Estella said hurriedly. "No more."

Mari furrowed her brows. "I am telling you the secret of life." She seemed almost offended that Estella wasn't taking her advice.

"And I would prefer it if we didn't. I know what to expect. We had a lesson in class."

"Oh?" She looked over at Lysander who was fussing with another servant. "He gave you the talk?"

"Yes." She nodded.

"It probably was—"

"Auntie," she chided, raising her hand. "I was given the talk, I know what to expect. I don't wish to hear about you and uncle."

A blush came over Mari's face. "Be gone." She laughed.

Estella couldn't wait until the awkwardness was over.

"So tell me about the king, is he nice?"

"Doesn't Un...Zeke tell you things?"

She gave a shrug as she moved onto the underside of her feet. "I hear some things, but your—" she shook her head, "Zeke says very little about how the king is."

"The king is nice to me."

She looked up from under her lashes. "But?"

Estella sighed, making it so she didn't actually move. "We got into a fight last time we saw each other."

"So?" Mari's brows furrowed before looking back at the bottom of her feet. "Couples fight."

"But Auntie, we fought about the other women."

Her aunt's brush stopped. "Oh? What did you say? Sometimes you are hot-headed."

Estella didn't know if she should laugh or cry. "I simply asked if I could have the women once we were married."

"Did he agree?"

"Not really."

"What happened?"

"He got mad that I asked about them. He started on about how I was assuming he wanted the other women, which is why I wanted them."

"Is that true?"

"No." She shook her head. "I don't actually believe he wants the other women. I think he does intend to do something with them, but I don't want all of them to end up in the nunnery."

"Just most of them." Her aunt nodded in agreement.

Estella chuckled. "No, I want to return them to their families. The king made a law against slavery. Keeping all those women here is a form of slavery."

"I see."

"Oh, Auntie, please."

"What?" She raised her hands in a sort of defense, and shrugged. "I agree, the women should be set free, but the king is also right, that it is not your place to ask for them."

"I am the queen, or going to be."

She shook her head. "Even though you are the queen, the women are under his care. He must decide what to do with them. For now, they should be content with being fattened up like prize cows."

"So I was wrong?"

Her aunt shook her head. "You have a right to know if he is to take on a mistress. Considering you haven't even had your wedding night, it is understandable. But he is a man, he probably forgot about them until you mentioned them." Mari went up to her hands now, dipping her brush into the bowl. "Remember, my Joy, he divorced his first wife, no children, rumors at every corner about her, he must have some scars."

Estella nodded in understanding.

"Here, I will tell you some good stories about Zeke when he was young and a fool in love."

Estella's face lit up as she grinned. "What did he do?"

"He climbed an olive tree to impress me, but the *stupid* branch broke under his weight."

CHAPTER 29

When the Bells Ring

A FLUTTER OF EMOTIONS swirled within Estella's stomach. She glanced at her hands that were now a deep red; love written on her hands from her aunt made her heart swell. This was a large event, one that was to last for days. Lysander had told Estella that their society was civilized wherein they didn't watch the king and queen on the wedding night like the other countries. It did little to reassure her that it would be an easy night.

A soft knock on the door pulled her back from her thoughts. "Are you ready, my lady?"

Estella looked behind her and saw her uncle Zeke there.

"Zeke, you're supposed to be protecting the king." Tears threatened to escape when she saw him. He was in his best suit for a guard. A dark, mulled blue with silver embellishments at the edges. His hair was covered by his turban, his beard cleaned and trimmed. As if he was going to be giving her away.

"The king is worried about you, so he sent me to escort you." He looked at her red silk dress, fit for a queen about to get married.

"Thank you." She was a little sad he couldn't be her uncle rather than a guard watching his queen at her wedding.

He nodded. "Of course, but I am glad I get to watch you get married."

"Uncle," she said loud enough for just the two of them to hear, "am I doing the right thing?"

He gave a heavy sigh. "I can't say I wouldn't be happier if I could have chosen your husband for you, but I am happy you will always be protected. He is a good king."

"Thank you." She swallowed as she held back her tears to not ruin her makeup.

"Ready, my queen?" he asked louder, gesturing to the door.

She nodded, adjusting her veil and taking a deep breath. "I am ready."

Estella walked with Zeke behind her, and yet, all she could hear was the crowds of people from the city. Zephyria was alive with celebration as they waited for their new queen. She wondered if she would be called the second wife; she definitely didn't think Amir would stand for that, but the town knew nothing of how the king felt about that title.

She kept her eyes straight as she continued to walk towards the wedding ceremony. It was to be at the entrance of the palace, where they could have the doors open to the public, though most of them would be outside in the sun.

Taking steady breaths, Zeke went to the door, giving a tearful smile to her. As the door opened, an array of flower petals fell before her. Estella was wearing a deep, red silk dress with a long train. It had lace sleeves, subtle red embroidery with some slight golden thread woven throughout. Her veil was longer than her dress and dragged behind her.

The grand wedding hall was a sight to behold, draped in flowers as far as the eyes could see. It was a sea of red, gold, and white. The gold was the marigold flowers littered everywhere. They were strung up as lanterns. White jasmine laid on the ground, leading her towards the altar. Red roses were placed against the walls, as if they were the wallpaper.

As she looked up, she saw Amir staring at her. His outfit was similar, his hair hidden behind a turban today. She took in the color of his eyes, seeing the melting color of amber rather than the cold look he had given her the last time they spoke. Now it seemed as if everything was behind them.

Amir gave a gracious smile to her.

Just breathe, she told herself as she walked closer to him.

Once she was in front of him, she gave the traditional bow. He offered his hand, and she stared at it for a moment; gingerly, she took his hand. Their eyes met once more. This was not how she thought she would get married, in front of the world, in front of Zephyria watching her every move, in front of her family without them beside her; and yet, she was here, marrying the king. She had won the contest, and won the king's favor.

The ceremony began, with them staring at a small man in a white outfit, adored with more jewels than the king and queen combined. He made a long, boring speech about Amir's family tree, the tradition that it held to have a queen with every king, and how traditions were to be upheld.

Estella was glad to be sitting for the ceremony.

"Will you be the Queen of all of Zephyria, be with the king till his dying breath, and show the world the might of the kingdom?"

"Yes," she said firmly. She did everything on cue as she had been taught. The walking, the sipping of the cup, everything that was not of her culture, but she was their queen now. It was her culture.

"May the King and Queen live forever!" the man said. His arms raised, and the crowds roared into cheers.

Amir was looking at Estella, and their gazes held each other. He helped her stand; after all, the fabric was heavy.

"I—" he started.

"Yes?" she asked.

He leaned down and kissed her on the cheek. Another cheer erupted, flower petals were thrown around. It was then that Amir took her hand, walking down the crowds as they threw more flowers. He gave waves, laughs, and a gentle squeeze to her hand.

Once they reached the end of the crowd in the palace, Amir started to gain speed, laughing as people chased the couple. He was headed towards his garden. Estella giggled as he looked so carefree, running through the gardens. It was raining flowers, color, and life.

The festivities that normally would last for days were cut short. It was delivered through a messenger that the borders were crossed by the foreign country. Amir left immediately to defend his kingdom, leaving Estella at the heart of the country in Zephyria. The wedding night never happened.

CHAPTER 30

Thirty Pieces of Silver

TWO WEEKS SINCE THE WEDDING

HOURS TURNED INTO DAYS, and those days were long, threatening to turn into weeks and months. Estella watched as the color of her henna faded little by little. She sat there in the throne room, thinking of her wedding. A messenger had run up to the king right after the wedding.

"My lord, the border has been burnt. The enemy attacks."

All wedding festivities ended right there. The king took his men, Lysander, Zeke, and Darius to the front lines.

Estella sighed as she looked at the fading henna on her hands, then she looked out at the people in the room. There were several servants doing odds and ends. Then there was Farid off to the side, writing something.

"Farid," she said softly, wondering if she should disturb him.

He stopped writing and looked up at her. "Yes, your majesty?"

"What are you doing?"

"I am keeping the records of the king straight."

"You aren't the bookkeeper, though. He is a different man."

He nodded. "No, I'm not. But I am the scribe for the king."

"How did you come to be the scribe? You're so young."

"The king found me in one of the kingdoms he conquered."

"How did that happen?"

"I was in the market, writing letters for people."

"How old were you?" She looked him over, and thought he only looked thirteen.

"I was eight-years-old, your majesty."

"Eight? How old are you now?"

"Fifteen," he said, matter-of-fact.

"Fifteen?" she gasped.

He nodded, his face very stoic.

"How did you learn to write?" Even though her uncle and aunt had been well off enough, she didn't have education in writing.

"I learned from a book that had made its way to the slums. I had nothing else to do, so I would practice the symbols over and over again until I could mimic the book. It was when I was five that my father realized that I had the skill of writing letters. Next thing you know, people are lined up to pay for my writing skills."

"So you have been working since five?"

He nodded. "Yes, it was a way for us to make some money. My father would make me bathe, and go to the nicer side of town. There he would try to convince people to get letters written by me. It wasn't long before war came to us."

"War with Amir," she said, matter-of-fact.

"Yes," his stoic face didn't falter, "Amir cleaned the country of its tyrant king."

"Was the king that bad?"

"He was a big spender. From the letters I wrote for other people, I remember a lot of people writing about food becoming more scarce, more expensive, and seeing if there was room for them to move out to other family members."

"After the war, he just asked you to join him?"

"Not exactly. He had won the war and was giving out orders for how people can still live there. He saw that I was writing a paper. I didn't even notice him, I was so busy."

Estella giggled. "How did that go?"

"He asked me for my name. Asked me if I knew what I was writing." He paused. "Next thing I know, he is buying me."

Her eyes widened. "You're a slave?"

He shook his head. "Seven years are up. I am free now."

Estella smiled. "Seven years, huh?"

He nodded. "Yes. I stay because I like my job. I'm no longer a slave by law, but I never really was a slave."

"What do you mean?"

"His majesty only bought me because my parents didn't want to let me go. Remember my kingdom was broke and I became a large part of my family's income. So he bought me."

Estella wondered for how much.

"It was thirty silvers," he said quickly.

"Huh?"

"That's what you were wondering right? How much I was?"

"Thirty pieces is fairly cheap."

Farid smiled. It was not a broad or wide smile, but one that had fondness attached to it. "The king said he would have paid thirty gold pieces for me."

"Why did the king want you so badly?"

"He said," the smile grew a little as he looked at some parchment, "he liked my handwriting."

Estella smiled. She would have to ask Amir about it when he came home. She liked the way Farid smiled, even if it was brief. He immediately went back to writing things down. Estella quietly stood up and began to walk out of the throne room. It appeared as if Farid had the only right to not stand when the royalty stood, as she quickly found out.

As Estella walked out, she noticed Hamid at the door. He smiled at her.

"Hello." She gave a reluctant smile back.

"Are you going somewhere?"

"To the gardens," she said promptly.

"Then," he gestured for her to walk ahead, "let us go to the gardens."

"I can go on my own."

"You're the queen now," he shook his head, "you can't."

Estella nodded hesitantly. "Very well."

She started to walk towards the garden. The sound of her shoes against the cobblestones echoed as she tried to keep her eyes ahead. Trying to focus on the tapestries on the wall, the paintings, anything but the face that Hamid was walking with her to the gardens.

It didn't take long before Estella made it to the gardens. They were lush, and somewhat bare after most of the flowers had been plucked for her wedding. Estella had asked that the petals stay on the grass until they withered. Most were still intact.

A twig snapped behind her, making Estella turn around. There was Cassia.

"What are you doing here, Cassia?"

She hugged herself, licking her lips, "I came to see an old friend."

"Hamid," she said quietly.

Hamid stepped forward. "Cassia, you need to leave."

Cassia smirked. "Why? I am visiting my old friend and our queen."

"Cassia, I appreciate you want to—"

"No!" she interrupted. "You stole the king from me."

"I did not," she snapped back.

"Listen, Estella," she ground her teeth, "I will not forgive you for this."

"Cassia," Hamid warned.

Tears rolled down her face. "You knew I wanted to be queen. We even talked about it at the party that night when we saw Queen Tabitha."

"I was thrown into this contest. I didn't want to be here any more than half of the other women."

"But I did!" She placed her hand on her chest. "I wanted to be queen, and here you got my wish. Now there are rumors you won't let the mistresses go to the king."

"That is not set," Estella said with conviction. "The king hasn't made up his mind, but I do have a plan should he give me lead on the women from the contest. You will not go into the shadows like you think. I will not have the women be nothing but ornaments."

"You're one to talk," Cassia said before storming off.

Estella felt as if all the energy left her as soon as Cassia stomped off. She let out a heavy breath. Hamid turned and grabbed her by the shoulders.

"Don't worry about her, Estella."

She continued to try to breathe, ignoring the fact that Hamid was touching her.

"Come on," he said, moving her towards her room.

Estella shook him off. "I will remain here. Send for my maids, please." She walked over to one of the benches, sitting down. "Now," she said in a tone that was more commanding.

Hamid's face pinched slightly before he nodded, then walked away.

She touched her forehead, sighing. She shouldn't be left alone, but at the moment, she couldn't be bothered to call for another guard.

"Your majesty!" A man came running up to her.

She stood on instinct and looked at the man. He was frazzled. Instantly, he knelt down.

"Is it the king?" she asked quickly, panic rose in her chest.

"No." He shook his head.

"Then what? Speak plainly," she said hurriedly.

"A king is on his way here."

Her brows furrowed. "What king?"

"The King of Zerzura."

CHAPTER 31

Echoes of Traditions

Darius was lounging on the pillows at the corner of the tent, eating some nuts. Amir was too busy looking at the maps to scold him.

"You know, Amir," Darius said as he ate the nuts, "you should have brought a mistress or two."

Amir now looked up at him. "What?"

"For entertainment, or you know." He looked at Amir, smiling.

"Mistresses are for creating heirs, nothing more," Amir said in a stern voice; however when he said it, it left a bitter taste in his mouth.

"You could do that here."

"With that logic, I could have just brought the queen."

"No, you can't risk her life here. Mistresses are easy to replace."

Amir put down the papers in his hand. "They are humans as well, Darius."

"But replaceable." There was a type of joy in his tone that made Amir narrow his eyes.

"Everyone is replaceable, even a king," he said in a low tone.

"No, my lord," Darius sat up now. "You are not replaceable."

"I will eventually be replaced; everyone meets their end."

"Amir, you're taking this too seriously. I was simply saying that you could have brought a few of the women here, release some tension you have, and enjoy yourself."

"I haven't even enjoyed my own wife, Darius, and yet you think I should have brought a mistress—when I haven't sorted any of them yet. Why would I have done that instead of just sending for my bride, my actual queen I spent so much time choosing, just to try for an heir with a mistress?"

"Didn't you like the other ladies?" Darius eyed Amir.

"If I had, do you think Estella would have been made queen? She wasn't of royal breeding. Though beautiful, she still is learning how to be a queen. Most of those women were bred for being the queen or a mistress to a king. I didn't want them."

"So will you sort them when you return?"

Amir said nothing as he went back to his maps. However, he wasn't actually reading anything. Which was irritating him because it reminded him of the last conversation he had with Estella. She had mentioned them, but Amir took no notice of what she actually wanted to do with them.

"Darius," Amir snapped, "go check on the men. Make sure everything is secure."

Darius didn't say anything, just stood up and left. Amir was finally alone, minus Zeke who stood at attention in the back.

"Zeke," he said as he slumped down into his chair. "What do you think of my having mistresses?"

"My lord," he bowed, "it is not for the common man to judge."

He waved his hand. "Don't give me that, we are alone. What do you think? Speak plainly."

"I think you are following in your father's footsteps, my lord." There was a calm, serious expression on Zeke. And it irritated Amir to be compared to his father.

"So by keeping mistresses, I am becoming my father?"

"You misunderstand me, my lord." He bowed low at the waist. "I simply meant this is a tradition. Traditions are important to people; they keep us close, and connected to our roots."

"I didn't keep many of my father's traditions, like mistreating my queen, or anyone under my control. I abolished slavery as best as I could. I gained more followers when I was a nobody prince, than I did as an adult and their king."

"You have many followers."

Amir sighed, knowing that Zeke was too well-trained to give the honest response he was looking for.

"What does your queen think about your mistresses?" Zeke finally asked, a question that under normal circumstances would never be uttered.

Amir smiled. "She wants them to return them to their families. Perhaps make one or two ladies-in-waiting. There were hundreds of women, I don't know what she wanted to do with *all* of them."

"Then my lord, what will be your own answer to your mistresses?"

"I want to keep them, but I can't for the life of me understand why I do. It is a tradition that is old, one that doesn't make sense. I remember the fights between the wives, and the mistresses and the servants that would help the favorites. My father did nothing to step in. I tried to protect my mother from some of the comments, but they always found a way to her."

"Did you want that kind of life for your queen?"

Amir shook his head. "No, I don't wish that life for Estella at all." He paused. "She is a bright light in the palace. I see the servants that love her, the way she touched them in their hearts. She talks to everyone as an equal; a true queen that doesn't need to be horrible to get ahead."

After a moment of silence, Zeke spoke softly. "My liege, it may be worthwhile to reconsider certain customs that do not align with your principles. Your fondness for Queen Estella is apparent."

"I'm sorry to interrupt, my lord," a voice echoed from outside the tent. Amir looked up to see one of his messengers standing at the entrance, a look of urgency on his face.

"What is it?" Amir asked, straightening up in his chair.

"The enemy forces are regrouping and preparing for a counterattack," the messenger reported, a sense of urgency in his voice.

"Thank you." Amir quickly stood up, all thoughts of mistresses and traditions pushed aside as the reality of the battlefield demanded his attention. He swiftly gathered his armor and weapons, his focus now on leading his men to defend against the impending assault.

Amir stood tall on the hilltop; his gaze fixed on the enemy's stronghold in the distance. He could feel the weight of responsibility on his shoulders as he signaled for his generals to call their troops to battle formation. The clash of swords and the pounding of war drums filled the air as the army mobilized with fierce determination, ready to face their enemies once more.

Amir's heart raced as he led his army onto the battlefield, ready to defend his kingdom and protect his queen. But as he raised his sword, doubts crept into his mind. Fearing he may never make it back to her, he was more determined than ever to make it back to her. Yet duty called, and he had no choice but to charge forward into battle.

"Let's end this war."

CHAPTER 32

Queen to King, Check

Estella ran to her room to change. She was well-dressed, but not enough to accept guests such as a king. A maid came running into the room after her, gathering up her stuff. Another set of maids came running, sets of dresses in their arms.

"What about red?" one asked.

"No, blue."

"Grab the white," Estella commanded as she checked her face in the mirror. She had to make sure that her meeting with Cassia didn't mess up anything. Earlier in the day when she got ready, she didn't feel as if she should get glamoured up. Now she was regretting it.

"The one with the long train?"

"The one you got engaged in?"

"Yes," she said flatly. "Someone ensure that the servant in charge keeps the king company until I am ready to be received."

A small child ran out as the queen commanded. After Estella had checked her face and hair, she jumped into her white lehenga. The long sleeves and train gave more elegance than the others. With the final adjustments, the women looked wide-eyed at her.

"Am I done?" she asked.

They nodded in silence.

"Then I will go to the throne room."

"You need an escort," one urged.

"Then walk behind me," she said in an even tone. Estella walked out of the room, and with all the grace she could have of a queen who was running, she headed towards the throne room. She reached the door, and Hamid wasn't there. She was happy, but had no time for that.

The guards were confused as she pushed open the door and walked with haste to the throne.

"Farid," she said loudly, but sternly.

"Yes?" He stood up, his face as stoic as always.

"We will have a guest. Tell me everything about the King of Zerzura while we wait for him here."

He nodded, then grabbed a book from behind him. Instantly, he flipped through the pages. Estella sat on the queen's throne. She looked at her dress, which now looked crumbled.

"Maids," she said hurriedly. "Fix the train so it looks like it is fanned out. I wish to look like I did not run here."

The maids ran to the throne, keeping their heads low as they adjusted the train. It was draped over the stairs, looking like a perfect seashell with it pleating.

"I have it," Farid said.

"Tell me," she commanded. "Quickly."

"Announcing the King of Zerzura," the guards said.

Estella had been briefly taught what to do when she is greeted by another king, but it was always taught when her husband, the king, would be beside her. She had no idea what was permitted on her own.

The king's head was shaven, save for the golden crown that adorned it. His tunic, adorned with intricate embroideries of silver and gold, draped over his broad shoulders and fell to his knees. His umber skin was tattooed with intricate patterns, each marking more elaborate than the next. His dark, sharp eyes watched her every move as he approached, assessing her with a keen gaze that seemed to see past the mask she wore as queen. As if he had some magical power to see she wasn't royalty.

Estella stood up and bowed her head. "Welcome, King of Zerzura. To what do I owe the pleasure of your company?"

"Where is your husband?" His voice was rich and deep. Sounding like thunder when it crashes against each other. He commanded the room, as a king should.

A small glint in her eyes appeared. "Has news not reached you, my lord?"

"Of the war?" He laughed a loud, blusterous laugh, "Of course. That is why I am here."

There was tightness in her chest. Was he here to take over the kingdom while the king defended his borders? Did he set up the assassinations? Did he set up the war?

He raised his hand. "Calm down, my queen. I am here to negotiate the terms of my kingdom. I said I would wait until after the marriage."

"Did you come here, knowing the king is gone, hoping that I would give you all you ask for?" She raised her eyebrow at him.

The king said nothing.

"I know what you seek. You are talking about the fish and wool you trade with us for the nuts and berries we trade with you," she said, more matter-of-fact than a question.

He gave a nod. "Yes, my queen. I see you're well-learned."

"I was made aware of the tension between the trades." She paused. "What would you like to happen?"

"You people think we just sit there and pluck the hairs off our goats, then sell the price high for no reason." He made no accusatory tone, but said it as fact.

"And I was made aware of some things that were said about our people in the market." She smiled knowingly. "How was it phrased? We sit in our palaces and pull nuts and berries from our windows, then sell them at a high price?"

The king paused for a moment before he laughed. "Ha! A queen with good humor!"

Estella gave a soft chuckle. "My king, I know that there is a lot in your country we know nothing about. You live by the seas, and when you turn around, you are greeted with high mountains where your goats live for safety. It is not an easy job to capture them, to brush their coats out, then clean and dye the wool to the beautiful colors you are known for."

The king nodded. "A very well-learned queen." He smiled in satisfaction.

"However," her smile fell, "we are a desert people. We grew an oasis in the desert with sands, rocks, and hard winds. We have little water springs, and during our rainfalls, though they happen, we must ensure we keep every drop. Do you think, even if we do pull the berries and nuts from our windows, that what we have to trade is any less valuable?"

The king scratched his chin, looking at the queen with a hard look. "You are not a dumb woman."

"I shall take that as a compliment." She smiled.

He continued to rub his chin. "What do you propose to do, your majesty?"

"Farid," she said softly, looking at him from the corner of her eyes, having the boy come running to her side. "This is the king's most loyal record and bookkeeper. There is no one better to negotiate with than him. Give your best, and let them settle the matter."

The king looked hard between Estella and Farid, then nodded. "Ack!" he snapped his fingers and a woman came walking up. She was older, and could have been Farid's grandmother. "Figure out a good deal."

The woman nodded.

"Farid, you may go into the library to discuss the matters."

He nodded, gathered some of his stuff, then ran off to the woman. "This way," he said, motioning out of the throne room.

Estella settled into a smile, "My dear king—"

"Oba," he interrupted.

"I'm sorry?"

"King Oba, or Oba." He smiled broadly.

She let out a nervous chuckle. "King Oba, since you are here, please enjoy Zephyria. There are plenty of things here I am sure you and your people would love to see."

His eyes bore into her. "How about you take a walk with me in the gardens? I wish to see the nuts and berries you people pick from your windows."

Estella was shocked for a moment, then realized he was making a joke. It was hard to tell since his voice was loud. "I would love to."

He extended a hand to her, being ever so patient as she walked to him. She took his hand; it was warm and large. She was sure he could break every bone in her hand should he want to. But he gently let her hand sit on his.

As they walked through the gardens, Hamid watched from a distance. The women from the contest had even come out, looking over the ledges, seeing who the queen was with. She felt more watched now than she did at her wedding.

"I hear," King Oba said in a low voice, well, as low as one with a loud voice could go, "that you did not get your wedding night."

She looked at him, aghast.

He chuckled. "Aye, don't fret, my lady. I know I missed the wedding, which is my shame."

"I'm sorry you missed it."

"It seems as if it was a good idea to miss it." He laughed. "Nothing happened and you are still on your honeymoon."

"What?" She blinked a few times at him.

"The markings on your arms." He lifted up her hand. "The marks of earth that show marriage."

"Oh." She blushed.

"You did not enjoy your wedding night." He chuckled. "How about you leave your husband? I will make sure you are well taken care of." He laughed louder than before.

Estella laughed with him. "I do not think the King of Zephyria would love that."

"Ack." He waved her off with his free hand. "We will be back in my homeland before the war is over."

She raised an eyebrow to him. "Aren't you married with several mistresses?" Estella silently praised Farid for telling her as much as possible about the king.

"So?" He looked offended. "I need a smart wife."

"I'm not so sure I am smart, my lord."

"Nonsense!" He slammed a hand on his chest. "I say you are smart, therefore you are!"

"Thank you, my lord." She gave him a genuine smile.

"Does that Amir treat you well?" His brows furrowed, his face falling into a frown. "I will go and beat him in front of his army if he does not."

"He does," she said quickly.

"Hmm," he looked at her suspiciously, "I still say come away with me."

Estella giggled again. "If he mistreats me, I'll run away with you."

Oba let out a loud laugh as he threw back his head. "Yes! I like you! You are a good match to that cat of a king."

"Cat?"

"Yes." He nodded vigorously. "He is sneaky, and has attitude like a cat."

She put her finger to her lip, looking up at the sky. "I suppose he is."

"Ah!" He pointed at her. "You see it!"

Estella enjoyed how much she had laughed with the king. "Yes, I see it now."

King Oba stopped walking. "My queen," he said in a soft voice, holding her hand with both of his. "I am as serious as the midday sun. You are a good match for the king. He is," he paused, "hurt, but you are like the north star. Even your name is of the stars." He gestured to the sky, even though it was midday. "I believe you will be good for him."

"Thank you, King Oba."

He smiled at her. "You're welcome. Come," he extended his arm to the gardens, "show me where the king keeps his plants he stole from me."

"Stole?" She looked at him, confused and shocked.

CHAPTER 33

To End the War

AMIR LET THE COOLNESS of the air fall over his body. It reminded him of the night he went with Estella to the festival. When they danced in front of a fire.

"Your majesty," Zeke bowed low behind him, "it is time."

Amir let out a soft sigh before he pulled the cloak's hood over his head. It was just long enough to conceal his face, but not obstruct his vision. He stuck to the shadows, with Zeke close behind him. Slowly, they made their way through the camp grounds, on the edge. Amir tried to keep his breathing as low and even as possible. He looked back at Zeke, and noticed the way he seemed to be in his element. Zeke was his most trusted guard—not the captain of the guards, but his most trusted.

Zeke must have felt the king's eyes on him, and gave Amir a curious look. Amir shook his head, and moved forward. Zeke silently followed, until they were at the area where there was nothing. Just dead bodies littering the ground and rotting, and the smell of decay beginning to swirl around.

Amir pulled up the mask he had around his neck to cover the smell. It was infused with the scent of dirt, not the worst smell, but Zeke, as well as Lysander, had said anything else would be discovered. He wasn't sure why Lysander knew; the man was a higher ranking servant, and one he allowed to speak freely. Perhaps Lysander knew the normal smells around him, and any new smells would alarm him.

Low to the ground, they made their way to the enemy camp, sticking to the shadows, and trying to not look out of place. Amir pulled down his mask, and raised his hood up a bit. It looked more suspicious to be concealed and low in the enemy camp. Amir straightened up, walking tall, as if he truly belonged. Zeke threw off his hood, and walked like a soldier. Several men looked up from their gambling and then went directly back to it.

There at the edge of the camp was a large tent that had golden tassels and deep red borders. Amir looked over to the right, at the small tent that looked like the others. Only this tent was alone, and rather close to the large, red and golden tent. Without a word, Amir motioned to the small tent. Zeke gave a nod to him before turning around and walking around the area. Amir made his way into the tent slowly and silently.

Just as he suspected, it was the leader's tent. He crept over the body and made a quick grab, his hand around their neck and another hand over their mouth. He saw a flurry of long black hair, and a pair of angry, almond eyes. Amir realized that he was staring at a woman. He quickly scanned the tent, thinking he grabbed the wrong person.

It wasn't a moment later that she elbowed him in the stomach and rolled him over, flipping Amir on his back. She was now straddling him, a knife to his throat.

"Where is the leader?" he ground out.

She smirked. "She has a knife to your throat." Her accent was smooth and was not of this area.

"How is that possible?"

"You looked for a man, that was your downfall." Her voice reminded him of a fox.

Amir said nothing, looking at how she held the knife, how her body was positioned to simply kill if he moved in any way. She knew what she was doing, and everything screamed warrior from birth.

"Move and I will kill you." She pressed the knife ever so slightly against his skin.

Just as Amir was about to answer, a blade came to the woman's neck.

"Release my master and I won't kill you," Zeke said from behind her.

Her smirk grew to a large smile as she dropped her knife, and raised her hands up.

"Slowly, get up off him," Zeke ordered.

"You have a good guard," she said as she slowly got up. She was wearing a type of cloth outfit that had high slits in her skirt on both sides.

Amir quickly got up and stood beside Zeke. "Thank you, Zeke."

The woman kept her hands up but at a more relaxed state. "So what now?"

"Leave my kingdom," Amir said.

"No," she said with a bored expression on her face. "That is not going to happen."

"We are here, and can kill you."

"You surprised me, and though you have been trained well, I'm certain," her eyes trailed Amir in a mocking way, "your guard here is more experienced and will probably kill me. However," she smirked, "one scream and my entire army will be here. How long do you think he would survive *them*?"

Amir and Zeke said nothing.

"Exactly." She put her arms down and placed them behind her back. "He might kill a few of the men, but in the end, numbers would win." She took a few steps to the left, then turned back, walking in a circle.

"What would make you leave?"

"The land," she said as if it was obvious.

"No," Amir said flatly.

She sighed, giving a shrug. "Then we will continue to fight."

"Are we able to leave without any problems?" Amir asked.

She gestured to the outside. "Surely, you got in here. No one thought of you. I'm pretty certain they won't bother you."

Amir didn't trust her.

"I won't scream out after you." She held up her hand, the other on her heart. "My honor as a warrior."

Just as he was about to say something, Zeke took a bow, sheathing his blade.

"Zeke," he hissed.

"She means no harm now, your majesty."

She gave him a gracious smile. "I like him. How would you like to come work for me?" she asked.

Zeke shook his head. "I apologize, my lady, but my loyalty lies with my king. I entered his kingdom, a foreigner, and he has allowed me to share his space. I will not betray the trust he has placed in me."

She gave a sigh. "Aw, so sad. I like you even more. Go ahead, I will let you leave alive."

Both the men turned to leave. Just as they were exiting, she called out.

"The offer is open indefinitely, should you ever change your mind."

They did in fact walk out of the camp without incident, and no one paid them any mind. Though his enemy, she was honorable, which made him fighting her all the more bittersweet. He would have liked to be allies rather than enemies, but fate wasn't so kind.

A letter came in the morning, along with the sleepy advisor Darius, the calm guard Zeke, and the panicked servant Lysander.

"What is going on?" Amir asked as he got out of bed.

"Your majesty." Zeke handed him a small letter.

Amir looked it over and saw the soft handwriting of a woman's. His heart leapt thinking it was Estella, then he realized it was not her seal.

Hello, King of Zephyria,

We have been ordered to pull out, by the order of my grandfather.
You were a worthy opponent, and parts of me are disappointed I
couldn't see just how much we could have drawn this out. However,
I am pleased to no longer be wasting the lives of my horses and men.
Perhaps one day, our paths will cross once more. Also, if you ever wish
to get rid of your guard, please send him my way. I would love to have
someone as loyal and well-trained as him.

Kashira

Amir sighed before smiling and closing the letter. "It appears, Zeke, you made a lasting impression on the enemy."

Darius blew out a breath. "How?"

"He snuck up on her. I don't know why that impressed her, but it did."

Zeke gave a bow at the waist. "To be praised by the enemy is an honor. However, I am faithful to my king."

"I'm glad of that. Too bad you are a married man, you might have had a real chance at her," the king teased.

Zeke gave a grimace. "Please, my lord, don't say that at home. If my wife hears it, I might end up sleeping in the palace."

Amir laughed before turning to Lysander. "I have a task for you."

"Of course, my lord." He bowed.

"Write a letter and hand-deliver it."

"To whom?"

"Estella." He smiled softly.

CHAPTER 34

Setting the Board

THE HORNS BLASTED AWAY for the third time. Estella made a dash for the gates, hoping for Amir. The horn was to signify his return. A small carriage, with soldiers seated at the front and in the boot area, pulled into the gate. With bated breath, she waited. The door swung open and out stepped Lysander, dressed in simple clothes for traveling. Though happy, Estella deflated a bit.

"I saw that," he hissed. "Not happy to see me?"

She scanned the rest of the men. "No, of course I am."

"Then why are you not looking at me?"

"I'm the queen," her eyes continued to scan each soldier, "I don't have to."

"My lady," his voice was flat, "he isn't here."

She looked down at him with her eyes wide. "What do you mean?"

"I mean," he sighed as he pulled out a letter, "he sends me, and his words in this letter."

"I heard the war ended."

"It did." His tone wasn't improving.

"Lysander, you are being cross with me and I'm not sure why."

"Because I am realizing I am now the nuisance man-servant to the both of you."

"You are not a nuisance," she said as she opened the letter.

Dearest Estella,

Forgive me for all that happened. I should have gone to you after the fight. I know that I never have wanted mistresses. I was still angry at Tabitha. The scars that she laid upon me are deep. I will explain more in person, but for now, I leave the handling of the women from the contest to you. I know you will be fair, and kind to them. Before I married you, I had all the servants who have served you tell me about you. Each one told me how kind you were to them, even after you were engaged to me. I will be home as soon as we bury our dead, giving them proper burial. Zcke is insistent about it being before the seventh day is up. Something about his creator's rules. I like the way he sticks to his creator, even in front of me. I shall be home soon.
I love you.

Amir

Estella reread the last line over and over again. He loved her. It was the first time she had heard him say that. And even now, it was written, but it was the first.

"My queen?" Lysander asked.

"He loves me," she said in a whisper.

"We knew that."

She snapped a questioning look to him. "I didn't."

He returned the look. "What do you mean? You had a fight with him and he still married you. Of course he loves you."

"How? We have had only a couple of meets."

"He liked you every time you met." He paused and then muttered, "Even the ones you didn't meet."

Estella giggled. "Well then, will you help me get ready for his arrival?"

Lysander gave an offended look. "What do you think I am doing here? I'm not a messenger boy. Yes, I had to deliver the message, but I also need to set up for his return."

"Yes, of course. But before that, I would like you to assemble all the women from the contest in the garden for entertaining large guests for me. I would like to tell them about their futures."

Lysander nodded. "Of course."

The chatter of women was loud and seemed to hold more venomous stares from several of the women. Estella was nervous, but tried to keep her composure as calm as possible. As the women continued to chatter away, Estella finally steeled herself, rising.

"Excuse me, ladies." She lightly tapped the rim of her goblet. Slowly but surely, the women quieted down, looking towards her. She gave them a sweet smile, and folded her hands in front of her.

"As you all are aware, his royal majesty is returning home soon, and I would love it if we could all be friends to a certain degree."

There was a murmur that went through the women.

"I know," she took a deep breath, "I won the competition which left a lot of you bitter since that meant you would be a mistress or something of the likes, but I am here to tell you," she paused, looking at the curious faces, "that by order of the king, you are all free from that responsibility."

A gasp erupted from the women, all of them starting to talk to one another, and the sound of them growing louder.

"Wait, ladies!" Lysander yelled out. "Please let her majesty finish before you start asking questions."

As always, she could count on Lysander.

"Ladies," she started again, "I know there are a lot of questions, rumors, and frankly, I know we will get through this together. Please bear with me. The king has left it to me on how to," she paused, wondering which word to use, "handle each of you so that we may come to an agreeable term without the king losing face with his alliances."

"How does that work?" one woman asked.

"I have thought of several ways for this to work. One, those who wish to become more educated, we will school to a certain degree. This will include writing, reading, reciting, and arithmetic."

A small murmur rippled through the girls.

"If you already feel you have been educated enough, you will be placed in a queue for potential suitors."

"So we will be auctioned off like cattle?" one woman said in a snide voice.

"No," Estella said firmly. "No one is auctioned off. You have already had your share of embarrassment and, so to speak, "auctioning," so I do not want you all to endure that. I was planning to host a ball when the king returned home, invite everyone, and let each woman choose whom they wish to keep company with."

She quickly held up her hand. "I must insist though, you all remain in the palace until you are fully married, and your houses are established. There is also a final option; if you wish to not marry and you feel like schooling you is pointless, you will become a lady-in-waiting for the other countries we have in our kingdom, or a higher rank servant in the palace should you keep a good standing." She gestured to Lysander. "And please be aware that Lysander will oversee you."

A silent hush fell over the group of women.

"I realize this is a lot to take in, and I will give you some time to think about it over lunch." She clapped her hands together and out came several servants carrying food and placing it on a long table on the back wall.

As the women began to make their way to the food, Estella sat down in her place, which was the head of the table, and motioned for Lysander. He quickly snapped his fingers and out came a servant with food.

"No," she shook her head, "I will eat what they are."

"Your majesty," Lysander gave a low hiss, "we have to make sure you're alive."

"Then have someone taste it." She smiled.

Lysander gave an inaudible sigh. "Very well, your majesty." He snapped his fingers and instructed to bring Estella a plate of food quickly. When she finally received her plate, after a poor servant tried every bite of her food, the seats around her began to fill.

Several of the women Estella had never seen before. *They must have been in another room*, she thought.

"Hello." She smiled at them.

"Your majesty," one girl beamed, "I would love to be educated but also married, how would I go about doing that?"

"I would like to be educated, but also, I don't want to be married or be a servant," another girl said.

"Since we are technically free, does that mean I can see my family as much as I want now?" another woman asked, worry etched on her face.

Estella opened her mouth to speak, but Lysander stepped in.

"Ladies, give the queen some time to eat, as well. It would do well for us all to digest the food and the idea of not having to be a mistress to the king."

The girls nodded, looking at their plates of food.

"Lysander," Estella touched his arm, making him bow and take a few steps back. "Ladies, I would love to answer your questions. If you wish to marry and have an education, you will be given the education first, and as you are learning, you will be allowed to go to the parties and gatherings that those who dismissed education will attend." She turned to the other lady. "If you wish to not be a servant but want an education, we can see about you possibly having a job within the kingdom walls. And finally, about your family, I would like to set up more possibilities for you all to see your families. We cannot allow it to be an all-day, every-day thing, but we can see about having designated days for families to visit."

Lysander cleared his voice in a low tone that only Estella could hear. "For safety reasons, we will have to limit it. I know many of you were forced into this as I was. You had no choice but to compete. I wish for all of you to be able to live comfortably here. Some of you will be moving to other parts of the kingdom, but fret not. Your lives will not be meaningless or less valuable away from his royal majesty or I."

Estella scanned the faces of the women before her, seeing a mixture of relief, uncertainty, and hope. She knew that this was just the beginning of a long journey to reshape the lives of these women who had been caught in the intense competition for the king's affections.

"I understand your concerns, and I promise to do my best to ensure that each and every one of you is treated with respect and dignity," Estella said firmly, her voice carrying across the room.

One of the women raised her hand tentatively. "Your majesty, what about those of us who have dreams beyond marriage and servitude? What if we wish to pursue other paths?"

Estella's eyes brightened at the question, a spark shining in them. "I am glad you asked that. Zephyria is a land of opportunities, and I want each of you to know that your dreams are valid. If any of you have any aspirations beyond what has been presented here today, please come forward. We will work together to explore avenues for you."

There was a hushed murmur that circulated the crowds.

CHAPTER 35

We Meet Again

MYRRH INCENSE DRIFTED THROUGH the air in an attempt to bring calm. Estella smoothed out the folds in her skirt as she looked in the mirror. This was a far cry from the original dress she wore to the first ball. Her pale lavender dress was a consideration, but she decided to go with a deep purple dress with small white pearls sewed into it. She had asked Lysander if it was too much, but after seeing all the other girls, she realized it was very plain. Some of the girls were literally dripping in gold; it was easy to tell who had money in terms of their outfits.

"Dripping in gold?" she asked herself out loud.

"Gold what?" Lysander asked, coming up behind her.

"Nothing." She forced a smile.

He eyed her. "You are beautiful, my queen."

"I still feel like I should be more glamorous."

He leaned back, looking at her fully. "Not at all, you are the queen now. You can't blend in anymore."

"I didn't blend in before." Her tone was flat.

"Yes, I know, but that was intentional."

"It's still intentional." She raised an eyebrow at him, chuckling.

He waved a dismissive hand at her. "It's a different intention. You are the queen. You need to stand out, but also, we can't have the king mad that you look like a golden statue. Now, let's get going. You have to be the last one to arrive."

"Why?"

"Because it's custom to make a grand entrance," he said as if it was a fact of life she should already know.

"I see, well then." She gave a half-chuckle. "Lead the way, Lysander."

As they walked down the hallways, she steeled herself for the entrance. Joy was not used to affection, but Estella was supposed to be. Two different people, but one person. She walked on, Lysander now pulling back, so she alone made the grand entrance.

"All hail Queen Estella of Zephyria!" the Master of Ceremonies yelled out before they opened the door.

Estella kept her eyes low; then as the door opened, she slowly raised her eyes and headed in. Step after step, the echoes of her shoes were the only thing heard as she entered the ballroom. She looked down, seeing everyone looking up at her. There was a sea of masks. Estella had set another ball for dancing and food. Only this time, anyone was allowed to wear a mask. She noticed how some of the women had no masks, but their faces were painted with cosmetics.

She graced them with a warm, soft smile. "Please, continue."

Clap! Lysander swooped behind her, saying something to another servant. The music continued; all of the people resumed their dance and talk. The room was full of noise once again. Estella knew she couldn't move officially until Lysander had her seat ready.

"My queen," he said softly from behind.

She gave him a slight nod, then followed him to the designated area. It was a set of thrones, both of them made of a dark wood, having some gold embellishments, and empty. As she walked up to the throne on the left, she knew all eyes were on her. She sat down, some of the maids running to set her dress just right as it fanned out.

As Estella looked on, she noticed that several women with masks were entertaining some men who were without masks. A soft smile formed on her lips, remembering Amir dancing with her on the first night.

"My lady," a familiar voice said behind her. "Would you like to dance with me?"

Estella lit up, turning her head around, seeing Amir smiling at her. He was wearing the old outfit he wore the first night together, but no mask tonight. His hair was combed back, and his beard smelled fresh with rose oil.

"I suppose I can dance with you, sir," she smiled playfully. "Before my husband comes."

He smirked at her. "Well, let's dance before he comes back." He grabbed her hand, and pulled her towards the dance floor.

The dress was heavy, but the way Amir twirled her on the floor made her feel as light as a feather. It didn't take long before everyone cleared around them. The dance this time was more energetic than the previous ball. Estella twisted her arms and bobbed her head, as the dance required. Amir did his part of the dance, moving his hips from side to side.

"Tell me," he said as he got closer, "who is going to marry whom?"

"I just got here," she hissed as she turned her head to the side before turning back to him.

He groaned, "You must have some idea."

"We are not going to be judging people again at this ball."

"Why not?" He laughed. "It is our entertainment."

She did a spin. "We are dancing."

He caught her in the middle of another spin, their faces inches from each other. "We were dancing the night we met. I would like to continue this tradition with you."

She took in a deep breath, her smile playful. "The ones in blue on the left."

He glanced to his left, seeing a man with a large belly, white turban and gaudy blue tunic. Almost as if they mixed it with another color, turning it to a sick color.

He was talking to a young girl who didn't look older than fifteen. She was in a pale blue outfit that allowed her dark skin to glow.

She leaned into his ear. "Farid hasn't stopped looking at her, but I believe the man is going to make an offer for her hand to you."

Amir's jaw tightened as he snapped a look at her. "She's young for someone that old."

Estella nodded. "Yes."

"Farid likes her?"

She shrugged. "I don't know, but his eyes seem to be fixated on her."

He scanned the room quickly, seeing Farid off in a corner, looking in the direction of the girl. There was a light in his normally dull eyes. Amir knew Farid long enough to know his emotions, and this was one he didn't know. It was only logical that it was some sort of infatuation. He looked back at the girl; she was clearly uncomfortable, but wasn't running away from the fat man.

"No," he said flatly. "Not approved."

Estella giggled. "I don't approve either. I had hoped," she started, "that we could approve of the women together. That way, they wouldn't be mine, or yours. They are our subjects and we will take care of them together."

Amir smiled at her, the softness in his eyes glowed under the lights. "Approved."

She chuckled. "Then, my lord, how about we continue to watch over everyone from our thrones?"

He looked back at the chairs; he hadn't sat there with a queen beside him in years now at an event like this. This was to be a tradition for years to come. Slowly, he led Estella away from the dance floor in the direction of the thrones. Estella began to reach for the chairs, when he pulled her back.

"Not yet, come on." He took her hand and began to walk around the crowds towards the curtains that led to the balconies.

"Amir," she hissed through her teeth. "We can't run away. Lysander will yell at both of us."

He smirked back at her as he continued to pull her. "Nothing I haven't heard before. Besides," he laughed, "it's good for him."

Estella couldn't help but laugh with him for a moment. It wasn't long before they reached the balcony. It was large enough to house at least half of the women from the contest. No one followed them, but Estella knew there were a few guards hidden somewhere.

Never to truly be alone, she thought.

"The night sky is truly the best sight," he said as he dropped her hand, walking to the railing.

She snickered. "Is that why you keep running off?"

He looked at her, narrowing his eyes. "Not in the slightest. I—" he cut himself off before taking a deep breath. "I am the first son of the second wife. I lived in the outer palace with my mother. By all rights, I shouldn't have been king. My father had mistresses, sons, and daughters. I got used to being alone, to staring at the stars for my comfort."

"What happened to them?"

"The daughters were sold off to other kingdoms as princesses at a young age. Most died in childbirth. The others, I never heard from again."

"And the sons?"

"They died in war. They were older than me by several years. My father didn't believe in going to war himself, but sending his sons out. I was still in training when they died."

Estella wasn't sure how to respond. It didn't sound as if they were all close as siblings. She didn't have any of her own, so she didn't know what it was like.

He looked into her eyes. "I never wanted mistresses. I never wanted to subject someone else to how my mother was treated. I didn't require love from Tabitha, but her constant accusation of having an informal mistress made me mad for so long. I was letting the scars bleed me of my joy." He cupped her face with his right hand, letting his thumb caress her cheeks.

Hearing him call her Joy without knowing it was her real name was bittersweet.

"So this is where the party is." Both of them looked over, seeing Darius with a drink in his hand and a smirk on his face. "I love this party, my lady."

"Thank you." she gave a single nod.

"Wonderful wife, Amir."

"Darius," he warned, "this is a party for two."

"Oh?" He blinked a few minutes. "I'm sorry, my lady, we won't be but a moment."

Amir sighed. "Not me and you. Estella and I would like to be alone."

Estella could see this wasn't going to go well. "Actually," she smiled, "I will go back to the party. Perhaps we can have dinner in your garden soon?"

His face lit up. "Yes."

"Ooh! I would love to join. Thank you, my lady." Darius bowed his head.

Both Amir and Estella's eyes enlarged.

"Um," she stammered, swallowing before continuing, "Of course, Lord Darius. You're welcome to join us."

He smiled broadly. "Just tell me when we are going to eat."

"I will see with Lysander when is the best time." She bowed. "Excuse me."

Once Estella was out of earshot, Amir glared at Darius. "You are not allowed to come."

Darius touched his chest, offended. "She invited me."

"You invited yourself. Don't come."

"Nonsense. The queen is now setting up the dinner for three. It would be a shame to make her rearrange the plans."

Amir's jaw tensed. "Fine," he said after some thought.

"Aren't you going to visit her tonight?" Darius said in a leery tone.

"No," he said flatly. "I want to rest, and I am sure she is still nervous about it. I will wait for the right time."

"Don't wait too long." He threw back his drink. "I heard King Oba was chatting things up with her while we were gone."

"I heard that, too, and I heard they were in public together. Nothing happened beyond a friend admiring my queen."

Darius chuckled. "You could always renounce your marriage and choose another from this bunch."

"Enough, and you've had enough to drink," Amir snapped. "I will not choose another. Estella is it. She is the Queen of Zephyria, and nothing is going to change that fact."

"You sure?" He smirked, licking his lips. "You should have found out more things about her, my friend. I heard some rumors, but I am sure you already know them." Darius walked back behind the curtain, rejoining the ball.

Amir stood there, looking up at the stars. "What should I do?"

CHAPTER 36

Into the Den of Vipers

LYSANDER TRAILED SLOWLY BEHIND Estella as she walked through the old palace. No one had been in it since the king's mother had died. It showed the scars of neglect. A faint smile graced Estella's lips as she looked around, thinking it reminded her of the king. Pretty, but wild and somewhat neglected. She touched some wild jasmine that had crept its way up the walls and pillars.

"My lady," Lysander whined.

"Lysander, why is that when I became queen, you are suddenly more whiny?" She raised an eyebrow at him.

He straightened up. "I resent that."

"You resemble that," she teased.

His brows furrowed. "We shouldn't be here."

"Why not? The king said I can have what I want as long as it wasn't his garden."

"He definitely didn't mean this place," he muttered under his breath.

"Where was the queen buried?" She looked around the courtyard, imagining the king as a kid—laughing, running around, and being silly. Nothing was expected from him, being the disgraced son of the second wife. She wondered how his mother looked, probably had his eyes, the warm brown that swept away her breath.

"The queen was sent to the mountain and let the birds take her flesh," Lysander said in a low tone, as he looked away.

Estella noticed the pain in his face and voice. She wondered if Amir was allowed to cry when his mother died. A small glint of something caught her eye, Estella walked over to it, and saw it was a small knife in a bowl. Probably having fruit once in it. She picked up the knife, picked up a piece of fabric from her dress, and...*CUT!* A three-inch slit was cut on the left side of her dress.

"My lady!" Lysander exclaimed. "What are you doing?"

"This is the least I can do," she said as she wrapped her hands around the cloth, placing her forehead against her hands. "May you rest in peace, my queen."

"Why did you cut your very expensive dress?" He stood there gaping at the cut.

"It's to honor the dead."

"Why is cutting your clothes honorable?"

"What makes feeding the vultures with a queen honorable?"

Lysander raised his hands up. "Hey, my people give coins and have a burn party."

"Why coins?"

"For the boat man," he said, confused.

"Boat man?" She raised an eyebrow at him.

He waved his hand. "Never mind, we can discuss that another time. Was cutting your dress really necessary?"

"Yes," she smiled before looking over to the middle, "is that a well?"

Lysander nodded, "Yes, I think the previous king covered it up because it went dry. Another reason why we shouldn't be here."

"Why are you so afraid, Lysander?"

"Because I know the king better than you."

She smiled as she rolled her eyes, walking to the well. There wasn't anything special about the well, just stones and mortar covering it up. Estella looked up, and just as she did, a cloth covered her mouth, and the more she struggled, the stronger the grip got on her. She didn't see who it was, but they were strong and taller than her. Lysander was already on the ground. They got him first. It wasn't long before she was knocked out.

Estella didn't know how long she was out, but when she finally came to, she felt wet, and her head hurt. "What?" she moaned.

Another moan came from beside her. She turned and saw Lysander slumped against the wall. She tried to get up to move, but her hand slipped on something slimy, and she winced in pain before giving a sigh.

"Lysander?" she groaned.

"Mm," he moaned.

She tried to sit up again, and this time, she had more control of her body. The room they were in was dark, but her eyes had adjusted well to the little light. She moved over to him, breathing heavy, checking to see if he was awake.

"Lysander," she tugged at his tunic, "you need to get up."

He groaned, turning over.

"Lysander," she said louder and more urgently. "Wake up!"

"W...what?" he moaned.

"Lysander, I don't know what happened."

"Este...Estella?" His breathing was labored.

"It's *your majesty*," she tried to joke.

His breaths grew shorter.

"Lysander," she swallowed. "We have to move."

"No." He shook his head a little.

"Yes." She gripped his arm, trying to pull up. "We have to get up now." Something told her if he kept staying down, he wouldn't get back up. She stood up, still holding onto him, then started to pull him up. She groaned as she pulled him. He felt like dead weight, limp.

"No." He shook his head.

"Yes," she commanded. "We need to get up."

Finally, after a few moments of Estella pulling and Lysander not helping to pull himself up, she finally got him upright, and leaned against the wall. Her breath became labored from the strain of pulling him. Lysander's breath was labored, but for another reason. She swallowed hard before looking around once more.

They were in a small space, and it was dark. No light beyond the little they had from their eyes adjusting. "Where are we?" she asked.

"I don't know," Lysander said as he held his ribs with his left arm.

"We got in here, and I don't think I have anything broken, so it must have a door."

"I think I have something broken."

She looked over to him, touching him for anything that might be out of place. She could see him, but not all that well. "I don't feel anything."

"It's my ribs, they hurt," he groaned.

"Oh…" She knew there was nothing for that. Her aunt had a lot of remedies for ailments, but there wasn't anything for ribs. Her uncle, very often from training, would come back with bruised ribs and not much besides an oil rub would help, and there was no ointment here for that. "We have to find a way out."

"Try something against the wall, maybe there is something there."

"Right." She nodded before making her hands touch every brick on the wall, as far high up as she could go and as low as she could go. She found that there was the thinnest amount of water on the ground in between the stones. Some of the stones were moist with something slimy; she suspected it was some sort of plant. As she moved onto each stone, she finally came to one where it was indented more than the rest. All the other stones were exact except this one.

"This one is more indented."

"Push it," Lysander said in a strained voice.

Estella pushed in, which wasn't easy since it was a little over her head. Once she pushed, there was a small whoosh sound and a small crack appeared next to it. Estella pushed against the door and light began to pour in. She turned back to Lysander, who was more pale than normal, and sweat was rolling down his cheek.

"Lysander," she went to him and wrapped his arm around her shoulder, "lean on me."

"Leave me, your majesty."

"No," she snapped. "We need to get out of here."

"We need to have you get back, then send someone for me."

"And leave it to chance that someone wouldn't come back to kill you? No."

He gave a chuckle, then coughed. "I doubt they would come back. They intended to leave us in there."

"I'm the queen," she said in shock.

"You are barely the queen," he grimaced. "The king hasn't consummated the wedding, so there is a chance to choose a new bride."

Estella grew quiet for a moment, then looked ahead. "Well, I'm not dead yet. Let's get out of here."

"Wherever that is."

"Right." She smiled at him, then slowly began to walk down the path.

Estella hated every step she took. The shoes she wore were meant to be lazing around the palace, not walking what felt like miles. On top of that, her dress was wet and very dirty from being in that cave thing. The wetness made the dress heavier. She should have chosen that teal, turquoise pants outfit and did her hair in the bubble braid. It would have been easier to walk in. Lysander's breathing was labored as they went in further into the depths below. Happily, or maybe not so happily, their path was lit with lanterns. She wasn't sure why they were lit, but she didn't have time to think about it. She needed to get to the end.

Finally, after what felt like miles, they reached a fork in the road.

"Please, Estella, leave me here and pick one."

Estella rolled her eyes, looking at the paths. Both of them were lit, so there wasn't a sure way to see if one was the exit. Plus, one of them might lead her to the people who threw her down the hole in the first place. "We have to choose one," she said at last.

"Well, leave me here and figure out which one is the safe one."

Estella looked at him, and noticed that he was sweating rather hard; his complexion wasn't well. "How about I let you rest for a moment while I scout ahead a bit. It will be easier to run away if I'm alone."

She set him down at the wall that split into the fork. Estella took off her shawl, which was the most dry item now, since it was thin and she was walking with it on. She thought about half a dozen times while walking to toss it to the side, but she thought better of it. Now she wrapped it around Lysander, hoping to keep him somewhat warm.

"Here, my friend." She smiled, trying to fix his hair a bit, feeling the cold, wet skin of his.

"Thank you, Estella. You truly are the star of the kingdom."

"And I intend to have you back there." She looked up and examined the two paths. She decided on the one to the left.

The floor went from stone to a smooth ground. It was hard, but it wasn't dirt. It helped quieten her footsteps, which she appreciated. She didn't want to run into the people who threw her and Lysander down here. She kept her breathing low, and finally, she came upon a door. Before opening it, she looked around, it was just a plain wooden door, with a golden handle, and light peeking out from the bottom where the floor was. She leaned her ear against the door, trying to hear any voices.

A small murmur of voice came, and as she listened, she started to make out what they were saying.

"Even if she were to escape, my main plan is still in action."

"The plan?" another person asked. Estella couldn't make out this person's voice very well.

"Yes," the first one chuckled, "and everything is fitting so nicely."

Her eyes widened as she stood there frozen. The words from their mouth spilled like poison on a plant—of betrayal. She kept all of her emotions and noise inside. She knew she had to keep listening. It was vital for her life, and Amir's life.

"I will finish him," the first voice said.

"But—" the other voice said.

"But nothing!" they hissed. "His reign is coming to an end. Then I will destroy those most loyal to him."

"You won't be able to kill him if Zeke is nearby."

They scoffed. "Zeke will be taken care of before the king is."

"How?" the other person asked nervously.

"With this." Estella could hear the rustling of paper. She wasn't able to see what was in it, but she knew it wasn't good when the other person gasped.

"But—"

"But nothing," they hissed again. "Everything will come to a head in a month's time."

"Why a month?"

"I have to make sure that there are things in place for me to take over the kingdom."

Estella held her breath, and grabbed her skirts as she quietly ran off. She didn't want to wait to see when the conversation ended, and then for them to find her. She heard all she could stand to hear. Now she knew who was behind the attacks, mostly, and she knew who was against her uncle. She knew she wasn't going to be able to speak about this to anyone.

When she came back to the fork, there was Lysander, slumped against the wall. He was breathing short shallow breaths, but seemed to be better. He still looked exhausted.

"Lysander," she breathed, "we have to leave now." She gathered up her shawl, throwing it over herself.

He heard the urgency in her voice. "What's the matter?"

"I know who is plotting to kill the king, and who threw us in here."

His eyes widened. "Who?" he breathed out, as if he was afraid to know.

She shook her head. "Not now, we have to somehow get back."

He pointed to the other side of the fork. "Shall we?"

She looked hesitant at it. "We have no other choice. We can't go back where we came from, and we can't go down the other path."

"What if it's a dead end?"

She swallowed hard. "Let's pray it isn't."

CHAPTER 37

Weight of the Crown

ONLY A FEW SERVANTS saw the state in which Lysander and their new queen came back. Lysander swore them all to secrecy as they bathed Estella. Washing her hair, massaging oil into her skin, and ensuring her nails were clean of all the mud and grime. Lysander was given a wrap around his chest and some medicine. He wasn't as pale now, and he had finally stopped sweating. Estella made them hurry as fast as possible. She had a plan.

"Lysander," she said softly.

He looked at her, his eyes weary.

"You know how I have dinner with the king?"

He nodded.

"I will find a way to tell him who is behind him, but I must have time to prepare it."

"What do you need?" he asked.

"Give me a week, ensure the king is occupied with all that he missed while he was at war. Call my..." she paused, "Mari, and have her come to reapply my wedding henna, then I need to see Zeke."

He furrowed his brows. "Why Zeke?"

"I feel as if I can trust him, and only him."

"Only?" There was hurt in his eyes.

"As a guard," she corrected. "I will always trust you."

He gave a weak smile. "I will get it done."

"I'm sorry I can't have you rest more, but I need all these things."

"What did you find out in the tunnel?"

"Who is behind this," she said in a dismal voice.

He gasped, then winced. "Ow, who is it?"

"I can't say," she said softly. "I need to figure out who is loyal."

"How can you tell if Zeke is loyal? He isn't Zephyrian."

She shook her head vigorously. "No, he is not the traitor. I heard of the traitors." She leaned closer to him, "I know who it is."

"Then why not just tell the king?"

"Do you think he would believe me if I told him that it was—" She bit her lower lip, "Never mind. When can you get things ready? I know you are hurt, and I am sorry for this. Perhaps the wait will help you recover."

He gave a grim look. "I'm not sure the king will enjoy waiting for a dinner with you."

"Actually," she smiled, "I would like two dinners for two different nights."

"Excuse me?" he squeaked.

"I need the first dinner to be for Amir, Darius, and myself. The second dinner, just for the king and I, in his private garden."

"And the first dinner?"

"Place it inside, in the king's entertaining room to make him comfortable."

"Should we have some entertainment?"

Estella nodded. "Yes, some of the women from the contest were singers. So please find them and ensure they are dressed as lavishly as possible."

"Lavishly?" he asked confused.

"I don't want the king's head turned." She smirked.

"Turned?" He gave her a deadpanned look. "Your jealousy is showing."

"Good," she said as she snickered.

He took in a slow breath. "Very well, I shall get all this done."

Estella stood on the balcony and looked out at the country. Her eyes went up to the night sky, looking at the deep blue that was glittered with stars. "What am I supposed to do?" she asked out loud. "Help guide me," she pleaded. Her head went down, her eyes closed tight, as she stood there in silence. Her people believed, as did her family, but did she believe it herself? What if she wasn't able to do anything? What if she was tossed aside like the previous queen? Or like the king's own mother?

Her breaths became slightly irregular as she bit her lower lip. The creeping feeling of failing, of being worthless, started to overcome her. The pain in her chest grew tight. Sounds were fading into the background.

"Please," she said in a sobbing voice. "I don't want to do this."

Suddenly, a warm hand touched her shoulder, and Estella whirled around to see her uncle Zeke. His eyes were glistening, as if he was going to cry. She had seen this look on his face when she was taken as the potential bride.

"Uncle," she sobbed, running into his arms.

He hesitated, his hands out, but after a few moments, he embraced her. His large hand soothed her hair, as she sobbed as quietly as she could in his chest.

"Joy," he said softly in her ear.

"Uncle, do you know who is behind this?"

He nodded.

"Then why haven't you done anything?"

"It is not my place."

"The person doesn't like you, which is why I had to hide who I was."

"Yes, but look at what you achieved. You are the queen of all Zephyria."

She frowned at him.

"You have gained favor on your own merit, nothing I did for you. No one can take that from you."

"Uncle," she asked softly, "how is it that they didn't know what I looked like before?"

His lips thinned into a line. "They know who you are now, which is why you ended up in a well." His eyes darkened. "I'm sorry to have still caused you harm."

She shook her head. "It is not your fault, but how did they find out?"

"There is a rumor going around your life before the palace."

She gasped; her hand went to her mouth. "No."

He nodded. "I'm sorry, my child. I have failed once more to protect you."

She took a deep breath and shook her head. "No, I know who is behind it. I will have to take care of it before I move forward."

Zeke looked curiously at her.

"Thank you, Uncle," she said as calmly as she could. She was raging mad, but knew she couldn't show it.

"Joy," he warned, "don't do anything that can be handled by those higher than us."

She smiled. "I will do all that is in my own power to end this." She took a few steps back. "Now, I must leave. I trust you will continue to watch over me?"

He nodded. "Always, my queen."

There was a bittersweet moment that hung in the silence between them.

"There will be a dinner in a week with the king and I. Please be ready for when that happens."

He nodded. "Of course, my queen."

"Thank you, Zeke."

CHAPTER 38

Time to Choose

ESTELLA SAT IN HER drawing room, where typically the harem would congregate with one another and gossip. She tried not to think how it was previously used by the last king's mistresses and his first wife, all talking about the discarded second wife. Knowing about Tabitha, the last queen and how she didn't have any competition, meaning she probably sat in here alone with maybe a few ladies-in-waiting.

A soft knock came on the door.

"Enter," she said in a stern voice.

The door slowly opened to a young woman with olive skin and long, light-brown hair cascading down her back. Her plump cheeks and round face were painted with cosmetics which looked to have aged her up quite a bit.

"Hello, Cassia," Estella said as softly as she could manage.

"Your majesty." She made no attempt to bow her head or otherwise.

Estella narrowed her eyes. "You are supposed to bow."

"You're no queen of mine. You're not even Zephyrian."

"No," she smiled coyly before letting out a soft sigh, "but I am queen. So I am given the respect as queen."

Cassia narrowed her eyes. "No."

"Cassia," she snapped. "I was friends with you before we were entered into this contest. I do not wish to punish you simply because you want to be a brat."

"A brat?" she yelled, some spittle coming out. "You stole what was mine! I should have been queen, or mistress. Then you come by and tell us we can do what we want? Well, I want to be queen."

"No," she said flatly. "That job is taken, and the king will not take a second wife or mistress."

"Then he should kill you for deceiving him."

Estella's eyes widened ever so slightly. She tried to keep it under control, but it was hard when someone had just said they wished you dead. She rose from her seat, and walked over to Cassia. Though Estella was older than her, Cassia knew what she was saying. Cassia made no movement of backing down or cowering as Estella approached her.

Estella raised her hand to slap her, this made Cassia stumble backwards, falling down on her backside. She cupped her face as she looked up and glared at her. As Estella looked down at Cassia, her eyes grew cold.

"Cassia, you knew me before the contest, and you have been spreading rumors around the palace. The punishment for this is death."

Cassia's eyes widened, her breathing quickening.

"However," she smirked, "I have no intention to kill you."

"Wha-what do you intend to do to me?" Her chest was rising and falling rapidly.

"You will be my lady-in-waiting. No one will be allowed to marry you without both the king's and my consent. Your parents have no say in what happens with you. You will live out your life in the palace. You will care for any of the children of the king and be referred to as your name. No title."

Cassia's face turned confused.

"If you abuse this opportunity," Estella's smirk grew, "you will be the latest cup bearer for the king."

"The king?"

"Of course, I wouldn't want you to kill me."

"But the king—"

"Just had some people try to kill him?" She nodded. "Yes."

Her hand went from her cheek to her throat. There was pain and horror in her face. "Why not just kill me?"

Estella chuckled. "Why? I can think of no better punishment than making you obey the rules and watch the king and I together. There is no better revenge than a life well-lived."

Tears began to fall down her face.

Estella cupped her face, pulling her to look at her more. "There, there Cassia. I am sure in time, you will learn to love your position."

More tears fell down her face as she whimpered at the feet of Estella.

"Lysander," she said calmly, pulling away her hand. "Clean her up and get her ready for the day."

"Are you sure? She did start some nasty rumors about you."

"Of course." She looked back down at Cassia with the smirk. "She will behave."

"Hitting does not become you—" Estella raised an eyebrow at Cassia, before she finished. "Your majesty."

Estella nodded. "See? If she betrays me, send her to be the taster of the king. With all these assassination attempts, I am sure she will find her way."

Lysander sighed. "Come, Cassia." He pulled her up, wincing a bit, then they walked out of the room.

Estella made her way back to her seat, and looked around. She was going to have to figure out more ladies-in-waiting to have. It wasn't a good idea to leave Cassia alone. She needed some that were going to be loyal to her and not Cassia.

"Time to see Farid." She smiled.

"You want what?" he asked, frightened.

Estella had found Farid alone for the moment and had cornered him. "I need you to tell me who is actually loyal to the crown."

"You should know, you spent time with them." He wrinkled his nose.

"I spent time with only so many of them." She sighed. "I know the king had you look into all of them."

His eyes darted around the room as if he anticipated the king to show up at that moment. "Okay, I know some of the women who want to just be ladies-in-waiting. One of them was just proposed to the night of the ball."

"Who?"

"Aisha, she is not looking for marriage."

Estella said nothing as she bore her eyes into Farid's.

Farid looked nervously. "Uh…"

Estella narrowed her eyes at him. "Aisha doesn't want to get married? How do you know this?"

"Well, some nobleman came and asked King Amir for Aisha's hand in marriage, and King Amir said he wouldn't allow her to marry yet. Aisha looked relieved."

Amir had agreed to discuss with her the women from the contest. "I see."

Farid looked away, his lips turning into a thin line.

"Farid, is she the one who was wearing the light blue dress the night of the ball?"

He nodded slowly.

Estella relaxed into a smile. "Approved."

Farid's brows furrowed. "What?"

"I'll have her as my first lady. She is young and she thus will be protected as my lady-in-waiting. Send a letter to the king about this. If he approves it, then I will have her join me immediately."

"Why not ask the king yourself?"

"I am preparing," she simply said. Farid was one she could trust, but she didn't know for sure. After all, being sold could have left a bad taste in one's mouth.

CHAPTER 39

Clearing the Air

Estella sat up straight and looked around the table. The ladies of multiple rooms were seated down, everyone chatting with one another. The women were dressed semi-formally as they sat down. Estella felt alone, looking up to see Cassia talking to one of the other girls, smiling. She caught Cassia's eye, which made her sit up pin straight and her smile falter.

"Everyone," she said before she gave a single clap.

All the women turned to her, settling down in volume.

She gave them a smile. "Hello, everyone, I welcome you here. You have already heard about the decision for your fate, so this is not that meeting again. Some of you will be the entertainment for the dinner with the king, his advisor, and I. This will be auditioned for. I want the ones who want it and will be respectful." She looked out at the faces of them. "I trust you all will do your best."

She turned her head, looking at Lysander who looked to be still in pain but with a smile on his face. He gave a single clap and several servants went to setting up the stage in front of Estella. The women went off to the side of the room.

"I need five ladies to do the traditional dance of Zephyria in as much unison as you can," Lysander said.

There was a murmur between the ladies.

"Who cannot do the dance?" Estella asked.

No one moved.

"Don't be afraid, you will not be punished. But it would be better to know than to embarrass yourself as you attempt to dance something you don't know."

Slowly, one hand went up. It was the girl from the ball, Aisha: dark complexion with braided hair, and large brown eyes. Estella smiled to her.

"Aisha, correct?"

The young girl nodded.

"Sit by my side. You were honest, and shall be rewarded."

A sudden spark and light were brought into her eyes.

"Come." Estella's lips curled into a kind smile. "You shall be a lady-in-waiting."

The young girl walked up to Estella, bowing low before sitting at the place Estella had motioned to. She sat in a lounged position, with a large smile on her face.

Estella looked over the crowd. "Anyone else?"

Several hands went up.

"You all may wait on the other side of the room. Thank you for being honest."

Slowly, the room shifted the women from one side to the next. Estella sat there, waiting for the women. In reality, this was a ruse of Estella and Farid to get Aisha to be her lady-in-waiting. When asked, Farid had said Aisha would be honest in her inability to dance. Lysander had mentioned how all the women had the basic ability to dance, but it's not beyond the balls. It was a risky gamble but Estella was pleased it worked in their favor.

Each set of women danced one after another. Only a few of them were outstanding. Lysander had been appointed to handle all the proceedings with the dance. Estella had taken note of some of the women scowling at her. Some of them were not even trying to hide their disdain for her.

"Cassia," she said loudly after the set of women with Cassia had finished their routine, "come sit with me."

Sweat beaded at her brow, and she swallowed hard. She said nothing as she walked up, gave her a bow, then sat on the other side of Estella. It wasn't as if she wanted to keep Cassia out of the fray, but she also wanted her out of temptation. Estella didn't enjoy threatening her old friend. The contest had changed their friendship; they had grown apart from each other. It wasn't just the one of them becoming queen, it was more. However, to ask her to change back to the naïve young girl she once was, was also naïve.

Keep your friends close, she told herself. *But make sure they don't turn into enemies.*

CLAP! Lysander stood in the middle of the room. "All right everyone, thank you for coming to the auditions. I will go around to each one who will be coming to the banquet for the dancing. You all did splendidly. The queen thanks you."

Estella gave a smile and nodded to them.

"Back to your rooms."

"Wait," Estella said, "I want to make one more announcement."

Lysander bowed and moved out of the way.

"There have been a lot of rumors lately, and I don't want to be a tyrant of a queen. I don't want false love, either, but I want to rule with the king in a gentler way. Please, as women, come to my side and know that I am not against you. Whatever rumors you have been told, know that whatever I did, I did as myself. I did nothing immoral, or improper."

There was silence.

"Ask," she said calmly. "I see some faces have questions on their minds."

"I have one," a blonde woman with olive skin said. "I heard your name is not your own."

"It was a name I was given by my family. Though it was not my name when I was born, it is something my family gave me."

"Is that the only thing you lied about?" she asked.

"As I said, it is not a lie, just the name I was given by a family member that I used for the contest. I have been my genuine self the entire time. My encouragements, my congratulations, my stories, they are all me."

There was a wave of murmurs. Estella didn't blame the women. Once a lie is told, it is hard to find the truth. Even though Estella didn't actually lie, it doesn't matter to some people. Half-truths can be seen as lies as well.

"Will you keep your promise that we can leave?"

Estella gave a gentle smile. "Did you all not find men who wished to dance with you? Who wished to talk to you?"

"Some of them believe we are the king's castoffs. So they like us as objects."

Estella gave a thoughtful single nod. "Yes, I observed that as well. Some people had less than honorable intentions with many of you. The king and I had come to the conclusion that we would—together—approve or reject the proposals of the men. I know we said you could leave, but as your queen, I dare not wish any of you to fall into a marriage where he will use you. I would rather you remain in the court, return to your family, or send you to another part of our kingdom. This is not for my benefit as much as it is yours. I want you all to be happy."

"What if we want to be used?" one woman asked.

Estella narrowed her eyes ever so slightly. "That would have to come up to why, and there would be appeals and written forms. Some marriages are political; not all are for love."

"Did you marry for love?" Aisha asked.

Estella turned her head to her new first lady. "I did."

"You had one date with him," Cassia cried out.

"Well," Estella smiled, "technically yes, I did. But also, the king is like a sandstorm when you meet him. So much happens."

"Tell us," another woman said from the back.

Estella chuckled. "You all want to hear about the time the king and I had a secret date?"

There was a procession of *yes* that rang out.

"All right," she giggled, "come around, sit. I'll tell you about the prince who jumped onto the princess's balcony. They went on a magic carpet ride together."

"Prince? The king isn't a prince."

"No, but he does act like a naughty prince a lot of the time. Someone who is free to do as he pleases."

The women leaned in.

"Now, this prince was valiant, and brave. But he was a naughty prince. He went to the princess's room in the middle of the night." She paused for dramatic effect. "Without an escort."

The women gasped, some placing their hands on their lips. Others were clutching their jewelry. Estella noticed how even the ones who were skeptical of her moments before were now invested in her story.

"Where did they go?" Aisha asked.

Estella leaned in closer to them. "They went to the Feast of Lots on the outskirts of the town."

CHAPTER 40

Last Page, First Kiss

AMIR HAD HIS FINGERS interlaced as he scowled out into the void. He was annoyed. He had not seen his wife in a week. At first, he thought it was the time of the month, but no. Lysander said it wasn't. This irritated Amir. But it was when Farid came with a letter from the queen, asking permission for her to have a certain young girl as her first lady in her wing, that he got angry. She could have sent the letter herself, or better yet, she could have seen him. They still haven't had a wedding night. It wasn't improving his mood.

Tonight was the night of the dinner. He was tempted to send Darius on a wild hunt or another kingdom tonight so he could have the dinner alone. When he asked Lysander about his plans, his man-servant told him it wasn't a good idea since Estella had planned for them to both be there. This also did little to improve his mood.

Amir wasn't trying to be controlling or be bound to his wife, but he wanted to see her. It was selfish but wasn't a king, or rather a husband, allowed to be selfish some of the time? He groaned as he cracked his knuckles.

"Farid," he asked, "what is the queen doing today?" He had started to ask Farid more and more about what she was doing. Farid had become attached to the queen, but Amir had a suspicion it was due to the young maiden that he approved of.

Farid didn't look up from his papers. The only one in the kingdom allowed to. "She is doing her bathing rituals today. Then she is going to be getting into her dress before the dinner."

Amir rolled his eyes and groaned once more. Estella was beautiful, so why was it a ritual to take beauty care? He didn't understand it. He thought she was the most beautiful when they were running around the town in common clothes.

"Is that why you are working now?"

"I am always working, my king."

"Not as of late. You spend free time with the queen's first lady-in-waiting."

"I now have a way to fill my free time besides learning how to write better," Farid said nonchalantly.

"My kingdom is turning upside down," Amir said under his breath.

"Not really, your majesty. It's just more lively now," Farid said as he continued to write, never looking up.

Amir grumbled as he quickly stood up. He didn't want to hear this from Farid. He knew he had work to do. Being a king of a vast kingdom wasn't easy as sitting down and doing nothing. He had to ensure laws were passed, anything that the judges didn't feel confident in—he had to rule in favor of someone—and he had to ensure that money was pouring in just as much as the country was spending. He had a lot of help with advisors, and treasurers, but ultimately, he had to do it. This is why he had bought Farid in the first place.

Farid wasn't a typical servant; in fact, Amir had even told him that he was free from his slave bonds when he bought him. Farid only cared about the numbers and the lettering. Farid wanted nothing else than to work with them. Amir used him to the fullest extent, but Amir also didn't want to abuse the relationship.

"Your majesty," Farid called out.

Amir looked back at him, almost at the doors now. "Yes?"

"My queen is in the library."

Amir wondered how Farid knew what was happening everywhere while remaining at his desk in the court room. He pushed the thought out of his mind as he made his way to the library. In reality, the library was the place to keep all the records, keep the art from the spoils of war, and to have some of the written stories down. More records than anything else.

He reached the door; just one small wooden door that looked almost unassuming. Amir had rebuilt the treasure door and the library door when he took over. The one thing people crave is treasure, whether it comes in gold or knowledge. He wanted them to be hidden in plain sight, something people would overlook in a panic.

He slipped into the door, seeing the four guards who stood on watch. They all were shocked and confused as they saw the king sneak into the room he could easily access.

"Is the queen in here?"

One of the guards gave a single nod, saying nothing.

Amir smiled. "Don't let the queen leave."

The four guards nodded their heads in unison.

Amir went to the door and slipped inside, silently closing the door behind him. He figured Estella might be towards the records, so he started there. Silently, he made his way around each of the large bookshelves. Looking around the corners, seeing if he could catch sight of her. Corner after corner he turned, finding nothing. He moved onto the arts area, hoping to find her looking at a painting. As quickly as he could, he moved around the area, losing hope of finding her now.

"They said she was here," he said to himself. "Did they all lie to me?"

He turned the corner and suddenly was met with her. She didn't notice him, and was staring down at a book. He hid himself, glancing at what she was reading. It was a small red book that had small golden embellishments on it. His eyes glanced up to her, the softness of her face, the way strands of her hair fell over her face as she looked down.

"Fun book?" He finally decided to say out loud as he stepped out of the shadows.

Like a startled rabbit, she jumped a little. Her eyes grew large and she slammed the book closed and brought it to her chest. "Your majesty," she said with a small squeak.

"Amir," he corrected.

"Amir, what are you doing here?"

"I'm impatiently waiting for my wife to put on the dinner."

"My lord," she started but he gave her a pointed look, "*Amir*, I am going to see you tonight."

"Tonight is too far away."

She tried and failed to suppress a smile. "My wonderful king, I will see you tonight."

"Yes, but I don't want to wait for my joy."

She paused and blinked a few times at him, "I was wondering actually..."

He raised an eyebrow. "What?"

"Would you like a dinner with just me and you tomorrow night?"

Excitement filled his eyes and face. "Yes," he said quickly.

"Oh, two dinners?" A voice rang out from behind them.

Both Estella and Amir looked over to see Darius and Hamid there.

"Why are you here?" Amir frowned.

"Hamid is my guard today, and I came for some documents. I found you two by chance."

"We are in the arts section."

Darius waved him off. "I know."

"Documents are over there." Amir pointed to the other end of the large room.

"Well, now I am curious about the dinner."

"You're already invited to the dinner tonight."

"Yes," he waved off Amir again, "but there is another dinner. I can't wait to go."

Amir was irritated. "No, it is for the queen and I."

"But what is better than having a party?"

Estella could see the anger in Amir's face. This wasn't going to go over well. She didn't want Darius to come, mainly because she wanted some time with the king alone. However, the idea of the advisor coming randomly thrilled her less.

"You are welcome to come again, Darius, but I am afraid the king and I will be discussing things about our marriage. It might be boring."

"Oh, we did that already when he was married to Tabitha."

The name hung in the air, and tension rose. It was warned to all the women to not mention her name ever, especially in front of the king. Darius just broke that rule. Estella wondered if it was because they were good friends.

Amir sighed after a few tense moments. "Darius, don't come. Your records are on the other end, now please kindly leave. I have something to discuss with my wife."

"Alone? I will leave Hamid here for protection." Darius said nothing else as he left Hamid.

Amir narrowed his eyes at Hamid, "Do not follow us." He quickly pulled Estella past a few bookshelves and turned a few corners. Once he was out of earshot, he looked hard at Estella. "Why did you invite him?"

"I didn't," she huffed. "I invited you, and he jumped in."

"I told him no."

"And I saw he wasn't going to come anyway. I don't want that. I would rather not be surprised."

Amir inhaled deeply before slowly reasoning his breath. "I suppose that's true."

"We can go for a walk in the garden, and be alone."

He smirked at her. "Really?"

Her eyes widened for a moment, taking a step back, only to find a bookshelf behind her. "Not like that."

He leaned in, pulling her chin towards him. "Are you sure?"

"Yes." She blushed; she liked him like this.

His lips brushed against hers. "I find it hard not to go to your room every night."

She swallowed hard, her breathing shallow. She squirmed a little.

"Mmm, my joy, are you not happy with that thought?"

"I-I..." she started.

Amir didn't wait for her response as his lips crushed against hers, the softest moan escaping her lips as he wrapped his arms around her waist, pulling her closer. The tip of his tongue pressed against her lips until she opened up. His hand went up to her hair, holding her as he deepened the kiss. Amir released the embrace for a brief moment, hearing the soft satisfied gasp of air from her lips. He tilted his head, kissing her once more.

Her arms wrapped around his neck, and she stood on the tip of her toes, feeling the warmth of his chest. The smell of vanilla on his beard tickled her as he pulled her even closer. She wasn't sure how he was able to, but she didn't care at that moment. He tasted of spice as his tongue danced with hers.

Slowly, he pulled away from her, his arms resting around her waist. Both of their faces were flushed, both trying to catch their breaths.

"I think I should go and finish getting ready," she said, swallowing.

Amir licked his lips, his chest rising and falling as he released her. "Yeah, Farid said you were supposed to get ready, but you are here in the library. Why?"

She bit her lower lip, looking away. "No reason."

"Estella?"

"I was looking up something for tomorrow. I won't have time tomorrow, so I thought I would today."

"What things?" He looked down to see that the book was still in her hand.

"Some..." she couldn't think of a lie.

Amir thought for a moment; he knew what the book was. It wasn't of records, but it did have some stories in it. They were the poems of his mother, the second queen. She wrote in her spare time; some of it was small stories of Amir, and her life as the second queen. Amir had thought of burning it when she died, but he also wanted to make sure she didn't get forgotten in history. He hadn't read it fully. Just knew what was the gist of it. He wondered how Estella got a hold of it.

"All right," he said finally. "I will see you tonight."

She grabbed hold of his tunic. "You're not angry with me, right?"

His brows furrowed. "No. I thought you must have wanted this badly enough to interrupt your beauty treatments, therefore it must be important."

"I don't need many. I've spent the last few months getting beauty treatments. How much more can someone need?"

He smiled. "I said the same thing."

She chuckled. "So you won't leave me the moment I become old?"

"I hope I make it to see your hair silver as the moon," his hand went up to her cheek, "to see the smile lines deepen, and to see the years we have spent together woven in your hands." He took her free hand in his. He leaned in and gave a kiss on her cheek. "I'll see you tonight."

Estella watched as Amir walked off. Once he was gone, she looked down at the book she was holding. She wasn't trying to hide it from him. Estella had stumbled across it when she was looking for something to present the king with as a wedding present. The book had fallen down, she had picked it up to see what it was, and it was then the king had showed up. She read some of the poems at first, seeing that the woman who wrote it was describing the flowers, the plants, and the sky. As the pages went on, the flowers were withering and the sky darkened. Estella wondered what happened to the poet to make them see the world as glum.

She opened to the last page, seeing if she could find something about the poet. On the last page, it read:

> *To the woman who marries my son, may you see things clearly and do all that is important. The hard path is not the one that is won with war, but with the right words. May those words find you, and may you love my son Amir as much as I did.*

Estella gasped as she looked at the name. Amir. This was his mother's. She looked up where she last saw him. "Amir," she said in a low whisper to herself, before looking back at the book, "I'm sure he knew what it was, and yet he allowed me to have it."

Chapter 41

Wrong Vintage

Estella was dressed in a lavender dress, similar to the one she went to the ball in. Only this time, it was simpler with a lighter silk skirt. The small embellishments were in silver and her hair was placed into a bun on the back of her head. Estella made sure she had the smell of vanilla and jasmine sprinkled into her hair.

Amir came into the main greeting room. It was large enough for several hundred people, but there would only be a dozen or so going to be there today. Estella had gone over everything with Lysander, who was going to be in his position to ensure it went well.

"Hello, your majesty." She gave a low bow.

"Estella," he said firmly.

She gave him a soft smile. "Yes, sire?"

"Amir," he corrected.

She intentionally sighed. "Amir." She gave him a smirk.

"Hello, you two," Darius said with a cheerful sound.

Estella smiled at him before bowing her head. "It is wonderful to see you, Darius."

"I heard there is some song and dance going to happen."

"A dance with music," she corrected.

He dismissed her with the wave of his hand. "It is the same thing."

Estella looked at Amir. "After you, my lord."

"Amir," he corrected once more.

"I'll eventually get it, so please be patient with me."

"I will be," he took her arm in his, "as long as you call me Amir."

She looked at him for a moment before seeing the humor in his eyes. She let out a small chuckle, which he joined in.

"What is funny?" Darius asked.

They both let out a small cough and tried to hide their chuckles. Darius looked them both over.

"Please," Estella motioned to the table set out, "sit and enjoy your food. As you already know, the dancers will be out when we are seated and well-fed."

The table was at the floor with pillows surrounding it. The overwhelming smell of meats and cheeses wafted through the room. There were three seats on the far end of the table. Estella had planned for Amir to sit in the middle, Darius on his left, and she on his right. What actually happened was that Darius sat down in the middle. Estella knew etiquette would not allow her to sit next to another man other than her husband.

Amir watched as Darius sat down and began to eat a piece of meat. Now Amir wasn't a bulky man, or even a fat man, but he was strong. He walked to Darius and pulled him by the shirt and into the left side.

"Amir!" he shouted.

Amir ignored him as he continued to drag him to his seat. Estella blinked as she watched it unfold. Amir sat down in the middle and smiled at her.

"Have a seat, my joy."

That nickname again came up. She wondered if he knew or was just trying to give her a sweet name.

"All right," she said as she situated herself next to him. There was a bell on the edge. She picked it up and rang it.

Little by little, servants brought out more food. There was silence between them as they ate.

"Estella," Darius said.

"Yes?"

"Where are the dancers?"

"I believe she said it would be after we eat."

"Then why not now? I am done."

"I am not," Amir said coolly as he ate a piece of bread.

Darius leaned back and sighed heavily. "I don't like waiting."

"You will."

Estella sat there in silence as she watched the two friends glare at each other. Amir didn't look to be finishing any time soon.

"So, Estella, how was the proposal?" Darius asked.

Estella burst out into a laugh. "Uh, the king," she gasped, "I mean Amir," she corrected herself. "It was a wonderful proposal, and I was surprised I was chosen."

"It shouldn't have been," Amir said softly.

"So you're not mad that he kissed you?"

"Kissed me?" she asked confused.

"I heard you kissed her, Amir."

Both of them shook their head. "No," they said in unison, blushes rising in both their faces. It was unlikely that Darius knew what they did in the library.

"I was surprised because we barely know each other."

"I know all I need to know about you." He smirked.

"And what do you know about me?" She raised an eyebrow at him.

"That you are fiery. You have a determination about something, I don't know what it is yet, but I will. You listen to direction, even from servants. You are humble."

She gave him a curious look. "What do you mean I listen to servants?"

He rolled his eyes, taking a grape. "You think I didn't notice that you were the only one dressed simple, while every other girl was dressed in gold?"

"That could have been my own choice."

"You were also told to behave, who else would tell you that? You have no family."

She gave a coy smile. "Sir, I am not so high in status that I should not take the advice of others, especially when they come from reliable sources."

"The servants?" Darius asked.

She laughed at him, "My own source of help."

Amir gave a shrug. "Call them what you want, but remember that Lysander is mine, not yours."

"I am an extension of you, therefore he is mine as well." She laughed.

Amir gave a look like he wanted to say something, but then didn't, and just smiled. Estella giggled as she took a bite of a grape with some cheese.

Amir snapped his fingers and out came a young boy with a goblet and pitcher.

"Wine?" she asked.

He shook his head. "A new type of drink without alcohol."

"Oh? Sounds delicious."

He turned to the boy, who was taking a sip of the drink first. The boy placed the goblet down on the table, and waited a moment.

Just as he was about to hand the goblet to his king, his other hand went to his throat, as he gasped for air, falling to the ground. His lips turned purple, and he seized up. Amir jumped up out of his chair, grabbing hold of Estella.

"Guards!" Darius called out.

Within a moment, twenty different soldiers came running out, surrounding the now dead body. Amir shielded her from the sight of the dead body.

"See that he is properly buried, dispose of the goblet, and the drink he poured from," Amir commanded as he led her away. Estella looked at Lysander, who had a pale look on his face.

The king was almost assassinated.

Estella took a deep breath as she looked around. She thought of last night, and the young taster she had seen die. She knew she had threatened Cassia with the job, but none of the tasters had actually died before. Now there was someone who was indeed dead. She knew the matter was swirling around the palace by now; she hoped it would keep Cassia in line.

The garden was beautiful as the low candle lights reflected off the glass dome cast a beautiful glow around. She had set up a small chess table on the far end as it was when they first officially met. The dinner was at a low table, with meats, cheeses, and fruits on it. Estella was nervous as she looked at everything.

"Is this enough?" she asked aloud to herself.

"I think it's beautiful," Lysander said from behind her.

She jumped a little, then relaxed when she saw him. "Oh Lysander, thank you. Are you sure?"

He nodded. "I think the king will believe I helped you, though."

"All I did was remember how it was set up on the first night. Nothing grand."

Lysander gave a teary-eyed smile to her. "I will leave you both tonight as you requested."

"Not quite," she said softly. "Darius had invited himself to this dinner as well."

"Why?" He frowned.

"I'm not sure, but he did."

Lysander gave a heavy sigh. "Well, there is enough food to feed three people, but it's not as romantic."

"No," she shook her head, "but maybe we can sneak away just the two of us."

Lysander nodded. "Yes, get Darius drunk, then sneak off."

Estella snickered. "I'm not going to get him drunk."

"Why not?" he asked, offended.

"Because it's not good to get drunk."

"You aren't getting drunk, you are making *him* drunk."

"Still the same thing." She laughed.

Lysander waved his hand. "People got drunk all the time in my country. It wasn't seen as bad."

"My people don't believe in it."

Lysander eyed her suspiciously. "Estella, did you ever tell the king to not drink?"

She blinked a few times. "No."

"Are you sure?"

"I would remember talking to the king, especially if I told him to stop drinking."

"Hmm," he mused. "The king must have had another woman tell him that."

"Tell him to stop drinking?"

He nodded. "The first night all the contestants came, the king got drunk. He said some woman told him to take up chess and stop drinking."

Her eyes widened, her mouth agape.

"Estella?" he asked, concerned.

"That *was* me," she whispered.

"What?" he hissed.

"I told the king to stop drinking without meaning to. I thought he was a guard. I didn't get a good look at him, and to be honest, I didn't even know what the king looked like even if I did see him fully."

"How did you not see him well enough?"

"Well, he got tangled in a curtain and I tried to help him. He was clearly drunk and I told him to take up chess since it's a game anyone can play, even the poor."

Lysander groaned. "So you are the reason the king no longer drinks."

"I didn't mean for that to happen. I thought he was a guard."

"A guard who gets drunk on palace grounds gets a death penalty. And yet you thought nothing of telling me?"

"I didn't think of it again," she said. "It wasn't important for me to remember telling some man tossed in a curtain to stop drinking."

He nodded. "Yes, I understand that. You saw it differently."

"Forgive me, Lysander."

He frowned at her. "I will not. Now I have to find other things to serve the king, and I am a servant, you are the queen. Act like it."

Estella giggled. "You know you are very familiar with me, Lysander."

His eyes flickered something for a moment.

She extended her hand out. "No. Make no mistake. I love having you here. I would do nothing to destroy that."

He relaxed a bit. "Thank you, my queen. I will take my leave now. As per your request, we will be nearby, but not here."

"I don't want to be all alone with the king and Darius."

"I know, but maybe he will be tired and fall asleep."

"Don't drug him," she warned.

"Good day, my queen." Lysander smiled as he quickly walked off.

Estella took in a deep breath. She must tell the king the truth tonight. Who has betrayed him, who is behind the attacks. All of it, including her name.

CHAPTER 42

Time for a Coup

ESTELLA SMILED AS AMIR was alone. He was dressed in a plain garment, with a white, loose shirt. His hair was combed back and his beard was clean. He smelled of spice and jasmine. Estella thought he looked more like himself than he did last night.

"Hello, Estella," he said softly.

"Hello, Amir," she replied. There was a moment of silence between them. They stared into each other's eyes.

"Hello, you two," Darius interrupted, cutting off the moment they shared.

Estella gave him a smile as well. "Hello, Darius."

"What is today's menu?"

"Oh well, I had planned this one some time back and I didn't have time to adjust it. So only some simple things the king and I love."

He scowled for a moment. "Oh well, I'm sure I will find something."

Amir sighed. "You're taking advantage of the queen's generosity."

"Not at all," Darius chuckled, "I'm just making myself at home."

"My joy, please," he offered his hand to her, "take me to our place."

She gave a smile to him, taking his hand as they walked to where the food was laid out. Estella noticed how there were no guards around and no servants. Lysander really did make them alone tonight. Something sent shivers over her body as they looked at the food. Nothing was wrong with the food, she saw the man try it himself. Darius was eating without caution with no sign of poison.

"Uh," she looked at Amir, "let us take a walk, just the two of us." She gave a nod to Darius. "Excuse us, Darius, I wish to stay as thin as possible."

That was the first time she ever said that, and she hoped it would be the last.

Darius nodded with his mouth full.

Amir gave a curious look to her as she led them away. She went down the path where they had walked their first official date. The garlic flowers were in full bloom and they made the air thick with their perfume.

"Estella," he said in a low tone, "what's wrong?"

Panic rose in her throat. She opened her mouth to speak, but it felt stuck.

His eyes trailed over her, as if he was looking for her injuries. "What's wrong?"

"I know who is behind the attacks," she said in a whisper.

He stopped looking for her injuries and his eyes grew large. "What?"

"I know who is behind the attacks, but you need to promise me that you will consider believing me?"

"Why wouldn't I believe you?"

"Because she is also a liar!" Darius cut in, stepping out of the shadows.

Both of them looked at him. "I am no liar," she snapped.

"Then tell him."

Her breathing hastened. She looked Amir in the eyes. "Amir, I love you, but Darius is the one who is plotting against you."

"See?" Darius let no time for it to sink in. "She is trying to turn you against me. Don't listen to her, Amir."

"Notice, he never calls you his king."

Amir's eyes darted between the both of them.

"You are a liar, and shall be hanged for this," Darius spat.

"I speak the truth," she said with conviction. "I heard you when I was thrown into the old well with Lysander. I am telling the truth."

Amir looked hard at her; his eyes bore into hers. He was looking for something. Lies? Truth? He said nothing as both Estella and Darius spoke.

"Amir, don't listen to her. We have been friends since boyhood. I am your only true friend."

"He is plotting to kill not only you, but those who are loyal to you. Please, Amir," tears rolled down her face, "believe me."

"Amir, she is plotting against you."

Amir looked over at Darius, who was now a bit closer. His arms were wide open, as if he was expecting Amir to hug him as they always had. Estella was pleading. She had made a grave accusation against someone of a high position. But as she pleaded, Darius also was calling him by his name. He wasn't denying it.

"Darius," he said in a gruff voice. "What is my position?"

"You're the king," Darius replied with confusion.

"Then call me the king."

"Amir," he laughed, "I have always called you that."

"Say *you are the king, your majesty*."

Darius said nothing. The moment hung between them. Amir took in a deep breath and nodded.

"The queen is telling the truth," Amir said, more of matter-of-fact.

Darius let out a groan. "I'm glad it's out. Now I can stop licking your boots for your scraps." He chuckled, "I'm still shocked how you managed to escape the prison I laid out for you."

"Scraps? You are the second most powerful man in the country, what else could you want?"

"I want it *all*," he said in a growl. His eyes darkened. "I will be king." Darius quickly drew his sword, swinging at Amir, who managed to dodge it, and then grabbed his own sword he thankfully decided to carry tonight. With the whoosh of his sword, they clanged against one another. Estella ran off to the other side, watching helplessly as the men fought.

Amir dodged the blow to the head; Darius was not play-fighting. He had every intention to kill the king. There was no witty banter; there was no taunting from Darius. This was pure hate coming from his eyes.

The blackness from them was overwhelming. He swung low and threw his sword in the air. He threw some sand in the air, caught his sword, and swung. Happily, Amir had seen this exact trick from Darius before. It wasn't against him, but it was so dirty that Amir had made a note to talk to him about not playing dirty tricks in training arenas. Darius had argued that the enemy will also play dirty tricks, and they need to learn now before they reach the battle. Amir never imagined this would be used against him in a real life-and-death struggle.

"Give it up, Amir," Darius said in a bitter tone.

"Give up what's mine? Never."

"Yours?" Darius blew out a hot breath. "You got it only because your brothers died."

"They died in a noble cause."

"They died because it was fixed." Darius laughed.

Amir stilled for a moment. "What?"

Darius stopped swinging his sword and pointed it at Amir's chest. "My family has been next to yours for generations. Slowly, we have been carving our way to make our way to overthrowing you."

His eyes widened. "Why?"

"Enough talk," he said in an annoyed tone. He took a step back and extended his arm forward, thrusting his sword.

Amir parried the blow, the swords making a clanging sound. He stepped forward and shoved Darius's sword aside. There would be little time before he could make contact. He turned and avoided a blow to the side. He made a thrust, only to get stopped. Thrust after thrust, Amir was able to keep up, but there was only so much a man could take. He knew he had to finish it soon. He wasn't able to focus on Estella and what was happening to her if he was focusing on not dying.

CUT!

Amir felt the warm sensation of blood pooling on his arm.

"Seems like you were focusing on something else," Darius said as he laughed.

Amir said nothing as he gripped his left arm. He lost focus for a moment, and it cost him a strike.

"Don't want to call for the guards?"

"This is a single man's fight," he said in a low tone.

"Do it," he gave a mocking bow, "I won't judge you...*my lord*."

Amir knew better than to play into the enemy's hands. He took a few steps to the right and struck hard. Darius anticipated it, and blocked the blow. However, Amir had a heavier strike so the block was only effective for a death blow. It grazed his shoulder and he let out a scream.

Blood trickled down his arm, mimicking the king's.

"Just like this fight, Darius, you will never be able to be anything more than a poor man's copy."

What you shouldn't do in a fight is enrage a person who is already used to playing dirty tricks—especially in a sword fight. Darius took no time and swung low. Amir jumped to avoid being cut. Sand flew in the air. Amir was unable to dodge it, making him fall backwards. Darius was now on his feet, with the tip of his sword pressed against Amir's chest.

"Call the guards," he said in a sinister tone.

"No," Amir said calmly.

"Do it," he snarled, pressing the sword more, a small drop of blood started to run down his chest.

"Guards!" Estella screamed.

Both the men looked over at her. Tears had run down her face and she was clutching her chest. She wasn't able to do anything for Amir in that moment. There was no way she could win against him, but she did what she was able to.

"Guards!" she cried out again.

Hamid came running in, panic on his face as he looked at the scene.

"Hamid," she plead, "arrest him."

"Are you all right, my king?" Hamid asked.

"I'm fine," both the men answered.

Amir and Estella's face contorted into a confused look.

"Hamid, who is king?" Darius asked.

"You are," he answered.

"You traitor," Estella said in barely a whisper.

"You see, Amir? I own the kingdom. I am no second best," he said with venom in his words.

Estella was standing there, her eyes wide, her mouth agape. Hamid had betrayed her, betrayed Amir, and even her uncle, who had vouched for him. Her skin formed goosebumps as she stared at him.

"Let's end this, Hamid. Get the girl."

"With pleasure," he said with a smirk on his face as he made his way to Estella. She closed her mouth and took a step back.

"Don't!" Amir said, but couldn't move.

"Shh," Darius smirked, "we will see how it plays out there."

He stalked closer to her, and Estella took a step back for every one he took towards her. Finally, she was unfortunately backed against a wall.

Estella had to think of something. Panicked, she said, "You betrayed everyone."

"I did what is best for the country."

"You are not Zephyrian," she said quickly.

"Neither are you."

"I am Queen of Zephyria."

He laughed. "Not for long. You didn't even have a wedding night, and soon you will be my wife. Then everything will be right according to the creator."

"I will not go with you." She tried to not make her voice tremble.

"You don't have a choice. I have been given permission to take you as my wife once the king is dead."

"I would rather die." Tears welled in her eyes.

"I won't let you." He reached towards her, grabbing her arm, giving a slight squeeze.

"You betray your own people."

Hamid smirks. "I will be spared."

"Your soul will not be spared. You will be judged for this day."

Darius laughed. "You married someone from the Ātash People."

Amir said nothing as he watched Estella.

"Stop trying to spare the time. I will marry you the moment Darius becomes king."

"No," she said as he brought her wrist up. He now had his hand around her wrist, as if he was an iron; chaining her.

The next part happened in a flash. Estella wasn't good with a sword, but she had watched her uncle train enough, and even had some lessons with him when she was a young girl. She pulled his knife from his side, the one she knew was there. She took hold of it and pressed it against his throat.

"Get away from me," she said in a cool tone.

Hamid chuckled, taking a step back, but still holding onto her. "Don't think he will trade me for your precious king."

"I'm not dumb enough to believe he will do that. You're of no value to him. You betrayed your own people, your king, he will kill you the first chance he gets. He," she paused, "does not trust you."

There was a flicker of doubt that ignited in his eyes. Estella pressed the knife to his throat more. His grip on her hand loosened, but he didn't let go.

"Let go," she said firmly.

"Hamid," Darius said, "don't listen to her. She is trying to get into your head."

The doubt in his eyes grew.

Estella wasn't going to lie to him, and tell him everything would be all right, but she needed him distracted. He could easily take her knife with very little effort.

"Why protect someone who is so easily able to betray the king?" she asked.

"I am..." He trailed off as if he was trying to think of a good excuse.

Estella took the opportunity to cut Hamid's hand that was holding her wrist. He let out a scream, letting go of her and gripping his own. Estella ran over to Amir.

"Don't!" Darius snapped. "I'll kill him right now."

"No," she shook her head, "you will not."

"Yes, I will," he sneered, his voice like venom.

"I don't believe you, snake," she snapped. "I believe you wanted Amir to do your dirty work for you, to kill Hamid, because you don't trust Hamid. It's hard to keep a kingdom if you kill those who helped your coup. Your reign is at an end."

"My reign has just begun."

Hamid turned and just as he was about to, he stopped.

"Don't move." Zeke stood there, a knife at the throat of Darius and a sword at his back. "Either one of you makes one move, I will not hesitate to end you for the creator and king."

Estella let out a relieved breath. "Zeke."

"Forgive me, your majesties. I had to take care of those in the palace that were plotting against you. I had sent someone who I thought would protect you." He gave a hard look to Hamid. "I misjudged."

"You are not at fault, Zeke," Amir said as he slowly got up. "We were all fooled."

More soldiers came running into the garden. Estella stepped towards Amir, panicking. She didn't know who they would plead their allegiance to.

"Be not afraid, my queen," Zeke said. "They are all good men. I have weeded out all the wrongdoers."

"Where is the captain of the guard?" Estella asked.

"He was unfortunately taken care of," Zeke said solemnity.

"You don't scare me, Zeke," Darius spat. "You are nothing but a stupid Ātash who believes a deity will help guide you."

"And yet," Zeke smiled, "I am the one with my blades on you."

Darius dropped his blade, as well as Hamid. Both men made no move as the other guards surrounded them. They were restrained and bound.

Estella ran to Amir, helping him up.

"Are you hurt?" he asked, looking at her wrist.

She shook her head, "No. Are you?"

"Just a scratch." He chuckled.

"You're bleeding through your shirt," she cried, tears rolling down her face as she examined him.

He chuckled. "I'm fine. He grabbed you, he scared you. I was so worried about you."

Estella opened her mouth to say something, but Zeke cleared his throat, pulling them to look at him.

"Your majesties," he bowed, "what would you like done with the prisoners?"

Amir looked at them. "Hamid was brought to me by you, Zeke. You vouched for him."

"Amir," Estella said in a pleading voice.

"He is from the Ātash People, so I will leave his punishment to your people. Do what you want to him, you have my full blessing and support."

Zeke nodded at him.

He took in a deep breath. "As for Darius," Amir's eyes went cold, "give him and his family to The Boats."

Darius's eyes went wide. "You wouldn't dare!" he cried out.

Estella looked at Amir. "Amir?"

Amir cupped her face, pulling her to look at him, "He threatened you, my family, my people. I cannot allow him to live and be swiftly killed. His family will also join him, as they also are guilty."

Estella knew that The Boats were for the worst offenders. Where two narrow boats are put on top of each other, exposing the head and feet of the person. Honey and milk are placed on the exposed areas, to allow the insects and vermin to feast upon the victims, slowly and painfully. This was to be a public execution for Darius and those in his family.

"What about the women in his family?" she pleaded.

He narrowed his eyes. "What about them?"

"Surely we can show mercy to them."

"Very well," he sighed, "have the women sent to someone."

"Who?" she asked.

"A worthy opponent." Amir smirked, which made Zeke shake his head. "Take him away, and send word to Kashira of Loajin."

Everyone took the prisoners out of the garden, leaving the couple alone. Estella did not envision this night going in this way. And considering that the king just put Darius in the worst punishment, she didn't feel brave to say the next thing.

"Amir, I have something to tell you."

He looked at her, his brows furrowed ever so slightly. "What's wrong?"

"I have been…" She trailed off. "I am not Estella, but my real name is Joy." She swallowed hard. "I know lying to the king is a punishable offense, but my family gave me that name to keep me safe. Also, my uncle is Zeke." She said it so fast that her chest was heaving.

Amir stared at her for a moment, then began to laugh. He cupped her face, pulling her into a kiss. A deep, warm kiss. He smelled of rich spices and of blood. When he pulled away, he lightly rubbed her cheek with his thumb.

"My joy," he smiled at her, "I already knew."

Epilogue

In the days following, Darius, his family and anyone who was tied to him was convicted of treason. Per the law, set down by Amir's father, the punishment for traitors was, The Boats method. Smearing the punished with honey, as insects and animals fed on them live; the average person taking nineteen days to succumb to death. It was Queen Estella who argued the women related be spared and sent away.

Zeke apparently had gone through the trouble to find all those who were against the crown behind the scenes. Zeke told Amir who had been conspiring against the crown. It turns out, the now previous Captain of the Guard was promised a promising position of power, such as advisor. The treasurer was told he was going to keep some of the riches from the vault if he turned against the king. Several men from Darius's personal guard did *not* know about the coup, thus were spared. Zeke was asked to betray the king on behalf of his people, however when he declined, a watchful eye was kept on Darius. All the attempts on the king's life were from Darius convincing others to do his dirty work.

In the end, Amir decided to send the guilty men to Zerzura instead, for it was discovered that an advisor was conspiring with them, helping break the ties to Zephyria. Amir and Estella worried themselves no longer once the trial concluded in Zerzura, and they were found guilty once more. King Oba was not known for being a lenient man when punishing those guilty of treason. Hamid was given to the elders of the Ātash People, and punished according to their laws. Amir did not interfere, and though the final judgment was not left to Zeke, Hamid, nor any of the other men, were never seen again.

Estella gently hummed as she stroked the hair of the infant in her arms. The young prince was soundly sleeping, allowing Estella to enjoy the moment with him alone. As she continued to hum, the doors burst open.

Estella snapped her neck towards the door to find a small girl skipping into the room. Her raven hair cascaded and bounced with each skip.

"Jasmine," she hissed, looking at the young prince, to see if he was still sound asleep.

The young girl put her hand in front of her, bowing her head. "I'm sorry, Mama, but I wanted to show you my flower."

Estella noticed the small, now wilted, yellow flower in her hand. With her free hand, she motioned for Jasmine to come towards her. With newfound glee, she skipped towards her mother.

"See, Mama?" she asked, holding it up. Estella took hold of the flower, examining it. The petals were large and round. They didn't look like many flowers that were currently in the garden.

"What is this one called?"

"Baba called it Zephyrian Rose."

"And Baba is—"

"Always right about plants," she said with a large smile on her face.

"What about anything else?" Amir asked as he pushed off the door frame.

Estella smiled at him before looking back at the prince. "Only sometimes," she said softly.

"Harsh, my joy," he said, leaning over, looking at the young, sleeping prince. "How is Jafar doing?"

"He sleeps, unlike his father."

Amir let out a deep, low laugh. "His father has a country to maintain to give to his offspring."

"Like me, Baba," Jasmine said, with her arms raised.

Amir picked up his daughter. "Yes, like you Jasmine. One day, you will be queen of Zephyria, and I want you to be like your mother. Strong, and joyful."

Jasmine giggled. "I want to be scary like Baba!"

Estella and Amir exchanged a look before Amir raised an eyebrow at Jasmine. "Where did you hear that Baba was scary?"

"From Lysander," she said with decidedness.

"You called, your highness?" Lysander walked into the room with a tablet, writing something down.

"Lysander," Amir narrowed his eyes at him for a moment, "just because you are my advisor now, does not mean you can tell my daughter that I am scary."

Lysander touched his chest with his hand. "I would never, my lord."

"Then," he looked at Jasmine, "did Lysander say I was scary?"

She nodded. "Yes, Lysander said Baba is scary when angry."

Estella chuckled. "Daughter, you know who Baba is scared of?"

"Mama?" she asked, tilting her head.

"Sometimes," he snorted.

Estella shook her head. "Baba is most scared of Lysander."

Jasmine's deep brown eyes looked between all of the adults, as if she was trying to figure out who was lying and who was telling the truth. Everyone had a serious, emotionless face on.

"I want to grow up to be like Lysander," she said proudly.

All three adults let out a laugh. Amir rubbed his nose into her cheek, making Jasmine squeal with delight.

"My lady, I would be honored if you became queen and took it seriously as I do." Lysander gave a low bow to her at the waist.

"Lysander," Estella said, "are you sure the laws don't stop her from becoming queen?"

He blinked a few times. "Of course, she will be the next heir. She is the first born, and therefore, she is the one who will inherit the throne."

"But the laws, Lysander," Amir urged.

"I can safely say that after reviewing all the laws with Farid, there is no such law that prevents the young princess from becoming queen. There isn't even a law that says she has to marry someone first."

"But there was a law for me?" Amir glared, but Estella clasped his free hand within hers. He turned to smile at her.

"It was for the best," she said.

"Mama," Jasmine asked, wiggling to be set down on the ground, which Amir obliged. "Can you tell me the story of how you and Baba met?"

"We met in the jasmine garden." She smiled, touching the tip of her daughter's nose.

"Wait, what?" Lysander snapped his neck to see Estella. "When was this?"

Amir and Estella chuckled in unison.

"It was the night before the grand ball your father had put on. He had to meet all the women in the country to find a wife."

Jasmine's eyes grew large as she leaned in on her mother's leg.

"In the morning, everyone was allowed to choose a piece of jewelry. I had one item, but I knew the king was fond of flowers. So I snuck out and plucked one," she made a motion of plucking it from the air, "but your father caught me, calling me an assassin."

Jasmine gasped. "Did you hurt Baba?"

Estella shook her head. "No, Baba let me go, but I never saw his face that night. It wasn't until the next night, when I actually spoke to your baba."

"Was Baba nice?"

"Yes," Amir answered. "It was Mama who was not nice."

Estella's cheeks turned to a red color. "I was nice, otherwise you wouldn't have married me."

"I married you for more than one reason." He smiled.

"Estella," Lysander whimpered, "you met the king that night?"

"Actually," Amir gave a broad smile, "Lysander caught Baba and yelled at Baba for sneaking out too."

Jasmine looked blankly at her parents. "You both like to sneak out."

"It never stops, actually," Zeke said as he walked into the room. "Your baba and mama still sneak out all the time, and Uncle Zeke has to follow them sometimes to make sure they don't get hurt."

"Uncle Zeke!" the young princess exclaimed as she ran over to him, hugging his legs.

"Zeke, you still chase them, even as Captain of the Guard?" Lysander asked.

Zeke nodded as he patted the head of the princess. "You know, princess, you look just like your mother when she was your age."

Jasmine beamed at him. "Thank you, Uncle Zeke."

"For being part of your mother though," he knelt on his knee, and held out his hand, "I present you with this necklace."

Jasmine picked it up, examining it. Smooth wood in the shape of a flame, on a leather cord. "This is beautiful, thank you, Uncle."

He took it from her and placed it around her neck. "Young Princess Jasmine, you are the future queen of Zephyria, but you are also part of the Ātash People. May the flame live inside you forever."

The End

Acknowledgements

As far as I could remember, I wanted to be a writer, from that one story written on WIN 98 to now. There is no way I could express my gratitude to my mother for allowing me to research, to write, to read my books since day one. All the bad ones, to see my craft form into what it is, and still growing to be. Thank you mom.

My siblings, to know this '*secret*' and be just as excited for my books as any fan. For helping me with this book and any book I was writing at the time.

To the team of English Proper Editing Services, Hannah was a dream for being an editor. I couldn't have asked for a better editor. I didn't dread her notes. I didn't believe she would tear apart my work or change my voice. This book is me, it is all of me, with Hannah's help I got it polished to the point I was happy with.

April, thank you. No thank you can be completed without you. The hours we spent trying to get the titles right, the hours I spent telling you not to read this books because it's not dark. Thank you for truly being there for me.

Thank you so much JC Robins!! If you hadn't told me to take a second look at my cover, I would have published it with the wrong name. You have been a wonderful friend and author friend.

To mon loup, thank you for the ISBNs. You did help in other ways but the ISBNs was the biggest help for my mental state. You saw me go mad with what to do about not having an ISBN to which, you provided.

To all my author friends who encouraged me, who helped me, who, even though knowing almost nothing about me, helped me believe in myself and my work. I am here today because you all did work in the background.

Lindsey Stirling who definitely will never read this book...probably. A girl can dream. I listen your music every time I write. Thank you for your music, it helps me write every kind of scene.

Afterword

This book is a work of fantasy, and while I drew inspiration from various traditions, cultures, and stories—such as Persian, Jewish, Iranian, Iraqi, Middle Eastern, and Indian influences—it's important to note that it does not aim to be historically or one-hundred percent culturally accurate. There are elements from real-world cultures included, but they are meant more as nods or *"Easter eggs"* for those who recognize them, rather than strict representations.

My intention was never to create a fully accurate portrayal of every religion or culture, but rather to celebrate the richness of these traditions in a way that serves the story. I pulled inspiration from tales like *1001 Nights*, *Arabian Nights*, *Aladdin*, *Prince of Persia*, the story of *Esther*, and various other sources that resonated with me during my research.

Since this is a fantasy setting, I hope readers will enjoy the imaginative elements of the story, with the understanding that it is a romanticized and creative interpretation. While I believe fantasy should be given more leeway when it comes to cultural and historical accuracy, I also understand that not everyone may share that view. Though there is mention of a creator, this was never meant to be religious book. The Middle East has a deep love of their creator, regardless of what they call their creator. I wanted to show their love through the writing. Even if you don't like religion or don't believe, I want you to understand it is very cultural for a lot of people in the Middle East. And I didn't choose one over the other.

While researching, I did come across some interesting cultural practices, like the Persian bachelor-style contests, which I incorporated as part of the story. It was a challenge for me, especially with the decision to not include magic, but ultimately I really enjoyed bringing this story to life.

Thank you for your understanding and enjoyment of this creative exploration!

9 781967 631018